EAS

For a while Ricari and I strolled along in the darkness and quiet between the Bon Marché and the Stud, not speaking. A big jock type and his giggling, wasted girlfriend, walking past, made some comment I didn't hear, but I saw Ricari's cheeks flame scarlet. "Hey, shut up, you fucker," I said ignorantly. I was almost too drunk to support my own weight. "He'll kick your sorry ass."

"What?" The jock stopped and started walking back. "What did you say?"

Ricari and I both stood still, silent. He darted me a look that I couldn't interpret.

"You better keep your bitch on a leash," the jock blustered, squeezing the Giggle-Jiggle queen possessively. She exploded with literally snotty laughter.

"She's not mine," Ricari said, not without some humor.

The jock attempted to rush and take a swing at me. He never got that far—Ricari intercepted, adeptly tripping the jock so that he fell onto the gritty, filthy sidewalk and ripped his palms on the pavement. The girl broke out laughing even harder at that, and it seemed to galvanize the meathead. He sprung up with truly impressive speed and assaulted Ricari instead.

It wasn't the best idea the jock ever had. Ricari took the jock's hands in his and gave a subtle twist; I heard, even at three or four feet's distance, the moist popping sound of shoulder joints coming undone. The jock couldn't even yell; Ricari clamped his wee hand over the jock's open mouth and fastened himself onto the base of his neck . . .

JEMIAH JEFFERSON

VOICE OF THE BLOOD

LEISURE BOOKS NEW YORK CITY

For Willow, who got me into Bauhaus in the first place.

A LEISURE BOOK®

February 2001

Published by

Dorchester Publishing Co., Inc.
276 Fifth Avenue
New York, NY 10001

ISBN 0-8439-4830-2

Printed in the United States of America.

Visit us on the web at www.dorchesterpub.com.

VOICE
OF THE
BLOOD

Prologue: Hematopoiesis

All the best tales begin with rain. In reality, this is the end of the story I am about to relate to you, but I begin here, because I'm sitting waiting in the pitch-dark parlor of my old house, bare feet with their long nightmare toes peeking out from beneath an appropriately literary white eyelet nightgown. The rain is picking up outside from a sleepy waltz to a tarantella, and often when it rains like this, my lover John returns to me for the night. My lover—the unfortunately feral and tragically beautiful—may join me here, for he hates being out in the rain in the mulchy graveyards and unwholesome underpasses where he ordinarily stays. I am calling to him without raising my voice. I envision him standing solid before me. I want him to come in to me tonight.

I am listening to the rain with all my senses. Synaesthesia is one of my great rewards—I can, if I wish, hear the raindrops hitting leaves outside with my skin, hear the molecules of wet earth opening and sprouting

7

with my nostrils; it seems as though time stops between raindrops distinctly hitting the slate roof tiles in groups of ten or twenty. Moments like this make me insist and insist that we vampires are certainly not undead ghouls; as I sit precisely balanced on my bare tailbone, which rests cool and damp against the wooden slats, sniffing the wet peat of long-dead, long buried Oregonians wafting from a mile away, I feel more alive than any human creature ever felt. I am now so *capable* that restraining myself is a pleasure. Morality is delicious.

Nonetheless, the sight of my skulking, fey, lupine lover would please me no end. I haven't seen him for weeks. A week to me is a long time; I am mostly solitary and often idle, and my human scientist colleagues interpret my moody demeanor as aloofness. I'm sure they think I'm just some frigid workaholic who never sees any sunlight, one of those ice queens who wears a leather jacket, but still spends the evenings in a cold white laboratory.

My dearest friends are dead or far away. Oh, Ricari—I long for him sometimes—I wish he were simply here to talk to, to tell me sad or freakish tales of his life, but he gave me almost two years of his guidance and companionship, and then slipped off quietly, in darkness of course, leaving behind him only a receipt for a one-way plane ticket to Toronto. He always did prefer his solitude. I think about Lovely's laugh, as he read in Chloe's big bed while drinking ginger tea, and I miss them so much it makes my chest hurt.

John's here, though, in some ways at least. I'm not sure if he made the conscious decision to not be my companion, or whether he's just wandering about compulsively, like a half-wild housecat. I don't know why he became that way, while I became thus; the vampire blood pulsing through what was a human brain can do some weird things to people.

John and I were engaged to be married once, in that

other life, that human life, so sane and silicone in comparison with this. It was about a million years ago, or maybe it was only five. I was then, as I am now, Ariane Caroline Dempsey, early twenties, American, of mixed race, molecular biology specialist, lover of plain black T-shirts and violent action films, and prone to sitting bare-assed in the middle of the floor during a rainstorm.

So I've been thinking about everything, reviewing it in my mind; we vampires have the unfortunate trait of having very sharp memories, even of things we'd forgotten when we were humans. We can remember every embarassment, every disappointment, every shitty little betrayal, as well as the joy of the first bite of fresh persimmon jam, or the sweetness of falling asleep after a night of worrying. Some get extremely testy, some stop caring about anything they've said or done, and some, like me, I guess, just step back and quantify. Thinking about the past gives me something to do while I wait, a back-process in my mind to pass the time, the inexorable time, the excruciating waiting room of being alive.

For all the beings in my extended hemophagic family, the transformation occurred at a particularly touchy time in a person's life, especially for those of us in the twentieth century—that time in one's life where living becomes an effort for the first time. I was not old enough yet to see life as a blessing, as something to be treasured and appreciated as it goes along. Like Ricari, I became long-lived right at the time when it no longer seemed like something to desire. The very young take it in stride, take it for granted in fact, that the immortality that they feel inside is the real thing. After the age of forty or so, some people grasp at it desperately, see it as a grand cure for their failing eyesight, graying temples, and temperamental bowels. All I saw before me was sixty years of degeneration, and the gradual loss of my youthful charms, which weren't that terribly many to begin with.

I'm not unhappy. Quite the opposite. I know myself now to an extent that would have been impossible otherwise, and I like what I know. I just wish it wasn't so hard, you know. . . . So many deaths already and how infinitely many deaths to come?

Ah! A scratching and a scribbling at my back door? I jump up and rush to the kitchen window and gaze out at the plaster birdbath in my backyard, bouncing with raindrops. A white sylph is materializing, indistinct through the veinlike tracery of rain on the windowpane—John, naked, discarding heaps of mud-dark clothes onto my lawn and stepping with great delicacy into the fountain. He tosses his head like a Macedonian prince. So I open the back door for him, and he glides in, half asleep seemingly, his beaded silvery skin icy to the touch. His dark eyes are impossible to read. Heedless, hungry, he touches me through my nightgown, wetting me—look away, won't you?

I'll distract you with pretty stories. I'll tell you with my sharp vampire video-camera memory how I came to see through darkness and John came to possess the four sharp tines that currently, sensually, pierce the skin of my shoulder.

Book One
Haemostasis

Chapter One

So who started it?

John and I had been quarreling for days, almost non-stop. As soon as we woke up in bed together, I kicked him for stealing the pillows; we fought about whether we wanted sandwiches or leftovers for lunch; we fought about what movie we were going to see at night, and where. It wasn't as though we had such great differences of opinion—the two of us were freakishly similar in tastes. But we seemed to fight as a main form of communication.

It had all started so sweetly between us. He was a new professor at the Northern California Institute of Technology, where I attended graduate school; this Dr. John Thurbis brought an impossible reputation with him—the *wunderkind* from the gutters of one of England's grimmest cities, Ph.D. at twenty-nine in the near-supernatural field of particle physics. I, innocent of the fate that was shortly to befall me, was on my way to the ChemQuad to attend a lecture of my least-favorite class when I was accosted by a tall, dark-haired stranger with glasses and beautiful skin, who proceeded to rant at me about the stupidity and beauracracy of the administration. I stood and listened patiently, having heard all of this many times before from students and staff, and I was about to excuse myself and go on my way when he sighed and said, "Well, fuck-all, I need a drink. Want to go have a few stiff vodkas with me?" It was three o'clock in the afternoon, so of course I said yes. There followed a great dinner, inspired sex, and a day and a half spent in bed watching cable TV.

That had been almost two full years earlier. Since then, we'd gotten engaged, put toothbrushes in each other's homes, watched each other's academic reputations blossom. Since I'd earlier made the choice to stay in animal biology and mutational analysis, rather than running off on the genome bandwagon, my star didn't shine out quite as obviously as his, but we were still a formidable scientific force. Once the head of the Physics Department came upon John and me in a restaurant, and made sure to announce to his cronies, "The combined I.Q. of that table approaches four hundred—and they still look cute together."

In September of that year, John had received his dream invitation—to be a guest fellow at Cambridge from mid-December until May. Essentially, that meant he got to eat a lot of Yorkshire puddings, drink a lot of aged port, and argue about unification theory in front of a roaring fire with a lot of overbred graybeards who wouldn't have given John's dad, a Welsh-born cannery worker, the time of day. Being a fool, he couldn't have been more thrilled—and he accepted the invitation before he'd even told me he'd gotten it.

I tried to be mature about it. I was twenty-four, a genius in my own right; I had my grants and my devoted students and my own place to live. I could get along without a lover for a few months. I didn't let it show that I cared one bit, and for some reason, that didn't sit well with John. His indignation didn't sit well with me, and so there we were.

There was a particular Thursday when we'd been fighting so badly that I hadn't slept the night before; my period was due, and my knotted muscles cried for one of John's big-handed back rubs. But there was no way I was going to ask for one, the way he was acting. I hated giving him even an ounce of power. I was also a fool.

I had gone to pick him up for a dinner date, and he baited me by being late. "Our reservations are for eight-thirty," I said through my teeth. "What does that clock over there say?"

John was absentmindedly puttering around his living room, one sock on. He loved playing the Einstein bit, though he was about a quarter century too young to be convincing. "It's fast," he said.

"What does it say, John?"

He glanced up at me from where he crouched over a pile of clothes on the floor. "Ariane, uh, you might want to check your hair. It's . . . sticking up a bit . . ."

"What?" I dashed to the bathroom and squinted at myself in the mirror. Of course my hair was sticking up. I had worked for almost half an hour rolling the frizzy dark-red curls into a bun at the top of my head. I fiddled with the combs holding it all together, sighing. My body sang a repetitive song of pain. I fumbled in the medicine cabinet and dry-swallowed two aspirin.

"Are you ready yet? It's almost eight-thirty," John said impatiently.

Dinner was strained. We'd blown our reservation, and the maitre d' took great pleasure in telling us that it would be almost an hour before the next table opened. John winced, but he had to pretend he didn't care, so he led me to the bar and bought me a cocktail.

"I'm starving," I said.

"You'll live," John said. He plucked at my hair and the bun collapsed. "Oops . . . Dreadfully sorry . . ."

"No, you're fucking not. You have no idea how long that took me. You asshole." I cupped my fallen hair in my hands. I felt like I was going to cry. I felt like an elephant had stepped on my birthday cake.

"Oh, sweetheart. It's only hair. I think you look beautiful with your hair down."

"But that's not the point. I put so much work into it."

He sighed. "Don't get bloody neurotic about it. Be more of a . . . free spirit."

"This from the man who made us half an hour late because he has to have matching socks . . ."

We finished our drinks in silence.

The meal was unextraordinary . . . some kind of chops, soggy vegetables. The pain was crawling inside me like a wicked animal, like a leering gnome armed with stilettoes. John was talking and I wasn't listening to him at all. He finally broke my reverie when he barked, "Where are you?"

"Outside," I said. I pushed my plate away. "I'm really not hungry. I think the aspirin has fucked up my stomach."

John spat out an impatient sigh. "I finally buy you a nice dinner, and you're not even here to eat it. Christ, Ariane. You never talk with me anymore—all you do is bitch. Why don't you just tell me the truth?"

"And what's that?"

"That you don't want me to go."

"Would you stay if I asked you to?" I said.

He lifted his eyebrows a bit. Behind his wire-rimmed glasses he wasn't looking at me as he spoke. "No, I wouldn't."

"Let's just call the whole thing off," I said.

"I don't want to. Jesus."

"I don't want you to stay here anyway," I lied, waving my hand. "You'd just hate me for it. It's a good opportunity—hell, they already say your name in the same breath as Niels Bohr and whoever those other brainiacs were—Tesla or whoever the hell. It's a great thing. John-John needs his tenure. And you haven't even given me a goddamn ring yet."

"Now you're just being stupid." He sighed again, tossing his napkin with a little splash into his plate. "Let's just go, all right?"

"You want a ride home?"

"What do you think?"

I dropped him off in front of his flat without a goodbye. He just unfolded himself from the passenger seat of my Geo and slammed the door behind him. I didn't watch him go.

I went back to the campus, not bothering to change out of my flowery dress and girlie shoes. There was always work to do, and it distracted me from the tattered, illogical puzzle that was my life. A light rain had picked up while John and I were in the restaurant, and the lawns of the campus quads squelched under the heels of my pumps. The warm lights of the library, located in the center of campus, beckoned through the mist that was all that remained of the squall.

I roamed through the library, dazedly selecting bound volumes of all my favorite journals. In the back of the book stacks I glanced around and, sure I wouldn't be seen, hiked up my dress and checked my panties for bloodstains. Nothing so far. I knew it was close—my periods were regular, mercilessly reliable, almost down to the minute. With the amount of pain I was in, I knew it wouldn't be long. I sighed. Time to check out.

One of my lab students was working behind the circulation desk, and she smiled at me. "Hey, Ariane, you're here late, huh? I should think you'd be home asleep by now. Don't you ever take it easy?"

"Not if I can help it."

"You look nice. Hey, d'you see the police cars?"

"No, where?"

She paused in the stamping of the cards to take another bite of her chocolate bar. The smell of it bothered me a little. "Over on the other side of the park, by the bike shop. I think somebody must have broken into the bike shop."

"Or somebody's robbing graves," said the other student library worker, adding a morbid tremolo to his voice.

"What?" asked my student dubiously.

"There's a cemetery over there too," said the young man. I thought I recognized him—a creepy premed who had once stolen the complete skeleton from the lecture hall and returned it dressed like Prince, complete with purple velvet coat and spike-heeled boots. He stole a rectangle of chocolate from the bar.

She smacked his hand. "You're high," said my student.

"Yeah? Wanna make something of it?"

"I'll see you guys later," I mumbled.

I wished I was high. My cramps had been slowly rising in intensity as I strolled through the library, and now, in the grassy center of the BioQuad lawn, it came to a head, a climax of full uterine spasms, and my knees buckled slightly as I entered the main bio building where my lab was located. Then it was all over. I drew my breath. A bubble of warmth swelled between my legs. There was no one around, so I hiked up my skirt again and touched my finger to my vagina— blood, fresh as a stab wound.

Oh, great, I thought. Well, I had some tampons and a washcloth in my offices; I would have to make do for a little while, at least. I didn't want to go back home to find a message from John on my answering machine, demanding an apology or an explanation. Not yet. I let the door to the building swing closed, trailed my hand along the bricks in the stairwell leading to the basement. All was very quiet in the building—I could barely hear someone playing Pink Floyd down the hall, just the faintest echo bouncing along the walls. No one there to bother me.

For some reason the door to my office wouldn't open. I struggled with the key for a full minute, my eagerness burning through to impatience, and I let out a stifled curse. Finally I shoved open the door with my shoulder.

My office was dark and filled with a damp wind speckled with rain. I couldn't see a thing for a minute; my hand fumbled for the light switch, but it had no effect. At last I made out some white things on the floor—papers, strewn all about, blown by the wind, and bulkier, oblong forms. They were my pet rats, not moving, their fur pink and wet and matted.

I remember screaming.

That was it.

Then I was lying down on a hard, narrow bed, covered with a wool blanket. I had been in this bed before—it was one of the sleep-lab beds, in which I'd done many nights for the pocket money before I graduated. I wondered why I was there; I hadn't done any sleep-lab experiments for months and months. I was cold and infinitely drowsy.

Before I could wake up completely, I heard someone implore me, "Don't try to talk, we're taking you to the infirmary."

I couldn't move anyway. I felt myself being half lifted and half rolled, then boxed in with stretcher bars. I wanted to tell them that all this fuss was unnecessary, I was fine, but I couldn't move at all. I felt no pain, just a chill that immobilized me. I opened my eyes. I was being wheeled away down bright corridors. I thought I smelled John—he liked a certain soap. I felt a hot hand against my cheek.

"You're gonna make it, don't worry."

I was confused. I went back to sleep.

When I woke up again, the pain came with consciousness, hand in hand, like death and taxes. I moaned out loud and grabbed for my belly. John was there beside me, and he stroked my forehead and my hand until I relaxed. He wiped a few tears away from my cheek. "You've had a miscarriage," he said in a whisper. He sounded broken. "Your neighbor found you—he heard you scream, and he found you in a pool of blood. Your office is a real mess. The window was broken, your rats are all dead, it's a shambles. I'm just glad you're all right."

"I don't feel all right," I said thickly.

"No, I'm sure you don't. You're on an IV and will be till morning. I'll be here tomorrow to take you home—you have to promise to take it easy for the next week or so—no school."

"I'll get behind," I groaned. The room was spinning as if I'd had far too much to drink—half turn, then stop; the same half turn, then stop, then the same again.

He squeegeed tears away from his own eyes, as if he were ashamed of them and didn't want me to see. Behind his glasses, his eyes were red and swollen, his dense lashes still wet. "Nonsense. You're the smartest girl in school. You'll make it up in no time—I'll bring you your lessons. Dr. Reid already said he'd take over your TA classes until you feel up to coming back. Everything's going to be all right. You just have to relax, OK? I'll come get you between the Astro and Particle lectures."

I looked at him, then turned over my arm, stiff and cold with the metal and plastic tubing hanging out of it, and let all my cells collapse against the rough cotton duck of the hospital sheets. The room was blessedly dim—late night lights were on. "Don't be late," I whispered to him.

That night as I slept, I had nightmares about it. Again and again I came into my office, each time finding something more awful to look at—one rat had had its head ripped off and the trails of flesh spread across the floor like a red feather boa; another was crushed into a white furry bag of liquid, horribly misshapen. Again I saw the lightning strike, illuminating the white papers flying about like some Hitchcock intro, the overturned office chair, the ruined stereo, and—what else?

I was convinced there was something else in the room.

A gynecologist came to visit me when I awakened in the morning. I sat up in bed, drinking a pint of nutritional milk shake, and she sat in a chair opposite me. "How are you feeling, Ariane?" she asked me cheerfully.

"Kind of like someone stepped on me."

She granted that a medically astute smile. "It wasn't really a miscarriage that you suffered," she informed me. "We didn't find any of the hormones associated with pregnancy in your bloodstream."

I didn't say anything, plucking at loose threads in the hospital blanket.

The gyn sighed and went on. "Ariane, you weren't attacked, you weren't raped, were you? You can say so, I won't say anything about it if you don't want— I'm just trying to make a diagnosis."

"I . . . no," I said truthfully. "I mean, I don't remember. I'm not a repressed-memories kind of person."

"I thought so. I mean, we didn't find any semen traces on you either—just your own blood. The only thing I can think is that you suffered a prolapsed endometrium, for God knows what reason. There's nothing left of your uterine lining now. It seems to be

21

reforming itself normally, which is good. It's a really rare occurrence, and it usually happens after a couple of miscarriages or abortions—"

"Never had an abortion."

"Yeah," she agreed with another shrug. "Just one of those freaky things, I guess. But you're healthy otherwise, so you're going to be just fine as long as you rest."

I finished my shake as she left the room, then gobbled down a few Tylenol and an antibiotic, and slipped into a twitchy sleep for a few hours.

Again and again I mentally visited the room, looked around, squinting my eyes against the stiff wind, and then screaming until my throat was raw. But at some point the scream had died away as if it had never existed. There was something strange about the time . . . perhaps I had never screamed at all. My hand struggling at the doorknob, then throwing back the heavy wood, staring into the dark . . .

John was prompt that afternoon to pick me up, both of us grimacing at the embarassing ritual of the wheelchair escort to the parking lot. He had brought me some sweatpants and a T-shirt to wear—my long flowered dress had been quite ruined. I settled wearily in the passenger seat, rattling my vials of pain pills and antibiotics, and John squinted at the dash as he started the unfamiliar vehicle.

One thing I can say about John is, though he drives like a half-blind Chinese grandpa, he's a wonderful nursemaid. He had a sickly childhood and an overprotective mother, and he knows all about soups, hot blankets, pillow fluffing, and Travel Scrabble. I was soon settled on the living room couch like Cleopatra with an array of light beverages, little sandwiches, and good books spread out before me within my reach. "Do you hurt anywhere?" he asked.

"I think you could punch me and I wouldn't feel it," I replied, smiling and sloppy with codeine.

He got on his knees in front of me and kissed the backs of my hands. "I love you so much, Ariane," he said. "I can't bear the idea of something happening to you. I'm sorry I was so beastly last night."

"Oh, honey, don't worry about that. I wasn't being too sweet myself."

John smiled against my hands. "You get much more Southern when you're drugged," he remarked.

"Surely, y'all. And don't worry about the ring. I'd only lose it anyway."

He shook his head and blushed. "If you need anything, call. Please, I mean it."

"Go to school," I urged him. "I'm going to sleep for a while. We can't both be slackers."

"Tell me you love me first."

"I love you, John. I love you—passionately."

He stood up and grinned. "I accept that," he said. "I'll be back after my last class."

"You're not going to drive, are you?" I teased.

He smiled crookedly. "Er, no, I think I'll walk. . . ."

At last he left me, and I leafed through the papers. As usual, all they had was item after item of horrors—war in Eastern Europe, war in Africa, police corruption, two young men found horribly mutilated in the cemetery across the street from NCIT. The kids had been robbing graves, it seemed, until some big-time psycho got to them and slit their throats and gutted them. No leads on who, but already there was some slight anxiety about yet another Jack the Ripper. I was usually dismayed by things like that in the news, but I read all the tales of woe and murder with druggy fascination. I read the news item again and again until I couldn't hold my eyes open anymore.

I slipped into a hypnagogic state. I spent years of my life perfecting the transition from wakefulness to half sleep, and thence to sleep; I can stay in this fugue state for hours without sleeping, especially when on some form of opiate, like codeine. It wasn't quite meditation—peace of mind was impossible for me after the scary stuff I'd read.

Naturally I went back to last night, like the tongue going to visit the recent dental work. For some reason I had a lot more clarity now, as if some fog over my memory was slowly lifting.

There *had* been something else in the room—a hunched and bony form, skinny as a Third World starveling. I'd thought to myself, *Homeless, malnourished, probably broke in to steal something to sell or barter for food.* I was afraid, but I advanced closer, knowing that I was possessed of some physical power, and a little bit of mental strength, and I had little cause for fear. The bones of the body were draped with a muddy, tattered, eaten cloth—a big coat, perhaps a rain cloak, dark in color. "Hey," I said cautiously, holding up my hand. "I know female self-defense."

The person turned its face towards me.

oh shit

I was losing the memory . . . must reel it back in. I shifted my place on the couch, then lay perfectly, perfectly still, slowing my breathing. Back to sleep . . . but not quite. At last the images swam back, coalescing.

The face of the—*creature*—I couldn't bring myself to think of it as a person anymore. Perhaps it had once been a person, but not much was left. The skin was dark, the color of the mud, dotted here and there with pinkish, livid sores, holes in the flesh. The skin didn't quite cover the cheeks—the strain of stretching over the high, rampant cheekbones seemed to be too much for it. The only thing I saw that didn't disgust me filled me with horror—the eyes, bulging and terribly bloodshot, large blue-gray irises, sentient eyes, eyes that begged, full of agony. It opened its mouth and hissed at me. The mouth was filled with yellow-orange teeth, four of them sharply pointed, two on top and two on the lower jaw. It hissed again and lowered its head to tear at something. It was one of my rats, squeaking in terror. The creature crushed it in one of its bony claws, and sucked out the blood that gushed from the rat's mouth. When the blood didn't come out fast enough for it, it crammed the rat half into its mouth and bit into it, sucking the juice out the way you would a slice of orange.

And yet I still hadn't screamed. I'd pissed myself, that was for sure—I felt it running down my legs in a steaming-hot stream. But I was silent, transfixed. The creature . . . it was in so much pain. It threw back its head and gave a hoarse cry, rattling in its throat. I realized why it had hissed—it hadn't enough flesh in its voice box to make any further sound. Somehow the blood was feeding it.

It was gazing at me now. (In my fugue I writhed on the couch, sick with fear, but the images came unbidden now, released from their floodgates.) Its eyes were truly terrible. It was weeping now, great painful tears that made the creature gasp when they ran into the open wounds on its face. *Salt tears!* I thought in wonder. Not blood or pus, but salt, simple sea salt like any decent mammal. The creature stood up. It was wearing a large coat, as tattered as its own skin, and some rags of what looked like a fine silk or satin, reduced to ribbons. It was so tiny and wasted that no flesh covered its bones, only that mud-colored, fragile skin.

I felt a subtle *push* in my brain, almost an actual physical pressure, a little squeeze.

Slowly I circled the room until I had my back to the desk. My hand slipped in rat blood and raindrops when I tried to steady myself. I wasn't thinking at all— merely moving my body to and fro, arranging it idly but deliberately. I lifted up my skirt.

In some other place, I felt myself squirming against the upholstery on my couch, groaning through clenched teeth. In the memory state, my mind raced while I was physically paralyzed, the negative of what I was remembering—my body moving without the action of my mind.

Opium is a funny thing—the fantastic things you dream up seem real, but immense; the real things you remember seem to go on forever, you recall every atom of detail. I didn't want to see it, but I did—I felt it and remembered it completely—raising my skirt and allowing the creature to lift up my legs as if it were a lover ready to mount me. It tore my panties off with one deft swipe of its right claw, the fingernails glittering on it like talons, and it put its head between my legs and began to lap up the drops of blood coming from me.

The tongue was rough, sweet to the touch, not cruel or stinging, hungrily penetrating me for more; I lay there passively, but not so passively that I felt no pleasure or fear. There was a screen up in my mind—I could see it clearly, but not around it. It said DON'T BE AFRAID. I NEED YOU. YOU ARE BEAUTIFUL AND KIND. The wraithlike hands gripped my buttocks, caressing them so that I felt the smooth texture of the bones and the clothlike shreds of skin. In a long moment, the licking and sucking became insistent, and I felt myself swelling towards an orgasm. I didn't want it. There was nothing I could do to stop it.

I had it—or it had me—the orgasm, intense as lightning, blistering through my nerves, forcing a great spurt of blood out of my womb into the creature's mouth. In my mind I felt an echo of my own reluctant ecstacy—the creature's sympathetic pleasure pangs. At that moment I felt its hold on me slip; I saw around the screen, I saw the corpses of my rats and smelled the stench of freshly turned earth, urine, blood, my own terrified sweat; and then I screamed. I screamed harder in that one moment than I ever have. In a panic the creature gave a great pulling suck on my cunt, as if to turn me inside out, and that is truly all I remember. I must have slumped to the floor, and there I was found, alone, slowly leaking what was left, my dress soaked with piss and blood.

I slid off the couch and crawled on my hands and knees to the bathroom, heaving dryly into the toilet until I slid down to rest on the bathroom rug, my cheek pressed to the sensual cold nubs of the tiles.

When John returned to me that evening he found me asleep there on the bathroom floor. He shook me awake and half carried me back to the living room. I drew him tightly to me and made him lie lengthwise on the couch with me. I held him and cried and shook for a long time, which he ascribed to too many drugs and not enough company. He held me tightly, fed me chili and saltines, and let me win at Scrabble three times. We crawled into bed and he held my naked body against his. "Are you cold?" he asked, eyes round with warm brown concern. So alive. My beautiful lover.

"No," I said, touching his warm, stubbly cheek. "I feel better now."

In a week I was back in school, back at the lectern, good as new. Of course, the rumor mill at the Loony Geek Farm was healthier than any of the students, and I was treated with delicacy and deference. I pretended that nothing had happened, and soon enough there were fresh scandals to take everyone's mind off my little accident.

John treated me like spun glass for a while, holding doors for me and bringing my lunch to my new office, but even he got over it in time. I assured him, perhaps a little too much, that everything was all right, that I was fine now. By the time the first of December rolled around, I could tell he didn't believe me. My empathic professor lover lay beside me at night while I lay awake, and I could feel his lashes brushing my back as he blinked, as awake as I was.

What could I have told him? Would he have believed me? I hardly believed it myself. I have a New Orleans child's healthy respect for the supernatural, but generally that extended to not cussing in cemeteries and knocking on wood. How could I possibly explain to a scientist that I had seen a dead man walking the earth—had let him touch me—had let him lick blood from my pussy until I came? I didn't want to believe it, and I had been there. I didn't think it would go over very well with anyone else.

He never did ask me about it, either. Sometimes he seemed about to ask. He would hang his head, fall silent at dinner, take my hand, and stare intently at me as if he could force me to volunteer what had actually happened. When John did this, I usually laughed, kissed him, sang a Beatles song, suggested cocktails after classes, and he would shake his head as if to say, *How could I ever suspect her?*

In the heat of the pre-finals weeks of classes, I had the double stress of doing my coursework and trying to look after John's travel arrangements. He and I spent hours on the phone long distance to England, trying to convince his mother that it was better if he stayed in the professor's apartments provided for him, rather than in her cold-water flat ten miles away. She would generally listen to me more than to John. To add to that, John had nothing in the way of clothes, and no eye for clothing or good shoes, and I had to shop for him, only occasionally convincing him to come along with me.

After one morning off, returning to campus with armloads of shopping bags from Oak Tree and the Gap, I tumbled into my chair in my office, praying I'd gotten my interlibrary loan requests in through the mail. I called my student lackey, Lola, and asked her to get my mail from the faculty mailroom and bring it to my office, and to score a muffin while she was at it.

Lola came in with an armload of documents and a

chocolate muffin. "I would have brought you coffee, but they were out," she said.

"Thanks, baby."

"How are you today?" She began to arrange the papers on the desk. I think she had a crush on me. She was a well-scrubbed Arizona girl in leggings and sweatshirt, her lips always perfectly pencilled in a subtle color.

"I'm fine . . . a little harried as usual . . . What's this?" I held up a Fed-Ex envelope and squinted at it. There was no return address legible on the outside.

"I don't know. It came just as I was walking out the door. Weird, huh? I better run off to Cellular, I've been late every day this week. See ya." She waved and shut the door behind her.

I took a crumbly bite of muffin and tore the perforated cardboard strip off the package. Inside the envelope was another envelope, this in a creamy pale brown expensive paper with rough edges, rather like an invitation to an art gallery opening or commencement at a hippie college. I slit it with my thumbnail and pulled out a slip of identical brown paper, with a scrolling, strange handwriting in dark brown ink. I read it once, then set it down, then picked it up and read it again.

To Miss Ariane Dempsey.

I would not blame you if you did not forgive me for what I did to you that night; I can certainly never forgive myself. I want to express my regret, my undying debt to you, my desire to set things right. If you are not afraid, allow me to apologize to you in person. Come to the Saskatchewan Hotel on December 12th. Come by eight, Suite 900. I say again, I am nothing to fear.

My eternal apologies.

I nearly lost the muffin in my anxiety.

It really had happened. I wasn't going crazy. I could

feel a special vibration in the paper—something in the handwriting, too careful, too old to have been made by a real person—but too sloppy to have been printed. I jumped out of my chair and paced the office, John's bags of new clothes falling unheeded to the floor. What could I do? How in the world should I react?

I was interrupted by the entrance of Dr. John Thurbis, bringing my lunch, hot from the PhysQuad microwave. "Spinach lasagna," he sang. "I bought it myself—Jesus, Ariane, what's the matter?" In a second he had set down the lasagna and taken me tightly in his arms. "Ariane!"

"I just . . ." I felt dizzy in his arms. "I think I'm just hungry."

"You look like you've just found out someone died."

"No, no, sweetie, I'll be OK. I stood up too fast." I squirmed away from him, shuffled my mail, and covered the brown slip of paper with some Xeroxes. John was staring at me, blankly hurt. "Thanks for the grub, sweetheart."

He sat on my chair and pulled me down into his lap. "Are you sure you're going to be all right without me?"

"I'll manage. Geez, John, I get a little light-headed, you think I'm about to have puppies. It's all right for you to calm down now." I kissed him on the top of his head and stuck my finger into his ear. He giggled. "I bought you some clothes. I hope you don't think they're too 'Liverpool gutter punk.' "

And so on. I led him off the trail. In a while he was heading off across the grass back to the safety and logic of the PhysQuad, and I was alone in my office with the lasagna and the letter. I read it over and over for hours, touching it until I thought I would rub a hole through the paper.

Chapter Two

I had already made up my mind to go. John's plane to Gatwick Airport was on December 12th. I don't think I could have given myself up to the unknown had John still been around—of course, there was no way of knowing what to expect, but perhaps my Southern clairvoyant streak had betrayed the future.

John's and my last night together was pretty unromantic—we stayed out half the night moving his things into storage and buying his last-minute items. At two A.M. we toasted each other with gin and juice at my kitchen table, took off our clothes, and got into bed. We felt each other up for a few minutes, but both fell asleep before anything more interesting could happen.

In the morning I drove him to the airport, and we shared coffee and flavorless blueberry muffins in a blond-wood airport cafe at seven. "I think this is a good thing," he said hesitantly.

"I agree. Don't worry. You'll enjoy yourself. And

then you'll be back." I gave him my sleepy understanding smile, and he cupped his hands over mine cupping the coffee cup. He looked into my eyes for a second, and leaned across the table and kissed me gently on the mouth.

"I'm still worried about you," he said.

"Please, don't. I'm going to be OK. You take care of yourself. You better hurry—they're boarding."

Bags were shouldered, and coats still damp with the morning's rain were doffed, and he kissed me again. I watched him jog-trot down the concourse to his gate, wave back at me with an uncertain smile, and disappear.

I actually don't remember the rest of that day. (Amend what I said earlier—it's the rule proved by it's exception.) I know I went home and probably ate something, and I may have taken a bath: I certainly slept most of the afternoon away. Everything else is gone in a haze of white noise, my mind's preoccupation driving off even the memory of what happened.

I woke up at around six-thirty, somewhat sweaty and with a faint headache that swelled if I bent over or turned my head too quickly. Not knowing what to expect—and deathly afraid of overdressing—I put on clean black pants, a black T-shirt with a faded Adidas logo, and a threadbare cardigan the green color of split-pea soup. It was a warm night for San Francisco in December, rainy in breaths, with a moon beginning to glow luminously through a thin frosting of clouds.

I had looked up the Saskatchewan in the phone book before falling asleep. It was in North Beach, the real North Beach where it converges with Chinatown, and not the nebulous ritziness that borders the Marina and Pacific Heights. I drove along Van Ness in the dusk, hoping that it wasn't some crack house filled with junkies, or Chinese child prostitutes, or both.

I parked outside a closed record store and walked up to the address. It was a tall thin brown building wedged tightly between a bookstore that was still open, and a dry cleaner's. The lobby didn't look too bad—like something from a Jim Jarmusch movie, a little seedy and old, but still slightly respectable, with a very old man behind the desk reading this week's *TV Guide*. He looked at me with vague interest, and I nodded to him as I went to the double elevators along the far wall.

Come by eight, Suite 900. I say again, I am nothing to fear.

It was all brown inside too, long empty brown hallways of old wood and brass gone dull from age and dust particles settling onto the polish. Nine was the top floor, and there were only four suites, kindly pointed out to me by the brass placard on the wall opposite the elevators. Suite 900 was at the end of the hall, on the right.

There was no sound at all save my footsteps falling onto the thick, flat, patterned brown carpet, and my nervous sighing and sniffling. I paused with my hand against the door of 900. What the hell was in there? Some terrifying obelisk? Corpses piled ceiling high? Or nothing at all? Was I being set up by some obscure Italian mafia?

The pressure of my hand pushed the door ajar.

From inside, I heard a faint clear voice call out, "Come in, the door is open."

I stepped inside, onto a polished parquet floor.

The room stretched out thin and narrow, with great Victorian windows hung with dusty venetian blinds, open to allow what moonlight there was. Pieces of antique furniture stood around without much eye for form, a secretary here, a tall thin lamp there, all of it emitting a faint incandescent shine. Over in the corner by one of the windows, a boy lay on his side on a chaise tongue. He looked at me intently, and the same voice, a deep throaty man's voice, spoke again. "Close the door, please."

I reached behind me for the doorknob, and drew it closed.

It wasn't a boy at all, rather a small slight man, interestingly proportioned; his wrists seemed too long for his shirt, his long thin athletic legs crossed casually at the ankle. There was something in his face that I remembered, almost as if from a dream. He sat up and languidly gestured to me with his forefinger.

Those claws. I remembered the claws. Now they were fingernails, smooth and oval and buffed to a high gloss, but still the claws from my nightmare, the ones whose scars I still wore on my thighs. His hands were long and seemed triply jointed with those silver-gray appendages on their fingertips, completely inhuman. I stared at his face for a long time, retracing the structure of those bones. Yes, that was him, all right, the huge staring orbs, now clothed in a delicate veil of eyelid and lash, the cheekbones smooth, the lips beautiful as if painted on in rose gouache.

"Yes," he said, "that was me."

I opened my mouth, about to speak, but nothing I was going to say would come out. He moved his face more fully into the light of the lamp, and ran his fingers through a few strands of unevenly ash-brown hair. He smiled, discreetly, almost shyly, not baring the frightening teeth that I knew were there. "Please don't stand there," he insisted. "Please, come over here, and sit down."

I did what I was told. How normal he looked! But completely unnatural. He wore a loose white satin shirt and brown velvet pants, very fitted to his shape. He wore them well; they showed off the girlishness of his body, the incredible delicacy with which he moved, quickly and artlessly like a deer. He took a very deep sigh, and looked around him. "Are you hungry? I could send for something for you to eat. Or to drink. Wine?"

"Yes," I said, "please."

34

He leaned over and picked up a telephone—a completely normal plastic telephone, not at all antique, beige and streamlined, and held it against his face. Next to it, his skin was as white as a freshly cut chestnut. "Room 900," he said. "Some cheese and olives, please. Oh, and bread. And a bottle of—" He held his hand over the receiver and looked at me. "Red or white?"

"Red," I said, after a moment's hesitation.

"A bottle of chianti. Thank you." He hung up, clasped his hands, looked at me.

"You're real," I said.

He had long sideburns, a disorientingly current fashion. "I am real," he agreed.

"You're a vampire," I said, the first part a whisper, aspirating the word for what he was.

He winced slightly, looking out into the corners of the room. "I know."

"You drank my blood," I kept going. "So what happens now?"

"What do you mean?"

"Do I become . . . one of you?"

As he shifted, I caught a glint of something hidden in his shirt, winking at me from the unbuttoned collar of satin. Before he could answer my previous question, I asked him, "What's that?"

He looked down, pulled out a string of polished pale beads, with a dull ivory crucifix dangling from the end. "My rosary," he answered.

"You keep a rosary?"

"At all times," said the vampire.

"For what?" I half laughed.

He smiled at me a bit. "I'm a Roman Catholic," he said.

"You go to Mass and stuff?" He nodded, once. "You take communion?"

"No," he admitted. "I cannot."

"Will you die?"

35

"I will have a stomach ache. I cannot digest. Also it would be wrong. A mockery of the things that I hold precious. I do go to Mass, confession, everything. I went this morning."

"Weird," I said.

"You will not become 'one of us,' " he said.

The room service came. A different old man came in with a wheeled cart, bearing a tray of bread, cheeses, and fat drab olives, and a bottle of wine that had already been uncorked. The vampire thanked the old man graciously and gave him a ridiculous tip, and the old man left with his wheeled cart, closing the door almost soundlessly behind him.

Once again I was alone in the room with the creature. He leaned forward and poured wine into one of the pair of glasses, and handed it to me. I took the glass and sipped at it, testing its flavor for anything strange, but it was normal good chianti, quite dry. I downed the rest of the glass at a swallow. The vampire refilled my glass without comment.

"Do you have a name?" I asked.

"My name is Orfeo Ricari."

"Italian?"

"By birth," he said.

"A long time ago?" I said, drinking another half glass.

"Very long."

"Why . . . why did you pick me?" The first glass finally hit me, burning through my empty stomach and hitting my bloodstream. It almost hurt.

Orfeo Ricari toyed uneasily with his rosary beads, counting them unconsciously off with pinches of his fingernails. "I did not choose you particularly," he said. "You were simply the first person I came to. Your university is very close to where I was buried."

"That . . . graveyard?" The one four blocks away, on the near side of Golden Gate Park, lovely, rather old, fenced in with razor wire to keep the kids away. "What are you talking about?"

"Can't you guess? I was buried. I was dead. I came back out. I was practically dead when I came to you—obviously completely mad, quite far from any kind of control. I was dead for seven months and then I was dug up again by some idiot schoolchildren."

I was getting there. That story, from the papers. "*You* killed them."

"I didn't know. I didn't mean to. I had no control; I was furious; they were there. I needed their blood. I don't want to. *I hate killing*," he said passionately. "Do you understand? I didn't mean to come to you—but I could smell your animals on the wind, and then—you came in—and your blood—" He stopped short, and gulped. "I wanted to apologize to you. I wanted you to know that I had no control over what I did that night, and I shall make it up to you."

Did he know? Did he know of my orgasms? And of the pain that lingered after the physical pain had gone away, the horrible longing to be taken again in his harsh and peeling hands and brought to his lips, like a bowl of wine? And now that he was no longer a walking atrocity of bones and decay, now that he was whole and beautiful again? I fell silent, not looking at him.

Ricari made another gesture with his hand. "Please," he said. "Eat. Eat and drink and enjoy. I like to see people eating. I cannot."

I picked up an olive and sucked it from its pit, washing it down with the end of my second glass. He refilled the glass again. I spoke with hesitation. "How could you . . . come back to life after you'd been dead and buried?"

He sighed. "I have done this before," he explained. "I am very, very old. I have lived through too much and seen too many changes. I am tired of being alive. But I cannot take my own life—it is a sin in God's eyes, and the ways that I can die, truly and forever, are so few and so painful that I hesitate. But, if I starve myself of blood long enough, I grow less and less animate, less like a living thing. I cooperate with, or I force the cooperation of, an undertaker, and I arrange for my death to take place. I rid myself of possesions, and the time comes, and I am closed in a coffin like any other dead man. Then I am buried—no one the wiser of knowing that there is still a flicker of me left. Rapidly it too dies, and I am at rest, as long as I am underground and the temptations of the world are far away. However, I am rarely allowed to rest for long. Someone digs me up hoping to find riches hidden in my coffin, or to dislodge me for some newer corpse. As soon as I reach the air and take a breath, I am here again. And unfortunately for him that brings me back, the reward is immediate death. I cannot stop until I have the blood of two or three humans in me, and I can think straight again and stop myself. You should thank your rats. They saved a human life—probably yours."

"I was just dessert," I commented.

He blushed. It was amazing—his face filled up with color like dawn spreading over the sky. "I apologize," he repeated. "*That* blood is richer. Goes further."

It was my turn to blush. I covered it up with immature blustering. "So if you were dead and stuff and you gave everything away, how come you get to hang out here with room service and everything?"

"I called my lawyer and told him there'd been a slight change in situation," said Ricari.

"So he knows about you."

"Yes."

"How many people know? Am I just really out of it?"

"I could count them on the hand of a three-fingered man," he said. "Including yourself."

"So—wait—" I waved the hand with the wine glass in it. "How do you live? If you hate killing? And nobody knows about you?"

"What I did to you," he mumbled. "Controlling with my mind. Usually it works. Usually they never remember anything."

"But I remember all of it. I do now anyway."

"With you I knew it wouldn't last, even as I was doing it—you did as I made you do, but you were still there, watching me, curiously, cautiously. You're different. I think it's because of what you do—what you've done. You make it your business to absorb knowledge without having to think about it." Ricari stared out the window. The moon was gone. "Usually my victims are asleep, drugged, or so weak of will that they would forget their mother's name if I told them to. One way or the other, they don't know what's happened, or they discount it altogether as preposterous."

"I almost did," I confessed. "I sometimes thought I was going crazy . . . I thought I'd made it up. But then . . . I know what I know. I believe in what I see."

"I wasn't sure whether you'd come," he said. "No. I was sure."

We sat in silence for a while and I ate bread and cheese and olives, whisking them down with chianti. I was getting kind of drunk, but things seemed to make more sense that way. He chewed his lower lip, and I noticed that his lips were slightly chapped, and a very faint mist of stubble had begun to darken his chin and his jaw above the sideburns. *How odd*, I thought, *his hair grows, and he sloughs off his skin.*

"I have," he began after clearing his throat, "something to ask you, Ariane."

"Yeah?"

"Will *you* kill me?"

"What?"

"End my life. I beg you. You are a woman of science. Death comes to you naturally. Surely you do not wish such an abomination to go on? Or think of it humanely. I want to die so much. Would you do no less for any stray cat, who cannot kill itself?" He leaned forward in the chaise longue, his eyes bright and passionate.

"I—I can't," I protested. "No."

"Ariane." He grimaced, and I saw for the first time in that angelic face, the bright sharp fangs, no longer than usual cuspids but very sharp, narrower than a human's teeth. The lower jaw had them too, but blunter, and a sleek little recess where the upper fangs rested, so as not to pierce the gum. Like an animal's fangs. "I am older than this building where we sit. I still talk of pianofortes and I clasped the hand of Wollstonecraft. Will you *end* this for me?"

"Oh, my God," I said softly. "No. Absolutely not. Absolutely not!"

"Why?"

"I don't believe you for one thing!" I jumped up out of the stiff little chair where I had been sitting opposite him. "How do I even know you're telling the truth? I'm drunk! You might just be some Polk Street hustler with a cheesy accent and a fucked-up sense of humor! You're not a hundred years old! I'm not going to kill you!"

"I will prove it," he said.

He stood up, and grabbing a London Fog raincoat from another stiff chair, slipped it on. He found some black wing tips under the secretary and stepped into them. He was perhaps my height, less weight than I for sure, his movements almost too quick to see. "Come with me," he said agitatedly. "Since you didn't deign to take off your coat, come with me downstairs."

I followed him out of the room and to the elevator. High spots of color dotted his cheeks above the sideburns. "By profession," he said as we got into the elevator and pulled the door closed, "I was a translator, in Paris, in 1812. I translated Italian into French, and Italian into English, and back again. Some of my works still exist."

He burst out of the elevator into the lobby and past the front-desk man, who barely glanced up from the crossword puzzle, and I trailed meekly after him, half lost in a cloud of wine. Ricari flung open the door to the bookstore so hard it stood open, its hinges bent, and sat down in one of the booky corridors, trailing his fingernails across the spines of old, mildewy antique books. I came to rest beside him.

After some minutes of heated perusing, he pulled from the shelf above us a small blue book, the spine ribbed in the old fashion, the pages edged in dulled gilt. "I found this last night," he said with a tight, defeatist pleasure. "If I could have killed myself then, I would have."

I stroked my way to the title page. *Elementary Treatise on Nicomanichean Morality, by Leonardo Gallimassi, translated by O. Ricari.* It was an eighth printing, 1888. I looked at him without comprehension. "This is not proof," I said.

He stared at me with pure blank exasperation. "Damned girl," he swore softly under his breath, and grabbed my wrist gently and pulled me from the bookstore through the shell-shocked door. We were going back into the hotel, he blazing with furious grace and me shambling after, bedazzled by his prettiness. Fake or not, I was beginning to think I would follow him over a cliff.

Back in Suite 900 he tore off the London Fog coat, and paced the room, deep in thought. I sank back into my chair and began mechanically eating olives. At last he came to a halt in front of me and began to unbutton his sleeve, rolling it back over his forearm.

His skin was the same delicate whiteness all over,

the veins standing bluely like rivers along the wrist and swelling into tributaries at the hollow of his elbow.

He seized the cheese knife and gashed his palm with it. We yelled out as one. Dark, viscous blood welled out of the wound and began to drip onto the parquet floor, like drops of molten chocolate. It was just not human blood.

And it was just not a human wound. Ricari stuffed the wound into his mouth and sucked at it, letting his saliva run down over his hand, then held it out to me. Almost visibly the wound was reducing in size and severity. The smaller it got, the faster it healed. "Can you do that?" he asked me saucily, drops of bright sweat standing out on his forehead. I looked into his eyes for a long moment, enjoying his expression of triumph, and when I looked at his hand again, the gash was merely a fat pink seam, pulsing as it closed the last gaps between the severed skin cells. Then it was a scar.

I looked at the drops of blood on the floor. They were black. I bent over to touch them; they were hardened, like disks of warm plastic, stuck fast to the wood inlay.

Ricari lay back onto the chaise longue, wiping his forehead with a handkerchief.

"You do feel pain," I murmured.

"I do. As much as you do." He was paler than before, and looked shaken.

I stood up then, and came over to the chaise longue. I sat beside him and touched his shoulder under the satin—he was very cool, not quite cold, but not warm—and then I touched his cheek. He was very smooth and soft, and there, cool too. "You didn't have to do that," I said, quite sobered up.

"Obviously I did." He looked up at me wearily. "It worked, right? You believe me now?"

"Yes." Under my fingertips his skin seemed to vibrate. "I will make you a deal," I said.

"Yes?"

"Let me know you," I said. "Study you. Hear your story. Then I'll . . . I'll do the humane thing."

He took my hands between his, and kissed my fingertips. "All right," he said. "Promise me."

"I promise," I said. "You promise you'll let me know you first, though. I must . . . lay you to rest properly. You can live on in other ways."

He nodded, closing his eyes.

Chapter Three

"I sleep during the day," he said, "but I can go about in the day so long as I take care. Sunlight hurts my skin—burns me. I simply like night better. Not so many people about. I can conduct my business without looking so strange.

"You mustn't bother with any old superstitions. Very little hurts me. Only prolonged sunlight, immolation, being dismembered. Most don't make it as long as I. I avoid conflict. I try not to get dismembered or set on fire—perhaps a bad impulse, for it's allowed me to go on for this long. Most meet violent deaths before this point. Some go on longer. I am reaching the end of what I can stand—I am probably already going mad.

"I like it when you have garlic on your breath—please eat garlic. I love its smell on your skin. It's good for your blood.

"I cannot eat; once I could, but I stopped a long time ago. It seemed wasteful—I who do not need to consume food, stealing food from the mouths of those who need it to survive. I do not care for the less delicate natural functions of the human body, and once I was rid of them, did not wish to have them back again. It is one of the few freedoms I enjoy in this form."

Ricari spoke easily and fluidly as we walked at midnight along the piers at the Marina. It was cold now, but the rains had stopped, and I had put on a long scarf and gloves and joined him on his stroll. The cold did not seem to affect him much, though he was bareheaded, wearing only the London Fog coat over some black dress pants and a turtleneck sweater. He gesticulated in the free Italian style as he walked and talked, and often turned to me with a knowing look that reminded me of the Italian grandmothers in New Orleans. He had come to meet me after going to an evening mass, and he was aglow.

"How long have you been in San Francisco?" I asked.

"Eh . . . fifteen years . . ."

"And before that?"

"Before that, New York City. Before that, Canton—Hong Kong now. Before that Cornwall. Before that—"

"Before that?"

"Berlin," he said reluctantly.

"When was that?"

"Nineteen-twenties," he said.

"That must have been interesting," I said.

"Yes," Ricari replied distantly.

Sensing a dead end, I switched the subject. "How long do you stay in a place before leaving it?"

"Oh, it depends. Anywhere from a year to twenty or thirty years. Before it was easier. Not so many photographic records and things to give away the fact that I still look like a youth." The lean boyish face pouted, odd against the weary pattern of his speech. "I am coming up on my time to leave this place—I died, after all, and was buried. If that poor undertaker sees me passing on the street, he'll likely lose his mind and be locked up. That is where you come in."

"Yeah, yeah," I said impatiently.

He smiled at me so sweetly that I put my head against his shoulder. He tensed at the contact and I removed myself, but then he took my hand impulsively, pulling off the glove and touching the bare flesh. His dry smooth skin tingled against mine, as if trying to make it a part of him. I shivered. "Thank you, Ariane, for your promise," he said.

"Oh," I said, embarrased, "no."

He pulled my glove back on, adjusting the fingers, and we walked along. The great black expanse of the Presidio was over the rise, looming up like something out of Joseph Conrad. "What makes you think I won't betray you?" I asked.

"Betray me? You cannot."

"No?"

"Who would believe you? And if they did believe you, I'd kill you. And then 'they' would kill me. That would suit everyone just fine. But I don't believe that is what you want, Ariane."

I said nothing.

"You will not betray me," Ricari said, pleased.

I got cold, and we left. Ricari adored my car. He was terrified of them, and didn't know how to drive, but he was as thrilled as a kid on a roller-coaster to be my passenger. He was fascinated by my CD player and piles of discs. "It's completely different from being in a taxi cab," he enthused. "I hate taxi cabs. I can walk faster than half of them can drive, what with them wanting to screw you for fares. What is this music— what is New Order? They sound very fascist."

"They are," I said, amused. "They aren't. They're just a pop band."

"Oh, I don't like pop music at all."

"What do you like?"

Ricari frowned slightly. "I like . . . tortured Russian composers," he decided. "And Debussy."

"Is there any music from the twentieth century that you like?" I asked.

"I don't know. I suppose I like the Beatles. I don't hate them. They're the only pop band whose name I can remember."

"I have Beatles," I offered.

"No, no, I don't want to hear them. There is too much music. Let us listen to silence, and car noise."

"I have Prokofiev at home," I said.

"Yes! I like that!"

We went to a late-night cafe and I had a mocha to keep me awake for the rest of the night, and then I drove him to my apartment. It was in disarray—I hadn't thought to clean it in the week or so that I had had Ricari in my life. I hadn't planned to bring him over, but I'd blabbed about Prokofiev, and I needed another sweater if we were going to be outside.

Ricari seemed to enjoy the mess. He moved quickly about the room, jumping between piles of cast-off cardigans and back issues of *Pathogenesis Journal,* the tails of his coat flying out behind him. He came to rest on my chair, peering out from under his flyaway bangs.

I put on Prokofiev, and water for tea to warm me.

"Ariane," he said, covering his cheek with his hand, "come here."

I approached him.

He took my face between his hands and gazed into my eyes. "I'm hungry," he whispered.

I pulled off my gray sweater and pulled up the sleeve of my shirt, exposing my wrist. The green veins sighed under the winter-paled, fine skin. Ricari looked at the wrist, and then he looked at me.

"Go ahead," I urged.

He took a few hesistant breaths, then lay his mouth against the skin of my wrist. His lips were icy cold and the inside of his mouth, when he opened it, chilled me where it struck. At first he only breathed against the skin, then kissed it, openmouthed, as you would kiss the lips of a lover. I closed my eyes.

The teeth hit me, plunging in between tendons, piercing me deeply. I gasped and staggered, and he pulled me firmly into him, bending my arm so that I had it around him and he could sip at the hot blood welling from the puncture wound. It would not be much—a puncture wound from a bite like that doesn't bleed until it's pressured. But then he sucked, turning the bites inside out, and how the fluid rushed from me into his mouth!

Then it was over. He was settling me back upon my couch; pressing his thumb, suddenly very hot, against the bite in the soft part of my wrist. I had fallen, I guess. I'd had my eyes closed, and so lost any kind of visual cue that I was losing consciousness. My body felt swollen with pleasure. Ricari kissed my forehead with blood-warm, blood-damp lips. I opened my eyes and looked up at him. He was radiant, his flesh a deep human rose, mouth red as berries. "Yes?" he said.

I managed a tired "Hm."

He got up and fixed the tea for me, and brought it to me, watching intently as I sipped at it while holding my wrist at a strange angle. "Look at it," he urged me.

I set down the mug and dared to peek at the wound. I am not a fan of puncture wounds—they are pretty gruesome, as opposed to the clean stern beauty of a cut. But there was only a trace of it there—some oozy plasma traces, rapidly hardening to a crust between the two cords of my tendons. "What?" I said. "How does that work?"

"I can heal you too," Ricari said. "My bite leaves no trace, if I taste. My saliva heals any small wound completely. You will, I'm afraid, have a slight scar."

It still hurt, but only vaguely now. I lay back and sipped my tea, praying it would replace my lost fluids. I had never given blood for blood banks, having indulged in unsafe sex with men of dubious heterosexuality in the past five years, and I had no idea how much blood I could lose before passing out. Not much apparently. Ricari stroked my forehead gently with his fingertips, the edges of his lethal claws lightly brushing my hair. Like an Irishman after too much ale, he began to speak to me in an intimate tone about himself.

"It's that you remind me of my sister, Elena. She was the eldest sister, with three sisters between us, but we were closest to one another. My mother was dusky, a southern woman, and some of the children turned out darker-skinned than others. Elena was one. She was dusky and had red hair, like you. Oh, she was beautifully tall, and strong-willed, and she wanted to take over my father's estate when he died, but since I was the only son, it was going to go to me. I didn't want it. I was irresponsible, I cared nothing about sheep or grapes or olives, and I still don't care anything about money. I wanted to lie around in the sun and listen to my sisters singing and paint and make up songs in Greek. Oh, don't get the impression that Elena was all bookkeeping and looking after servants and doling out responsibilities. She was also quite wild. It was the red hair—that Gallic influence—and she was the eldest, and she was very proud, and she felt slighted by my father, who was dense and very stern and always did what was right. Elena encouraged me to be the way I was, she thought I was pretty, I was her little darling, she had always been the one to carry me when I was a baby."

"What happened to her?" I asked Ricari softly.

He sighed. "Oh, dead, long, long ago. I think she married and took the estate, and she didn't love the man she married, of course. I broke my father's heart, you know. I ran away rather than be a man and take the estate and run the vineyards. I ran away to Geneva to be with the Shelleys."

"Did you get there?"

"Oh, I did, but I was too late. There was no news media in those days to keep one updated on which celebrities were where. I fell in with the other admirers, and we 'hung out' as you say, on the shore of the lake, and encouraged each other's childishness." Ricari looked down at me fading on the couch. "I shall leave you now. You should sleep. The sun will come soon."

"Not that soon," I insisted, rising off the couch. This time the visual warnings were right there—the world divided into chips of color and form—and I sank back onto the couch, my head resting on my green cardigan. I was so tired.

"Yes, soon. I will leave. It's stopped raining. I won't melt." He leant over and pressed his warm cheek against me—he was warmer than me now, his cheek glowing bright. His stubble was a pleasing texture. "Sleep. Sleep, little one."

"You're littler than me," I mumbled, and he sank away into the sweet dull depths of my sleep, and I could watch as he disappeared into the rising dark. I felt my arm slip off the couch and dangle, but I had no strength to lift it and set it to rights.

It had been less than forty-eight hours since I'd seen Ricari last, and he had supped on the blood from my wrist, but it didn't seem like enough and I wanted him to have more of me. I thought to myself that he must be terribly hungry now, poor moral creature, and it would be a whole night and day and night before he could attend Mass again. I thought of him in the church, pinching off his prayers with the words that must have been in his mouth like taste buds by now, and I wanted to arrive at Mass in a flowing white dress, and for him to ravage me upon the altar. Crimson spots on the white lace. Jesus Christ would weep to see his little girl so defiled.

I wasn't a Catholic and I never had been. My mother's family had been Catholics, that New Orleans brand of Catholic, weaving habit and superstition into a cloak that barred the cold wind of agnosticism, and kept my mother and her sister, Wilemina, out. My aunt was too skeptical for religion and my mother, too unstable.

I never knew my mother; she ran away weeks after I was born and nobody knew what had become of her. My Aunt Willie had her theories, sacks full of them— Mother in San Francisco, hippie consort of Hell's Angels, and dying alone by the side of the road gasping for junk and pills; Mother in the Southwest desert, schizophrenic, looking for angels and devils in the windswept mesas, finally dying alone of thirst by the side of Route 66; Mother, most likely, still in N.O., haunting the dank caverns where my father was last seen, trapped into a life of white slavery in one of the innumerable rotting hotels, dying alone and confused, schizophrenic, gasping for junk and pills.

I couldn't confess to Aunt Willie that all those prospects seemed hopelessly romantic to me, orphan mulatto child, bereft of religion and chemical releases. Aunt Willie, so patrician and practical and academic, caring only for the *New Yorker* and PTA meetings and dusty 78's of the Haskins Vocal Group, told stories designed to disgust and straighten me out. In a lot of ways they worked. I didn't so much blossom as shoot up like a brainy weed, a self-disciplined schoolgirl, a science freak who was allowed to dissect grasshoppers on the dinner table. I didn't touch drugs or alcohol or men until I left home and went to college.

At Tulane, when I was sixteen, I "went bad," as they

say. I buzzed my barbecue curls down to a fuzz, dyed what was left poison-green, memorized the Dead Kennedys album *Frankenchrist,* started drinking whiskey and dropping acid. I was always alone. People thought I was awfully strange. I found myself strange as well— too young to be in college, but able to instantly transform myself into the freak I always felt myself inside. And on top of that, having a lineage that included madwomen and slick, untrustworthy pimps who slouched, Tom Waits style, along the swinging doors of N.O. dives—I was afraid of myself.

I had never even seen a photograph of my father. Aunt Willie told me that none existed. My father, she'd said, was an unwholesome specter, unphotographable as swamp mist, vague, flaky, yellow of skin and of character. My mother had fallen into his seduction as inevitably as dinosaurs fell into the La Brea Tar Pits. She had played around with bennies and reefers before she met him, and in the three weeks that they knew each other, he gave her smack, crabs, and motherhood, and vanished into the alleyways that spawned him. My mother dully endured the pregnancy in Willie's parlor, staring out the window to the street below, which was wilting with kudzu, then coughed me out painfully, pulled out her episiotomy stitches, and blew town in the middle of the night.

Aunt Willie never really minded having me. She was unmarried, homely, and uninterested in hearts or flowers; she mainly tended to vegetables, math, and little inquisitive minds. She told me on a spring break before I went to Stanford that she had enjoyed molding me. "You were a pleasure," she said, her teeth still white in the putty-gray of her face. Cancer had claimed her hair and mobility, but she still did the *New York Times* crossword puzzle every day. "You weren't a little girlie, all Barbies and tea sets. You brought home dead birds and asked me why they went stiff, and when you had that compound fracture—remember?—you didn't cry. You looked at the bone sticking out and asked me why you couldn't see the marrow."

That was just how Aunt Willie was. She died that Christmas. I didn't go to the funeral—I had to study.

The semester was as dead as ancient Greek.

I sat alone in the room that was supposed to be my office and wasn't. When Ricari came and slaughtered the rats, all my things were moved down the hall, to a fallow room, and set up exactly the way they had been before. That was Dr. John's doing. He knew nothing of bereavement. I was bereft of the tiny crawling and snuffling life of my pet lab rats and of the sanctity of the space where Ricari had tasted me. He had pulled out of me not the concentrated cells and tissues of my painful month, but the very essence of who I was, who I had been, my lost potential to be, to create. I couldn't write, I couldn't read, I couldn't even doodle.

I had to get out of there.

I drove for a while, listening to the pop music Ricari despised. Joy Division, David Byrne, Hüsker Dü; nothing cheerful or plaintive, but the roughest voices, the thickest rhythms. I knew where Ricari was. Was he asleep during these last moist hours of the day, or was he awake, watching California sink into mists? How terrible to never feel the hot Vitamin D of the sunlight penetrating your skin, or the smooth gouts of a latté in your stomach. But he had the blood. He had power; he could divine the workings of my mind, and change them, and he could take a bullet and stop it, and vomit it up later for inspection. I needed to see him and speak to him, reassure myself once again that he was real.

But I was too shy to actually come round.

Was I? I was driving around Pacific Heights now, the smooth curve between it and the sickly throbbing heart of the City, the blazing nexus of restaurants and shops and crime and leopard skin that was Chinatown, North Beach, Tenderloin, Nob Hill. Night was getting there. The sky was already blue rather than gray. Friday night—the streets were clogged. I stole a parking space from a fish van outside Go Ran Chow Market, and began doggedly walking toward the Saskatchewan.

The old man at the desk looked up at me rather sternly. "Yes? Can I help you, young lady?"

He made me feel like some grungy kid. I looked like some grungy kid—jeans and dirty hiking boots, and a sweater with holes between the knittings, hooking my thumbs agitatedly through the holes in the sleeves of my winter coat. "I was—" My voice croaked out, destroyed from lack of use. I hadn't spoken in two days and I'd smoked six packs of cigarettes. "I was wondering if you could buzz Suite 900 for me, and see if he's in."

The desk clerk eyed me for a second, then slowly leant over and tapped a plastic phone console, which, though outdated by about ten years, was startlingly modern in the dull brown Victoriana. He held the phone receiver to his face. "Someone here to see you," the old man said after a time.

A pause.

"He don't want to be disturbed," came the old man's reply. He began to replace the receiver on its cradle.

"Wait! Tell him it's Ariane. Ariane come to see him."

He arched one white brow, then repeated, "She says she's named Ariane."

Another pause. I rubbed NCIT mud off the toe of one boot onto the back of my jean leg. There was no way I could face going home and being alone with the television and my tea and rolling papers and the lonely sound of rain on the windows.

At last the old man hung up the phone and settled

back down to his magazine. Without looking at me he said, "Go on up."

I praised whoever, and ran for the elevator.

The door to 900 was unlocked again, and I came in quietly and shut the door as softly as I could. I turned the lock and slipped the chain bolt together, whisking silently along its carriage like the piston of an arcane train.

Ricari was not in the front room, and I had to walk along the wall to the inside room, intoning softly "Ricari?" beginning to doubt that he actually was there. He had become invisible. I was sure he had heard of my coming up, and slipped out one of the windows, dropping soundlessly and weightlessly to the street below, startling a bevy of Filipino tourists.

But no, he was in the back, in the bedroom, in bed, wrapped in a heavy gray silk robe, his hair finger-combed only, and his face thin and white. "It's you, is it?" he said. He looked ill and sad.

"Yeah," I said, embarrassed.

"You look filthy," he commented.

"I sort of am. Muddy out there. Cold too."

"Why don't you wash and get into bed with me," he said coldly, calmly. "There is a bath through there."

How intriguing. I moved into the bathroom and shut the door. White light bounced cruelly off the polished white tiles. I thought about John as I began unlacing my boots and shedding layers of sweaters and T-shirts. He hadn't called me, and I hadn't expected him to. John was terrible on the phone—inarticulate and heavily accented, and not at all filled with comforting pronouncements of love or social interest. He was a letter writer if anything, and I checked my box every day, waiting for his fat dull envelopes filled with scathing anecdotes about the food and the other professors. Was what I was doing immoral in any way? Was I betraying the special trust that we shared as lovers by bathing in the vampire's hotel room, and planning on getting into bed with him, and attempting to warm my cold toes against his inhuman body? At any time the vampire could kill me, I thought as I stepped into a hot shower and wet my hair; at any time Ricari could rescind his agreement and snack on me, leaving smears of me across the white froth of bedsheets, and the old man downstairs, probably his blood-bound ghoul, hypnotized to do his bidding, would bundle me up in the sheets and sell me to the organ banks.

I washed myself with hotel soap, dried off, and bound myself with a hotel-issue white terry-cloth robe, satisfyingly rough and impersonal, and walked back into the bedroom. It was dark in there, lit only by ambient street light and the shining whiteness of Ricari's face and the translucency of his eyes. I knelt on the bed, and he parted the covers for me.

We lay alongside each other. Ricari was wide awake, but languorous. He stretched out one spidery arm vertically along the pillowcase, the same paleness of his skin; only the pillowcase lacked the Nile of veins that merged up his gray silk sleeve. I touched his throat experimentally. He was very cold to the touch. No toe-warming here.

"What do you want?" he demanded.

"I just wanted to see you," I explained.

He sighed. "Why," he said.

"What have you been doing?"

"Nothing at all," he said with a sigh. "Reading poetry journals. Talking to vagrants in the park. To my lawyer, who may be a vagrant in the park soon enough. He's going to give up law as soon as I'm taken care of."

"Have you fed?"

"No. I have no interest." As he said this his jaw tensed, and a colorless vein rose at his temple.

"Are you going to stay in bed tonight then?" I asked.

"That was my plan," he said.

"Why do you want to die so badly?"

"Can't you imagine? How dull it is to be me! Nothing is new to me. It's all the same. Paris; Topeka, Kansas; Johannesburg—it's all the same, human selfishness and greed and stupidity. Yes, I'm staying in bed today, and not getting out of it."

"You're so filled with self-pity." I smiled. "Come on. Get up. Put on sexy clothes and we'll go out, see the town."

"I've seen it."

"Do you want me?"

The quick shock of what I'd said traveled through both of us, like a shared earth tremor. It came out of me so naturally, I wasn't sure afterwards how I'd meant it. He stared at me for a long while. His face was very cleanly shaven and smooth, the skin texture like powdered velvet, and he looked a few years older, his eyes prominent. He hadn't had blood since the last time, and he aged, ever so slightly, when he hadn't had the blood to keep him plump and keep his hair and skin lively.

"You're mad," he said finally.

"No," I said. "I offer myself. I'm not selfish. I'm something other than that human greed and stupidity. I want to make you happy. I want to make you alive."

"No," he said. "This was not our agreement."

"It doesn't have to be. I would do no less for any stray cat."

He seemed to crumple, and he turned his face away and buried it in the pillowcase. I wanted him so badly then. The tensing of his wrists was like a religion to me, the curl of his fingers and his claws piercing the smooth cotton and tearing the fibers across, and the visible tension of his back like an African sculpture. How I wanted him. I touched the narrow stretch of tense gray silk with my fingertips.

He rose half up and picked up a small scalpel from

the table beside the bed, where it had rested naturally, like a travel alarm or a bottle of pills or a set of earplugs. I lay back and closed my eyes. "No, watch me," he breathed, "see what you're getting yourself into." So I watched him bare my arm above the elbow, to the fat reservoir in the crook of my arm. He kissed and licked and sucked the spot, making it tender and sensitive, and making the pinkness rush to the surface. He set his lips and drew the scalpel across the vein with a quick expert stroke, opening an incision perhaps two millimeters wide. It didn't hurt until it was long over and the hot trickle ran out and caught in the spikes of terry cloth.

He clamped his mouth on the wound and drank the blood into his mouth. I moaned out loud, begging him for something wordlessly, meaninglessly. He sighed like a baby at the breast, moving closer to me, embracing me, snuggling his head against my rib cage, resting as he drank with slow calm swallows. Almost immediately joy rushed into me from my arm, quite warm and cold at the same time, as if the blood lost was replaced with pleasure. The longer he drank, the intenser the pleasure became, until he was gripping my body tightly with one knee and one arm, and I convulsed slightly beneath him, my disassociated cunt seizing up and shuddering down, gathering itself up in a great tensile knot and striking loose.

And he was done. He lifted his face with a great breath. His mouth was lipsticked in the bright vital orange-red that is oxygenated blood, and traces of it daubed his chin and the tip of his slightly upturned nose. He looked a good three or four years younger than he had when I came into the room, and his face was quite red, shading to a pale human tone. He smiled and licked his lips. Together we brought my arm up and rested my wrist against my shoulder.

"I don't understand," I murmured, dizzy from the orgasm.

"I do," he said. "I know why you came tonight."

"Do you?"

I slid my leg between his knees.

To my surprise, he frowned and moved away, sliding to the edge of the bed and hooking his coltish legs over the side. "Did I make a pun? Sorry, I didn't mean to. Yes, let's do go out," he decided, informing me over his shoulder. He wiped his nose. "You must change, though. I won't go anywhere with you dressed like a lumberjack. Do you want new clothes? I could buy you new clothes."

The gash in my arm soon faded to a throbbing, clean incision. We put a Band-Aid on it. He dressed behind a paper screen and we went out.

He insisted on buying me something to wear, but the only places open were the most expensive shops in Union Square. So he bought me a rich velvety long dress of a green-blue that I would have never chosen for myself, and black suede shoes, paying for it with a credit card he handed over with a distracted aplomb. I didn't want to think about how much it cost. Ricari nearly ran out the door without the card, though, and he took a great deal of time signing the receipt, fiddling with the cheap plastic pen as if doubting his ability to write with it.

Ricari then proceeded to take me to dinner at a tiny restaurant where we had to linger at the bar for two hours before we could be seated; and the headwaiter gave Ricari a look of absolute poison when Ricari refused to order anything. He bought me soup, appetizers of delicate calamari, vegetables, fish and rice, tiramisu, and coffee, and enjoyed my swaying determination to get through such a meal after having had three vodka martinis.

After that, he dragged me bodily to a café-bar, and

ordered me cocktails of evil-tasting cinnamon liqueur.
"You eat and drink well," he commented, nearly the
first words he'd said since we left the Saskatchewan.

"I guess," I said, my head lolling upon the red vinyl
booth cushions. I had great difficulty lighting a cigarette, which I needed intensely.

"You are not like a modern girl at all."

"How so?"

"You are not tall. You are neither grossly fat, nor
bony like a peasant. Your face has soft angles."

I leaned back and took off my new shoe, the heel of
it already worn down and the suede soaked through
with rain and sweat. "You have a lot of money," I said.

"It was all in banks in Hong Kong. I gave almost all
of it away. I intend to give the rest away to you." He
placed his hand gently over my mouth to stifle my
protests. "No, it is settled. You agreed. Now. How shall
it be done?"

"How do you want it to be done?"

In the red smoky light of the bar his smooth boyish
skin was luminous. He gazed away into space as if
contemplating which pair of shoes to wear to the dance.
"I don't know. The least painful way would be to sever
my head."

"Mmm-mm, Ricari."

"No, really. My body will not be a burden. It will
quickly dissociate itself. You could bury me in your
backyard. No bones will be found. It is quicker, more
humane, than burning me. That, however, would be
total, and you would not have to deal with the problem
of how to sever my head completely with one blow—if
you missed I would not die—"

"No. I don't want to talk about this."

"You must." He frowned at me.

I resisted mutely, swaying my head back and forth. I
reached for my cigarette, upsetting my tiny cocktail glass.
It appeared between Ricari's finger and thumb—he caught

it faster than my eyes could follow. Not noticing that
he'd done anything wondrous, he set it back upon the
table almost out of my reach, touching the sticky rim
with fascination. I licked my lips, wondering if he
could feel the traces of my tongue and mouth when I
did this. Lost in thought, I stroked my belly and my
breast through the fabric of the dress. Ricari watched
me. "How would you like to do it?" he asked me.

"I guess I'll burn you," I said distantly.

"That is for the best. I will only hurt for a little
while."

"Incinerator at school."

"Yes . . ." he agreed.

"Did you ever dance the quadrille?"

"Many times," he smiled.

"Orfeo," I said to myself.

He caught up my wrist where the two scars had
faded as if years marked them, and pressed it against
his mouth. He kissed up my arm until he reached my
sleeve, pressed his cheek against the velvet. "You smell
of sin. My darling."

"I want you to take me home," I said.

"Are you tired?"

"I'm wasted." I tasted the sticky-sweet dryness of
my palate, and laughed. "I love you."

"You cannot." He laughed too, and rose from the
red vinyl booth.

I sat there and watched him stand and stretch his
lilylike body, arms reaching out under the white satin,
satin stretching across his tiny tight belly, and satin
dropping to a voluptuous mass at his waist where it
tucked into his black trousers. He saw I had not moved,
and he slid back into the booth and tugged gently at
my shoulder.

The cocktail waitress, who had been watching us all
night as she made her rounds, returned to our table.
"Your check?" she offered, slipping a black plastic tray

61

onto the table next to my half-full thimble of Gold-schlager.

Ricari accepted the ticket, and brought out his card again. As he handed it to her, she caught sight of his hands. "You have really cool hands," she remarked, her icy reserve evaporating in wonder; then she took a good long look at the joints and the claws, stretching out impossibly, more the joints of the wings of a bat than a plump ordinary man's hand, and I saw her face lock into a blank incomprehension. She glanced up at Ricari's eyes in a slight panic.

Ricari rose again and took her by the arms, smiling into her face; she was taller than he by many inches and stiletto heels, and he had to look up to fix her with his eyes. I felt the emanations of his presence radiate outward like heat, until it roared through my head and I could barely see; and I *heard* him, heard him say to her sotto voce, "Completely ordinary." But his lips never moved. Or perhaps I was drunk and I never caught an after-image of his mouth. I felt sick. I slumped in the red booth and closed my eyes.

The cocktail waitress was at another table, bending down in her tight black satin chamseong, a beautiful serving mannequin again. Ricari was pulling me from the booth. "Come on, sweetheart," he said, "let's go now. Now, please."

I dimly remember a taxi; Ricari bending in and saying something to a driver; my building presenting itself from the mists, walking inside without paying anything to the taxi driver and no hassle. I don't remember taking off the dress and shoes and getting into bed, but I was there, alone, queasy, the room spinning as the gray dawn rose again.

Chapter Four

"Hi, honey."

"Merry Christmas and all that."

"Thanks."

"How are you? What time's it there?"

"Mmmmmmmm. Um, it's um, eleven-twenty."

"I thought I'd call now—I figured you'd be awake."

"I'm sleeping in today."

"I wish I could." Transatlantic clicking—crystal-clear fiber optics my ass. *"I'm at Mum's house. It's snowing. You were right."*

"Wearing your boots?"

"Yeah." He laughed, and there was more silence, more clicking. *"How are you?"*

"I'm kind of unhappy."

"Yeah? Miss me?"

"Yeah. Yeah, a lot."

"I think about you all the time."

"Yeah," I said.

"Doing anything later?"

"I'm just gonna sleep. I've got a pot hangover."

"Now, don't go to the dogs now I'm away, right?"

"I've been to the dogs for years, hon. I do miss you."

"I, er, couldn't think of a present for you, I'm sorry. Is there anything that you want? I could pop it into the post on Tuesday—"

"No, don't worry about it. I don't need anything. I'm glad to hear from you."

Silence. *"I ought to go, it's Mum's phone, and there are relatives calling in all the time. I had to wrestle the phone away from her. I love you, though, darling, don't forget that. I love you and I think about you every single day. I'll be home soon."*

"It's all right, John. Take care of yourself."

"You too," he said. *"Don't smoke too much dope."*

"Okay. Don't drink too much."

I rolled over and turned the ringer off the phone.

The suite in the Saskatchewan glowed with candles. Ricari moved among them, touching his fingertips to the bright ends of the flames. Blisters rose upon the skin and were rapidly reabsorbed into the lines. "Imagine," he said, "having the same fingerprints for two hundred years. You would think they would have worn off by now."

"Come lie down with me," I said impotently.

He ignored me. He had had a haircut, and the clipped strands lay smoothly along his head, tucked behind his wide ears, like those of a young listening rabbit. He had a new shirt too, black, crisp, as if it had never come off its cardboard skeleton.

"How did you become a vampire?" I asked.

"The same as any vampire does," he said.

"Who made you?"

"Women," he said.

"Which women?"

He sighed and looked over his shoulder at me. His flesh was bright and hot and smooth today, though he hadn't tasted any of my blood in a long time. "Two women," he explained. "A noblewoman and her lover. Maria and Georgina. Polish, one of them, the other Swiss . . . or French . . . I don't remember. They took me in when I had no money and I was very hungry and just short of selling my body on the streets. I was their pet, their servant. I had no idea what they were at the time. They killed stacks of men—only men for them. They were lesbians, but they enjoyed young men, like myself. At first they had the intention of fattening me up and killing me like a goose for the foie gras, but they liked my poems, and my paintings—Georgina came upon me one day painting a portait of Maria, which she thought was beautiful, and then I was made a permanent guest in their house."

"Where was this?"

"Paris."

"Two unmarried women together in a house—"

"Not uncommon, not in 1813. It was assumed by those who may have minded that they were spinsters sharing the space—Maria was very rich anyway and no one cared—and almost everyone knew about them. They made no show of hiding it from anyone. Such things were far more ordinary then—women kissing in the parlor, stroking, making love. No one thought twice about it if they were rich—who was hurt by it? And I was their plaything. Little Italian boy from the country. *Trés au courant.* I fell in love with Georgina, and she was fond of me as a companion."

"You say that so coldly."

"I will never forgive them," he said vehemently.

"Have you never enjoyed yourself for what you are?"

He tightened his lips over his teeth. "Every monster enjoys his brutality now and again," he surmised. "That does not erase the horror of it—and every monster lives an eternity of horror for his crimes. I will not forgive Georgina for her impulsiveness—nor Maria for giving in to her—nor the decadence of the times for thinking it was a witty idea. Together they made me. Together they brought me up as a young monster, sheltered me, taught me their ways."

"Did you know they were going to do it before-hand?"

Here he paused, letting the candle wax drip over the hand that held one of the tapers, not feeling the heat burn its way into him. "I don't remember," he said. "I . . . think . . . not." He turned and looked at me sprawled on his chaise longue, drawing sonorous clouds of smoke over my tongue into my lungs. "I don't think I would have stopped them. That was not how I was then. I too thought it was a witty idea— Romantic and strange—I would become what Lord Byron only fantasized of being—a true monster, consumed by darkness, laughing in the face of gods and devils. I did not much change for a long while after that. I just played the coquette to men and ladies and killed them for their blood, rather than sleeping with them or painting their portraits or writing them love sonnets, for the benefit of their coin or a place to sleep and a hot meal."

"You were such a punk."

Ricari smiled sheepishly. "I was a fool," he said, "and a murderer."

"What happened to Maria and Georgina?"

Ricari set down the melted spike of candle and began pulling the wax from his skin. "Maria was old and mad," he replied. "She was not jealous of me, for I was only a man, but another woman came in between them. A mortal woman. Maria killed her in a rage, and Georgina left, she ran away alone, I don't know where, to this day I don't know where. Maria killed all the ser-

66

vants, made me take her blood, and sat in the fireplace where we used to turn lambs on the spit, calm as you please, her skirts bursting up like onionskin. On fire. I couldn't watch. I ran away too, and hid. They boarded up the house where we had lived."

"Is it still there?"

"Oh, God, no, paved over long ago."

"Were they beautiful?" I asked.

"The women?"

"Describe them to me," I said. I pulled out my bag of tobacco, and the box where I kept my grass, and began twisting the strands together on a translucent paper.

"Maria was very lovely—regal-looking, rich blond hair and white, round, soft shoulders. She must have been a hundred years old when I came into her house, and she looked perhaps thirty. She would not tell me who made her—it was a terrible secret. Also she would not tell me where her money came from, since she had never, in anyone's memory, been married.

"Georgie"—he said it in the French manner, all Zh's—"Georgie was like a beautiful witch. She was tall, tall for those days anyway, taller than I was, and very thin, like a wraith. She had wonderful eyes— black and sharp and always rolling like this." Ricari threw back his head and dramatically rolled his eyes around in the sockets like an indignant Valley Girl. We laughed. "She wore red too. Always red and white. She was the Pole, I remember now. She had a voracious appetite for women. Sometimes she brought home two or three, when Maria wasn't home, and the women would roll around in her bed, naked, groaning so loud I couldn't sleep. I slept in the servant's room outside the bedroom so that I could run in and warm their bed in winter."

"Did you sleep with them ever?"

That swell of color stained his cheeks again, and he

smiled like a schoolboy caught picking a daisy for his girl. "I was Georgina's lover," he said. "Maria did not like men at all. Georgie said I was hardly like a man, my skin was so soft. We were like brooms in a closet, the two of us, so thin."

"Did you love them?"

"I did . . . love them. Yes."

"And yet you can't forgive them," I reminded him.

"No. I cannot. I am angry at them, for doing this to me. That's the problem with vampires. They don't think. They forget that they aren't humans, and that their decisions will last so long as to be nearly permanent. Your momentary whims—your lonelinesses—they don't mean the same. You have to be serious, and compassionate, not just to your own needs, but to the needs of humankind."

"That's impossible," I said.

"It is not impossible. I do it."

"How old were you when you were made?"

"I'm not sure," he said. "I was raised on a farm where birthdays are not important. I was . . . twenty-two or twenty-three, I think."

"Come lie down with me," I said again.

"I heard you the first time."

"Don't you want me at all?"

"I need you, Ariane, that is all."

I laid my head on the arm of the chaise and put out the stub of my joint. Ricari lit a new candle, turning it this way and that, studying the flame until he tired of it too, and stabbed it into the pin at the center of one of the candlesticks. "Shit," I said.

"You're stoned," he said.

"Mmm. Yep."

"I remember that. Nice sensation."

"You've been stoned?"

"I've taken blood from many of the stoned. Not so much now. Seems to be passing out of vogue."

"Actually it's coming back in again."

"It's very late," he said, "or early, as the case may be."

"Happy New Year," I said.

"Why aren't you out with other people? Drinking and carousing?" Even nine floors up we'd heard the great roar when the clock struck twelve; the din had died down a long time ago.

"Not interested. New Year's boring. All the idiots feel like they have a real reason to celebrate. Being alive one more year, I guess. I don't buy it." Ricari's sleek dark form passed in and out of focus, blurred with the uneven light of the candles. His presence, though, was palpably strong, and in my leaden state it throbbed through my temples like a headache. "Anyway, there are a lot of drunk drivers out, and it's dangerous to drive."

"Why did you come then?"

"You know that," I said.

"I suppose," he said.

"You've been called beautiful before," I went on, "even when you were a little Italian love slave, haven't you? And even now that you're a monster as you so enjoy calling yourself? Haven't enough people told you that you're beautiful that you don't need to wonder why I came?" I opened my eyes; he stood very still, hands in his pockets. "I thought you might be lonely. Holiday season's hard for people alone. New Year's might be especially for you."

"I don't like 'em," he admitted. "Closest thing to a birthday I have."

"More'n two hundred candles on your birthday cake." An image of it crept into my mind—a fourteen-inch grocery-store party cake, being lit with a flame-thrower.

"Quite a cake," he said acidly.

I sat up dreamily to take off my cardigan, but without realizing it at first, I continued shedding clothes until I sat on the chaise in my black cotton exercise bra and blue silk panties. My skin at the thighs was so pale it inspired me. I could see the green vein tracing up into the twirl of reddish hairs slipping from the bunched elastic of the panties, the vein John had rather liked to run his finger along just before licking my labia and my clitoris, before jumping on me with boyish embraces. I meant to explain that perhaps I had undressed because of the excessive warmth of the room, that I hadn't meant to take off all my clothes, I wasn't coming onto Ricari like a horny high school nerd, hoping to wow him with the sight of my unshaven armpits or the appendix scar on my side; but all I managed to say was "Warm."

He looked at me, and sniffed a faint laugh. "You are lovely," he said.

"I didn't . . ." I shook my head.

"Come on, get into my bed, you'll get cold like that."

I stood up and went through to his dark bedroom and sank into the clean soft cotton sheets. Ricari followed after me with a candle, setting it onto the night table next to the scalpel and a heap of crumpled credit-card receipts. He sat next to me on the bed. "I have no idea what you think of me," I said. "I don't know why you don't kill me."

"I think that would please you too much," he said, still smiling. He moved the covers aside and touched the skin of my belly with his fingertips. I reached up and took his wrist, rubbing my thumb along its underside, like the tummy of a dolphin, and he arched his back, his fingers slipping down till they met the wisp of hair that came out of my panties to rest on my stomach.

"Kiss me," I pleaded.

He moved; hesitated; moved; then finally sat back and shook his head. "No. Go to sleep."

"Aw . . . you suck."

"Why then do you love me?" he said, cocking his head. I closed my eyes, and when I opened them again he was gone.

He came back before morning, smelling of second-hand alcohol, very disheveled. I had slept a little, slept a little of the marijuana off, and I bolted upright in bed to see him. The dawn was just beginning to violate the darkness between the slats of the blinds, and he was wearing a black shirt and ducked behind the screen, but I got a glimpse of his chin, streaked with a dark, definable substance.

"Ricari! What have you done?"

"None of your business," he said from behind the screen.

"Did you just kill people?"

"No."

"What then?"

"Nothing! Leave me be!"

I got up and went over to the screen. He knocked the screen over with his hand and stood there, shirtless, glowering, his face bright red. "You must leave now," he said crisply, authoritative, little sleek fellow with hard pink nipples, to me, mostly naked, shivering, barefoot on the parquet floor.

"Why?"

"I need my sleep, you little fool! Now go away." His speech was slurred.

"You've been boozing up," I said, and began to laugh.

"Not my fault. Out!"

"Why can't I stay? I won't molest you. I promise. I'll be a good kid."

"That is the least of my worries." He sighed heavily. "Please. Go quietly. I don't want to get angry with you.

You are so annoying sometimes. Go. Don't come again until I call you."

"I'm sorry," I said.

"Please," he said. The color in his face was subsiding, but he looked exhausted, his flat muscled belly rounded like a fed kitten's. His voice sounded very young, and deep, and tired.

I went and put on my clothes, gathered up my various things, and looked back into the room. He was swaddled in the gray robe again, lying his head upon the pillow. "I won't come until you call," I told him.

He did not respond. He seemed to be asleep already.

"You wanted to see me, Ariane?" Helen Troutman, the chair of the Department of Biology, let me into her office and closed the door. "You want a cup of coffee? I just made some."

"Oh, no, that's OK." I stood in the center of the room, hands in pockets.

"What's up?"

"I know this is really late notice, but . . . I, um . . . think I want to take the semester off. Emergency leave."

"What? Why? What's the matter?"

I was so close to just dissolving, so tired and bottled up, that I thought I was going to explode all over the modern carpets and the white bookshelves, but I just ran my fingers across my head. "I'm . . . I . . ."

"Jesus, sit down. What's the matter? Is it John?"

"No . . . well partially . . . I just think it's really time I took some time off. I've never even had a summer off in twelve years . . . I'm starting to . . . I'm showing the strain. I'm afraid I might get burnt out. I don't have any more ideas about my rats, I don't have any decent lesson plans, I just can't . . . face . . . another semester of lectures and labs. I just can't."

She rubbed her cheek with her palm, and took a solid

gulp of coffee. "Sometimes I wonder what's the matter with you driven types," she said. "You go like blazes until you finally crack. I for some reason thought—we all thought—you were going to keep up this insane pace forever. You are too hard on yourself, Ariane." Helen smiled at me. "It's your decision, of course. We can't force you to do anything. I for one think you should have taken some time off a long time ago. It's kind of bad timing, but we do have more than enough TAs to smooth over the cracks."

"I know. I'm sorry."

"Enough apologizing. It's OK. We don't want to lose you. Your kids will miss you."

"Yeah, I know."

"Take some time off. You can always come back. Keep in touch, OK? You all right for money?"

"I've got plenty. Thanks."

"Jesus Christ, take care of yourself. You're incredibly pale. And you've lost weight. Don't worry about it." She got up and put her arms around my shoulders briefly, in a strained, professorial intimacy. "I'll pass it along. OK? You should probably talk to Carole, you'll have to fill out some leave forms, but it shouldn't take too long."

I stumbled out of the office gratefully, spent the rest of the afternoon filling out forms. In the space where applicants were to fill out their reason(s) for leaving, I wrote in big letters, "GENERAL BURNOUT."

Ricari had me meet him in a trendy cafe south of Market. He was sitting patiently at the espresso bar with a humble cup of Americano in front of him, sketching on a napkin with a black felt-tipped pen, and he looked up at me as I came in and shook the rain off my hat.

I sat on a stool next to him. "Well," I said, "I did it."

"Did what?"

"Quit my job," I said.

"Why?" His voice broke it into two parts—one plainly interrogative, the other quizzical.

"Because," I said.

There was a long silence between us.

"I wanted to be with you as much as possible," I appended. "Before we die."

"We?" The same two-part voice.

"I don't think I can keep living without you," I said. "Knowing I killed you."

"You plan to kill yourself?"

"No," I said, "just stop living."

He did not quite laugh. "Don't say that," he said. "It is quite impossible to do. Don't commit suicide. Your soul is God's; only he has the power to take it away."

"Or you do, if you choose."

"What is your implication?"

I glanced up at the countergirl, her whitened skin and spiked dog collar, her fresh, delectable young face and rows of hoop earrings. In a mumble I ordered a double mocha, short on the milk. I knew it would make me sick, for I hadn't eaten all day. When she had turned to the steaming machine, I looked back at Orfeo and told him, "I want us to go away together. Make a new life. Make *me* a new life."

He scoffed. "Preposterous."

"Really? You're so consumed by loneliness—I need you as badly—I—this is my chance to become something else. I'm tired of my soul as you persist in calling it. I don't believe in souls. I only believe in life—life *forms*—"

"Too much *Star Trek*."

"No, shut up, listen."

"I will not listen. I thought you may have come to your senses in the interim. Instead I find you gibbering like a crackhead—"

"You may not love you, but I do!"

74

The countergirl peeked at my shout.

Ricari gave her an oily glance, and moved us to one of the tables near the back. The scent of wet wool and the fashionable perfume of the season overwhelmed me, and I felt a pang of nausea. Once we sat, he pinned me with his vast, liquid bright eyes, staring out of his thin face, and began to whisper to me like an angry mother. "You must rid yourself of this inane notion. I have no intention of repeating my mistakes—"

"You've made others?"

The espresso girl interrupted again. Cute or no, I wanted to knock her down and crush her windpipe under my hiking boot for breaking Ricari's gaze on me. She brought the mocha in a clear tall mug, and had my hat under her arm. "You dropped your hat," she explained. She kept looking at Ricari hungrily, interested in his black severe garb, his coconut skin, his Shelleyan sideburns. I stared at her until she went away.

Ricari stared into the separating depths of his coffee. "Once," he responded.

"You're kidding. I can't believe it. It must have been a long time ago."

"It was," he said. "Earlier this century. A long time ago."

"What happened? Was it really traumatic?"

He grunted and peaked his eyebrows. "Yes," he said, his mouth twisting with irony.

"What happened?"

"I let myself be seduced by loneliness and decadence again, and it exploded in my face. I made a terrible mistake even speaking to that person, let alone making him into a horrible creature like myself. I regret that more than any act in my life—and I won't do it again, so you can just forget about it."

"You have to tell me about this," I insisted.

"My goodness, you're sober," Ricari said.

"I'm frequently sober. Thank you very much."

"When did you last eat a decent meal?"

"When did you?"

He relaxed in his chair, smiling at me. "You want dinner? I feel generous."

"Why can't you just say you missed me?"

"All right," he sighed. "I missed you."

"Because I'm annoying?"

"Because, in your way, you are Christian."

"What!"

"You turn the other cheek. You give balm to lepers."

"You crack me up sometimes," I said.

I took three swallows of the mocha and we left.

After we went to a Chinese restaurant and I had set to a lovely chicken hot-pot and some clear soup, Ricari settled into his narrative mode, gesturing with a china cup of tea, which he held to keep his toothpick fingers warm. "I ended up in Berlin out of boredom, hearing that amazing things went on there. Until then—I had spent the First War in Switzerland, ignoring the whole thing. But Berlin was filled with fascinations—I particularly wanted theater, which I had been starved of for many years—not much theater in Switzerland. I certainly got what I came for, and then some. The place was lousy with Americans then, that was almost literally the first time I had ever met Americans and I thought they were enchanting really—"

"Is this other one an American?"

"Oh, no, German. I was merely prefacing. But I went to see a lot of Brechtian plays and performances, and became rather well known as a patron then. I had lots of money, which was not in very large supply, and I had stopped eating food, mainly I spent it on plays and buying rounds for other people. I get very popular that way.

"At any rate, there was one young man with a wide reputation for being the strangest fellow in Berlin—he was a great student of the Dadaists, and he seemed to glory in destroying things and horrifying little old ladies as they went to buy cheese. This interested me. Everyone else's decadence, as will happen after a while, gets rather boring and trite and you find out quickly how conservative they all really are. So I set out to meet this young man—not knowing that he had also set out to meet me.

"I went to one of his performances in a little theater—a garage really, with some wooden crates stacked on end to form a narrow little stage, and it was all quite dark, lit only by some tallow candles which smoked horribly and made everyone cough. There on the crates was this tall skinny man with very, very long hair—for that time anyway, even the homosexuals had their hair cut short—wearing a tattered tuxedo and a tin crown, playing an out-of-tune piano like the house was on fire. I wasn't very impressed, to tell you the truth, and afterwards I tried to leave. This young man jumped off the stage and ran and caught me by the shoulder, and said, 'Please—do stay—shall I put out the candles? I've wanted so much to meet you, Herr Ricari.' I swear on the Virgin that he said it exactly like that. He was not a beautiful creature or anything, but his passion impressed me, and so I stayed."

"What's his name?"

"Daniel," Ricari said with a little sigh. "Daniel Blum."

"And?"

"And . . . he insinuated himself into my life. He was a real sociopath—everyone did as he said because at any moment he might fly off the handle and start breaking things, only to come apologize later with a smile and a stein of lager and say he was only being artistic. He got me so turned around I didn't know day from night, and he discovered I was what I am, and he fell completely in love with me."

"Did you return the love?" I poured myself the last bitter dregs of the tea.

Ricari did not respond for a long time. "I shall not lie," he said. "Yes, I loved him completely, consumingly, we were as one. He acted out my most monstrous impulses. He never minded anything I did, he loved me totally, and he clouded my head so much that the thought of going a single day without him by my side was terrible. It seemed . . . inevitable that we would be together, he made it seem so, he told me every day that as soon as I made him we would be unstoppable, that we could do whatever we chose, we could be madly in love forever." He sighed heavily. "So, I did it. Regretted it instantly."

"Instantly?" I doubted, smiling.

"As soon as he took his first breath as a vampire, I felt fear and shame and loathing and remorse and all those good things. I thought to kill him at once—I, being older, was far stronger—but he was too young and naive, and it would have been like killing a baby. I thought that I could change his ways—that once he saw through these eyes that he would learn compassion and remorse and learn morality—but exactly the opposite happened. I learnt that I cannot change anyone by my powers, I can only destroy them, make them mad, or add fuel to their madness. God has given me one chance to redeem a single human being, and that is myself. I plan to do exactly that."

I sighed. My back hurt in the stiff restaurant seat, and the cold had seized up my muscles. The garlicky hot-pot had helped somewhat, but not altogether. "So what happened? Why aren't you still with him, wallowing in your regret?"

"You like to mock me, don't you? We ended it, after a few weeks together as blood-drinkers—his methods disgusted me, and he had only gotten worse in his iconoclasm. He is one of the most strident anti-Christians I have ever known—not merely atheist, but emphatic about the absence of a Christian God. He used to delight in crucifying rabbits and chickens and baby birds upside down on my wooden crucifix, until it became putrid from the blood and I had to burn it, much to his pleasure. He made airplanes out of the pages of my family Bible. I couldn't handle seeing him with other people either. He was infectious in his evil. I am not jealous by nature even slightly, but if I saw him cuddle up with barmaids, with American soldiers, drag queens, even little children on the street, who were his favorite victims—I would fly into a rage and we would fight. With fists and everything. I smashed his cheekbone once, but the next day it was healed, and he drove a pointed stake into my chest, not knowing it would not kill me. I pulled out the stake and threw it across the room and kicked him between the legs—what are you laughing about?"

"That is awesome."

"No, it's not. It's terrible. Have you any idea how much being staked in the heart hurts?"

"Probably about as much as being kicked in the family jewels."

"Anyway, you morbid child, I went away, since Berlin was becoming an awful place for anyone who was not a Nazi. Daniel wasn't a Nazi either, he despises government of any kind, and his father was a Jew and was killed by those bastards; but Daniel liked to prey on Nazis as well as their victims. He stayed. I went to England and holed up in a university tower with the books. After the war, Daniel tried to follow me, but I found out about him coming there, and I fled again, this time to China, where I knew he would not find me."

"Is he still alive?"

Ricari pursed his lips in thought, then looked up at me and nodded.

"Really? Where is he? Still in England?"

"I don't know," Ricari said.

He was lying. Like so many moral people who rarely lie, his lies were transparent; I saw the vein at his temple flutter and his eyes dilated. So like a human being in so many ways, yet still possessed of those fingers, those odd claws, those four pointy teeth that flashed when he laughed out loud. I loved him completely too. And he had done it once.

I felt a little weird. A twinge went through my side and came out my back, then cycled back through as intense pain. A cramp. I dropped my spoon.

"Are you all right?" Ricari asked.

"Yeah, I'll be OK." I fumbled in my satchel for a bottle of aspirin and swallowed two, washing them down with green tea. Ricari watched me with steel-eyed interest. Had he given me the cramp to distract me from his lie? I did not put it past him.

The waiter disappeared with Ricari's credit card, and I cracked open my fortune cookie. *Good fortune awaits you.* "You never even wanted to make another?" I asked.

"Not since then."

"Why not before? You were a hundred years old when this happened, if I'm not mistaken."

"I often had others around me before," he said. "I had been without other vampires for twenty years. Before then, I had Georgie and Maria, and later, some others."

"Who?"

"Later, child."

He came back with me to my place afterward, to listen to Prokofiev. I put on Bessie Smith first, though. "You like this music?" I challenged him. "American music?"

"Interesting," he said.

"I like it. I like the crackle and hiss of the recording coming through digitally." I stared at the disc whirling rainbows under its plastic cowl. "My lover gave me this a long time ago."

"Where is your lover now?"

"England," I said. "Cambridge. Physicist." I shrugged. "I'll probably never see him again . . . and I'm not sure that I care."

I sat down on the couch. My back really hurt now. Ricari was at my side, gently rubbing my shoulder, then my lower back. He lay his cool cheek against mine, and when I turned my head to kiss him, he didn't move away. I tasted his lips for a moment, sweetly, then moved away, not wishing to press it further for fear all would be taken away. He tangled my hair in his fingers and kissed my chin, drawing me close to him, brushing his lips against the hastily licked dampness of my own.

He and I pulled off my clothes. I was nearly paralyzed with excitement, stiffened with intermittent spasms of pain. I watched him the whole time; his face was completely blank, calm, bloodless, as if he were somewhere else. He unbuttoned the pristine white drapery of his satin shirt and dropped it onto the floor beside us.

I was naked from the waist down, half under him. He began kissing my belly, exposed under the white rim of my T-shirt, so much more exposed than if I were completely nude; I had no innocence in which to clothe myself. My nipples hurt under the tight cotton of my bra. Ricari's chest was smooth against my thighs, the demure twists of silvery hair under his arms brushing against my hipbones. I opened myself to him.

I could smell the blood.

Dazed, astonished, I glanced down at him wiping the smear of new blood from between my thighs and licking it off his forefinger, then going for more, touching me, then penetrating me, gathering thick droplets under his fingernail. "Oh, please," I whispered, "Oh, God."

It was not at all like the first time. Now he licked, suckled, lapped at the flow that his sucking increased. He had time now, he had no need of urgency; I was not going to save his life, nor was he going to take mine. I could not know what he thought or felt. I was hot all over, regretting taking aspirin rather than ibuprofen; the blood was flowing out of me as if I were a spigot. He sipped the uneven rich flow like a snake tasting the air. I grabbed one of his hands and slipped it under my shirt, to one of my breasts, and he felt it, ran his thumbnail over the nipple.

For hours this continued. At some point I got up and put on the Prokofiev disk; at some point we got up and moved to my bed; at some point the rest of my clothes came off and I lay there under him helpless and naked, while his dark tousled head weaved between my legs with a drowsy rhythm. At some point I came; and he helped me, I know he did; he increased the frequency of the strokes of his tongue, their insistency, until I moaned and twisted and my toes curled like ferns; then he slowed, breathed, pointed his tongue to catch the blood loosed by my spasms. He was still licking hypnotically when I fell asleep.

"When are you going to kill me?"

His face was a confrontational mask. I glanced up at him, then back at my Goldschlager cocktail. "Eventually," I said.

"You promised."

"I will," I said. "I'm not ready yet. Neither are you. You still have more to tell."

"What more do you need to know? I had a blueberry tart and Turkish coffee on the day that I died! Coleridge's breath stank! I have killed over seven thousand human beings! What else is there?"

"I want to know where Daniel is," I said coolly.

"I told you, I don't know."

"You do know. I thought Christians didn't lie."

"Damn you." In the red light reflecting off the booths he looked satanic. He genuinely hadn't had any blood in a very long time, save mine; I kept him functioning, but I couldn't keep him from looking deathly white, thin as a mantis, terrifyingly static in repose and jittery in movement like an old film. Anywhere else we might have gotten stares, but he had the whole staff of the cafe-bar so thoroughly hypnotized that he could have killed the bartender and poured his blood into a wine glass, and not gotten anything but the check. Ricari showed the strain in other ways too—like a fasting human, he was easily irritated.

"Yes," I said, "damn me."

"Stop acting so superior."

"I am superior, Orfeo Giuseppe Vittorio Ricari, 'cause I have the power to kill you, but you refuse the power to kill me."

"I have refused it. I may rescind this agreement."

"Really?"

"If you love me so, why do you not give me what I want? Why don't you do as I say?"

"I don't know." I was wearing the dress he gave me again; it helped keep the staff hypnotized; if things were as they had been before, the mundanity of the whole situation was assured. I put my face in my hands. I hadn't eaten this time, deciding to go straight for the liquor. I knew he was going to ask me about death again tonight—we had had too many weeks of conversation, sweetness, my blood freely given and his kisses unshy. "I need more answers, Ricari. Please. Like why won't you let me sleep with you? Why don't you want me?"

"I do want you, Ariane."

"Then why—"

"Have you never loved a moral man before? I will not violate your body in this way, or let you violate

83

mine. I have sinned enough in that way long ago—I don't want it anymore. It only leads to trouble—heartbreak—lies and broken promises, and death. I don't want to have this kind of relationship. I don't see you as a cheap woman, who gives away her womb to the first man who knows where it is."

"But you still—"

"I don't want to talk about that."

"I just want to, you know, take a nap with you."

"Don't be absurd. I know what you really mean."

"You infuriate me, Ricari."

"And you me!" Ricari slammed his hand down onto the table hard enough to crack the varnish. The other patrons looked at us in panic, but the staff continued on merrily as if they had heard nothing. The patrons went reluctantly back to their drinks, figuring we were some rich VIPs, perhaps the owners.

"I hate you," I said in a little voice. "I'm sick of doing things your way."

"Look," he said through his gleaming teeth, "I'm older than you. I know better."

"It's not your world anymore," I spat back. "You're a relic. Your morals are a relic."

"You sound like that damned Daniel."

"Well, maybe he's right, have you ever considered that?"

"You are sick in the head if you think that I would ever make you into anything like him," Ricari said. His white cheeks were stained with crimson, as if someone had dashed him inexpertly with rouge. "The last thing you need is power. More power. All you would do would be to persecute and repress. Let me be myself! Let me worship God and walk a moral path! Why does this inconvenience you so much?"

"Because I love you," I said, disappointed with how it sounded already. "I want you."

"Oh. And I'm to let the child touch the stove because

she wants to? Drink the pretty poison because it looks as though it tastes nice? What kind of person would I be?"

"As you're so fond of saying," I said, "you're not a person."

I expected a horrible row—perhaps blows—but I didn't for a million years guess what he was going to do next. Ricari burst into tears and buried his head in the creche of satin formed by his crossed arms on the table. "Stop it!" he sobbed. "Stop this attack!"

I was aghast. I put my arms around his shoulders and murmured to him, "I'm sorry," covering his delicate ears with kisses. He lifted his head and stared with enormously reddened, flowing eyes.

"I'm sorry," I said again. "I'm not worthy of you by any stretch of the imagination—"

"Let's go," he said miserably.

We drove about for a long time, crossing the Golden Gate into Marin County, coasting along the highway that wound around immeasurable secret towns, towns that existed on no maps and that tore down signs that directed motorists to them; along ochre cliffs that sparkled in the moonlight, and rain-soaked phosphorescent beaches. Ricari cried for a while, and I didn't speak, mortified at how I'd spoken against him. He was so delicate! I could not stand the idea that I had been cruel to him. At length he finished with his sobs, and leaned back, spent, while a few stray tears marked his pallid cheeks.

I stopped the car on the side of the road. I took his icy hands in between mine and gazed at him. "Orfeo," I said, "Orfeo, please, please forgive me."

"There is nothing to forgive," he said. "You are absolutely right."

"I don't know what the fuck I'm talking about. I'm an idiot. I hate to hurt you!"

"You don't," he scoffed, but his tone was lighter.

We looked at each other.

"I'll do anything you want," I said, "anything you say. You hypnotize me. I just ... don't want to live without you."

"You are enamored of an insect," he replied. He blushed.

"And if I am?"

He giggled faintly, then burst out laughing. I took him into my arms and he pressed his face into my breasts. "My child," he purred, "you are seductive."

Chapter Five

We had been thus for days.

Ricari sprawled against me, naked but for his rosary, his cock swelling tightly against me and then receding again, his mouth closed over my nipple, which he periodically bit, then suckling the blood that seeped from it. I writhed, feverish, half conscious from hunger and delight, falling asleep at times with his feather weight on me. I would wake at times and he would be gone, crouched in my living room, investigating my possessions, playing a single track from a CD, then discarding it for another. As soon as he saw that I had waked, he would spring back onto me, tussling virginally, caressing me, kissing my face and neck and my swollen breasts. He would lick open the healing wounds that were my nipples, bringing fresh streams of blood.

When I reached for his cock he would swat my hand away. "I am for you," he said, "you are not for me to take."

But I was, night and day.

Jemiah Jefferson

*   *   *

I sat at my kitchen table with a pen and a sheet of blank white paper.

Dear John, I wrote.

I tore up the paper and dropped it into the morass of unpaid bills, past-due notices, empty paper cups, vitamin bottles at my feet.

My phone had been cut off.

I took up the pen again. *My most dear sweet John, I am in love with another man.*

This wouldn't do either. More fuel for the dormant fire.

Another clean white sheet. *John—you will not believe this, but vampires exist, and I am in love with one.*

Shit. No.

It was daylight; warm daylight, stinking of cut grass from the park. I found it hard to think. I was so rarely awake at this time of day. I had to tell him something. I had letters from him—dull things in his incomprehensible hand, the paper on mesons he was writing, the old friends he had come across. The last two or three lay unopened on the couch next to the front door. I hadn't the energy to face his wonders, his queries about my vacation, why I hadn't written him more than a hasty scribble on a grocery receipt, and that in February.

My love, I would never want to hurt you, but I guess I had better. I have become involved with someone else—and it's not some random greasy intellectual or horny undergrad, but the most incredible being I have ever met. Sometimes I wonder if he really exists, and I also wonder if you exist, whether or not my life up to the point at which I met him wasn't all just a dream. It's so much worse than finding Jesus Christ or becoming a lesbian at the last minute or even deciding that I don't love you because I do—I still do—sometimes I miss your ordinariness, little things, I miss driving you around and stuff, I miss school—but I will never be able to escape this thing that's happened to me. I am in too deep to even make sense of anything and I am losing my wits—you would laugh to see me now—I'm a mess of bruises and I eat and eat but he takes it all— and he won't even fuck me or anything, but I swear it's real, he's real, you would fall in love with him too if you were here, if this was happening to you. It's like meeting an extraterrestrial or waking up one day to find that everything was suddenly on its side or stepping on the moon—this doesn't make any sense but I had to tell you something.

I folded up the sheet before I could tear it up and stuffed it into an envelope. I scribbled his address at the school on the front and put it into the napkin holder, and left the kitchen, endeavoring to forget all about it.

The doorbell sounded, startling a yelp out of me. I thought to ignore it and go back to bed, but it might have been Ricari. I put on a bathrobe over my T-shirt and pajama bottoms, and went to the door.

It was Carole, the admin from the Bio Department at school. I stood dumbly looking at her from behind the grate, my hand on the knob.

"Ariane," she said surprised. "You're home."

"Yeah," I said.

"Can I . . . come in?" she asked.

I nodded, and unlocked the grate so that she could come in. She shouldered her purse and looked reflexively around the room; she had been here before, ten months ago, for a party celebrating my grant for the year. The place was a wreck now. I hadn't felt like cleaning it. Ricari tended to make a mess at my apartment; I had so many things, and he didn't seem to care what he did in someone else's space. I sank down onto the couch, conscious of how this must look—four o'clock in the afternoon, me in pajamas, house a mess.

"I was just wondering how you were," she prefaced, moving a heap of magazines and CD covers onto the floor so she could sit. "Whole department's kind of worried. I tried to call before coming over, but it says it's disconnected?"

"I forgot to pay the bill," I said with a wan smile. "I know, I usually never forget anything, but . . . I've been really tired."

"Are you sick? Don't let people tell you chronic fatigue syndrome is a crock—"

"I don't know," I said. "I'll try to get the phone back on again next week."

"You have lost so much weight," she said.

"Looks nice, huh?"

Her face was a cartoon of concern. "You want to come to the park with me? It's a gorgeous day out, you could get some sun. You're"—she laughed—"you're starting to look like a white person."

I shook my head and failed in my attempt to smile. "I should really get back to sleep," I said. "I've been . . . I haven't really been the same since . . . um, since my miscarriage. I've been kind of keeping myself doped up . . . it's kind of hard. . . ."

"Oh, yeah, I totally understand. Hard to be bouncy when you're bleeding all over the place." That explanation seemed to soothe her, and I mentally patted myself on the back. "If you need anything, call me, OK? A lot of people are really concerned about you. We all thought you'd be hanging around the lab this semester, and nobody'd seen or heard from you in ages."

"I'll call you if there's anything," I said. "Thanks."

I showed her out, my knees nearly buckling with fatigue. She gave me a quick hug as she went, and glanced back over her shoulder at me, obviously not quite convinced. Oh, well, too bad. I locked the grate. I wished to hell that people wouldn't give a shit about me, so I could just disappear and nobody would even notice.

*   *   *

"The cruelest month," Ricari said languidly.

I looked up briefly from the room-service tray, then back at it again. A haphazard heap of roast beef, medium rare, stared back at me, and I took up the two-tined serving fork and began stuffing slices of it into my mouth.

The old man was still in the room, having not yet uncorked the wine, and he gaped at me. "Want your veggies?" he asked dubiously.

"Yeah, yeah, leave me alone. Spinach?"

"Creamed spinach. All we had."

"Cool," I said. "Now could you please get out of here?"

He placed the cork on the tray, sighing theatrically. Ricari gave him a twenty-dollar bill and shut the door behind him. Ricari returned to his place on the chaise and watched me eat. "When you're done we can go out," he said.

"You don't look so human," I said.

He was very bony and his eyes were like rained-on metal. He shrugged. "When you're done we can go out," he repeated.

I hadn't seen him for a full week. When I called the Saskatchewan from the pay phone at the 7-11, he was never in; when I went there, the desk clerk told me without looking up from his *People* that Ricari was not available. I spent nights at home in front of a candle, almost praying to him to listen to me, to get me out of this lonely hell I'd worked myself into; at last, earlier that afternoon, he'd sent over a florist's delivery boy with a silver-white hothouse rose and a card that said simply, *Come tonight*.

I had jerked off until I lapsed into a dizzy half sleep.

The candlelight ran over the panels of the parquet floor like melted butter. I sopped up the last of the creamed spinach with a crust of bread, and washed it down with a mouthful of wine. Ricari stared fixedly out the window. "Need an aperitif?" I asked, leaning into his sight.

He looked up at me without seeing me. Then a slight smile curled his lips.

"Tell me something," I said.

"Yes?"

"How is one made into a vampire?"

"By blood," he said. He moved away from me.

"No, but how."

"I've told you," Ricari said. "Shall we go?"

In a systematic fashion, we did the clubs south of Market. We began at DV8, at this early hour not yet filled with gyrating, leather-clad fashion students, waiters, and methedrine dealers. In the bluish light Ricari insisted that I drink four gin and tonics, using the power of his mind so gently and skillfully that I was halfway down my third before I suspected I was anything other than painfully thirsty. I protested in a mumble, inaudible over the pulsing of deep-house, but Ricari heard me. He only smiled. "Drink up," he said, and my arm lifted the fourth cocktail glass and filled my mouth with the bitter fizz.

I followed him in a haze from DV8 to the Endup to the Bon Marché. I had no idea what he was doing; he wasn't there to dance, certainly; I couldn't imagine Ricari getting down and funky with the ravers. I think I remember dancing a little, helplessly drawn into the beat, but he wasn't watching me. His eyes were elsewhere.

After my fifth drink, I sat still and watched him stare into space. He wore a white shirt with a slightly lacy collar—a woman's blouse that struck his fancy on his last shopping expedition for me—and plain slim dark trousers. He didn't fit in at all with the golden youth in their saucy neon colors and daisy appliqués, but nor did he look awkward among them. He was a tiny, perfect creature, delicate, a *capodimonte* porcelain sculpture of a melancholy poet. I put out my hand to touch his, and he drew it away, not quite startled, but disliking the contact.

I was confused.

For a while we strolled along in the darkness and quiet between the Bon Marché and the Stud, not speaking. I didn't dare ask anything, and he volunteered nothing. A big jock type and his giggling, wasted girlfriend, walking past, made some comment I didn't hear, but I saw Ricari's cheeks flame scarlet. "Hey, shut up, you fucker," I said ignorantly. I was almost too drunk to support my own weight. "He'll kick your sorry ass."

"What?" The jock stopped and started walking back. "What did you say?"

Ricari and I both stood still, silent. He darted me a look that I couldn't interpret.

"You better keep your bitch on a leash," the jock blustered, squeezing the giggle-jiggle queen possessively. She exploded with literally snotty laughter.

"She's not mine," Ricari said, not without some humor.

"You're a fuckin' asshole," I muttered, and spat at the jock's feet. I didn't manage to remember that I'd gotten beat up once in New Orleans, drunk and acting like a badass. It must be something with the red hair, the diluted heroic Celtic blood, half poisoned with alcohol and determined to have the last word, even if it's spat out with a mouthful of blood and teeth.

The jock attempted to rush and take a swing at me. He never got that far—Ricari intercepted, adeptly tripping the jock so that he fell onto the gritty, filthy sidewalk and ripped his palms on the pavement. The girl broke out laughing even harder at that, and it seemed to galvanize the meathead. He sprung up with truly impressive speed and assaulted Orfeo instead.

It wasn't the best idea the jock ever had. Ricari took the jock's hands in his and gave a subtle twist; I heard, even at the distance of three or four feet, the moist popping sound of shoulder joints coming undone. The jock couldn't even yell; Ricari clamped his wee hand over the jock's open mouth and fastened himself onto the base of his neck, which was as far as Ricari could reach, standing on his toes. The drunk girlfriend watched all this silently, baffled into calm, but not yet into sobriety.

She woke up, though, when she saw the jock slump narcoleptically to the ground. Ricari gazed up, his face blushing almost violet and his eyes brilliant, and gave her a look I will never forget—a kind of intent, pure even beyond the animal, beyond instinctual, something others might describe as pure joyful innocent evil. She had barely turned and began gathering her muscles to run before Ricari had her.

I bit my hand to keep from crying out. I swear to God, I thought he was going to kill her. Instead, he gripped her by the throat and the belly, turned her around, and looked fully into her face. He didn't say anything aloud, but she gasped as though someone had plunged a needle into her. Then she relaxed in his arms, and her head fell limply back.

He settled her gently in a sitting position along a concrete wall, frisked her, and produced her wallet from her little white leather purse. He pocketed the wallet and rejoined me under the streetlight. No one had seen; no one had driven by closer than a block away. "Is the guy dead?" I asked Ricari as we walked away.

"Almost," he said coolly. "I think he'll live, with help."

Despite myself, I glanced back, licking nervous salt off my lips. The girl was regaining consciousness, feeling with her hands along the pavement. No sound came from her. "And the cheerleader?"

"She won't remember . . . anything," Ricari said. His voice was strange, bizarrely lighthearted, as if he were no longer himself. He was as pink as a clover blossom.

"What do you mean? She won't remember what happened?"

"She won't remember anything at all. A clean slate. She can start all over again."

"Ricari," I said, horrified despite myself.

"Your moral judgments," he drawled. I realized that he was now almost as drunk as I was, his feed saturated with liquor. "Your moral judgments mean nothing here. These are the politics of the damned. I'll hate myself in the morning." His giddy cheer collapsed and he began to weep and bite his lower lip. "I . . . hate myself now . . ."

I grasped his arm. He had not gotten a single telltale drop on his pristine white blouse. "Don't think that way," I said, embracing him. "You were—you were—defending me. That asshole would have turned me into ground beef. You did it because you like me. Didn't you?"

He glanced at me, and a faint sloppy smile crept over his face. "Yes," he said, "keep believing that. Perhaps I too will believe it, in time."

He scattered the contents of the wallet in various dumpsters along the street, and then embraced me with one arm and pressed his cheek against mine. In our final destination, a quiet jazz bar on Market and Valencia, we kissed hungrily for hours. I could taste the luscious blood in his mouth.

There were still too many things to know.

Ricari made me consent to fixing a date wherein I would put him into the incinerator and lock the door. It was to be April 23rd, a Saturday night, when there wouldn't be very many people around to see us. We would slip in at about two in the morning, make sure the oven was fired up, then I would open the door, Orfeo would climb in, and I would shut the door and *leave*; he made me promise I would leave immediately before I heard him scream. Unlike luckier fictional vampires, Ricari assured me that he was not highly flammable and would take as long to burn through as a human being would. "Think of me as you would a log of oak," he imagined. "You have no remorse about throwing a log onto the fire, would you? That's all I am is old firewood, branches from a dead tree."

He made me make this promise in the red-vinyl cafe-bar, the staff so accustomed to us that they no longer made Ricari pay for my drinks. I sat with my back to him and he brushed my hair until all the frazzled brown-red curls lay smooth in his palm. "Orfeo," I said, struggling against the lump of sadness in my throat, "promise me you'll answer all my questions before then."

"I will not promise," he said lightly. "I will try to answer. I don't have answers to everything." He dropped a kiss onto the side of my neck.

"Why won't you let me sleep with you? I mean really sleep?"

He hesitated. "You don't want to know."

"Duh! That's why I'm asking."

"All I will say is it's not very nice."

"Do you turn into a bat?"

He laughed. "No, my dear, just a sleeping version of myself. My dreams are contagious. I don't want you to have to share my nightmares."

I smiled as the waitress brought me another cup of coffee—no alcohol tonight, I wanted to stay awake with him for as long as I could. I had less than two weeks left. "How many of your kind are there in the world?"

"I have no idea. Maybe a lot, maybe only a few."

"Do you know of any others in town?"

"Why? Do you want a new one when I'm gone?"

"That's not funny." I pulled away from him and poured some sugar into my tea.

He caught hold of my hair again, and stroked it back into place. "I'm sorry. I don't know. I'm sure there are—they have never made themselves known to me. We are solitary ultimately."

"What makes you think you'll die when you go into the fire?"

His hands stopped on my head.

"What makes you think you'll cease to be, go to heaven, whatever? How do you know your consciousness won't go on in those ashy little bits?" I continued.

He had resumed his brushing, and neatly rolled the smooth curls into a bun, securing it with a thick comb. "Because I believe in separation of soul and body," he replied coolly. "As do you."

"I believe in nothing. I only have theories."

"My child, you will never go to heaven if you don't believe in anything."

"I won't go to hell either," I said. I turned to face him and smiled. He took my face between his hands and kissed my forehead.

"Lack of belief is a sort of hell," Ricari said.

I put my hand on his chest and gently seized his nipple between my first and second fingers. He watched me, removed my hand, kissing the fingers, put my hand against his head so that I could appreciate the fine texture of his hair, and kissed me on the lips. "I think mystery is better than fact," he continued, "and waiting is better than getting."

"So what you're telling me is that you'd rather die than have sex with me." I kissed his chin.

"Ah, Ariane, you are lovely when you're pigheaded and deliberately stupid."

"I know when I'm beaten, don't rub it in."

"You are not beaten, my dear. You only think you are."

"Mmmmmmm . . ." I swayed against him. "Please stop being so superior."

He didn't reply. He sat back against the red vinyl and watched things go by. I wondered what it would be like to need no food, not have the maddening urge to pee, no dull craving for cigarettes or for the distraction of sexual tension. Ricari was a pure being. He needed only blood and God, and to die someday. No wonder he treated me as a psychologist treats a disturbed child.

"Did you pay my rent?" I asked suddenly.

He lifted his eyebrows at me. "Should I not have?"

"I was just wondering . . . because my landlady was bugging me for a long time . . . and then she stopped . . . I barely remember now."

"It was nothing," said Ricari. "I still have money left. I'm trying to get rid of it."

I kissed his hand, licking him, tasting the vampire skin. It tasted of nothing at all—perhaps of my hair conditioner. His flesh was the temperature of the room. I did adore an insect.

Despite this sweetness, we quarreled again as soon as we returned to the Saskatchewan.

"Darling . . ." I said, sitting on the gold divan and crossing my legs. "Look, I know you were lying when you told me you didn't know where Daniel is. I could see your pupils dilate." Across the room his back tensed. "Why don't you just stop playing games with me, which I don't appreciate, and just let me know what city, what country—"

"I will tell you nothing more of that creature!" Ricari exploded. "Why do you love me if you find me such a liar?"

"I know you have reasons for wanting to keep me away from him. All right, he's dangerous. Perhaps I should find him and kill him."

Ricari paled so when I said this that I shut up immediately.

"You will do no such thing. You would not survive such an attempt."

"Ricari—Orfeo—it's only that I want to have some part of you after you're gone—"

"He is no part of me," Ricari spat. His color was high. "He is the most evil, thoughtless creature I have ever known. He is a demon, hunting for fresh souls. He burns in hell, and he wishes for more innocents to fuel his fire."

I began to laugh helplessly.

Like so many Christians, Ricari could not stand it when people laughed at him. He flung down a crystal candlestick and it shattered against the parquet. "Will you listen to me?" he shouted.

This made me laugh even harder. I was not really amused—in fact, I was frightened by his vehement description—but I was helpless and hysterical, collapsed on the gold chaise longue.

He picked me up and shook me. "What's your problem?"

"Do I . . . do I . . ." I struggled for breath. "Do I have to promise not to crawl into the incinerator with you?"

Idly he stroked away the tears that were running from my eyes. "Yes," he said, all violence gone. "You must go on without me, or there will be no point in anything. Anything, you see."

"I can promise you anything but that," I said.

April 20th came.

I had slept on the chaise at the suite, wrapped in Ricari's silk robe, while he slept in bed. I got up and tiptoed to the bedroom door, intending to look in upon his sleeping naked form, but the door was bolted shut.

Ricari got up, as usual, at about five o'clock in the evening. He let me bathe with him, a nice chaste bath in the big hotel bathtub, with the water painfully hot. His skin under the lights was uniformly silky, the whitish color of unbleached cotton; in contrast, I was golden yellow, mottled with freckles, birthmarks, scars from various accidents and incisions. I carefully shaved his face with a straight razor—he didn't like safety razors at all, he always cut himself with them. "I used to bathe with my sisters," he confessed, washing my hair.

"Was it this sensual?"

"Oh, quite. We didn't know it or think of it at the time, of course. My sister taught me to kiss in the bath. It was completely innocent."

"Was this the redheaded one?"

He smiled at me.

Ricari was attempting to blow as much money as he could, so he bought me a violet linen suit, which he made me wear from the Italian boutique, and took me to dinner at a skyscraper restaurant. I was morose as hell. The more he spent, the lower I got. I spent the whole first course staring out the window, wondering if this or that fall would kill Ricari, what kind of things the same fall would do to me. The appetizer was eventually whisked away untouched.

"What's the matter?" Ricari asked, touching me on the chin. "Are you not hungry?"

"I don't know," I mumbled, peeling the skin off my cuticles, softened by the hot bath.

"Don't be depressed."

"The one thing I love more than anything else in the world is going away soon," I said, "and I'm gonna be the one giving it the ol' heave-ho."

"Please don't think of it that way. Be happy for me."

"It's just gonna hurt so much."

"Please, Ariane."

I was quiet then, and sipped a little of my soup to be polite, but mainly I ignored that too. Ricari, in his blue silk blouse and black jacket, watched me through the whole disappointing meal, his eyes gleaming with pity.

After he paid for the meal that I'd had maybe ten

bites of, we went walking around the deserted Financial District, its gray and barren streets filled with warm breeze and streetlight. We walked towards Market Street, the great band of piss-colored light, the spine of San Francisco.

"I can't do it," I said, balling my hands into fists.

"You must," he replied.

"No, I mustn't. I would only be doing it because I love you—and maybe I don't love you enough to throw you onto the pyre."

"You would do anything for me," he scoffed.

I shook my head.

We reached Market, and crossed it at Fifth Street.

I stopped him on the sidewalk, and gazed into his eyes.

"Tell me," I insisted, "where Daniel is. I have to go to him."

Ricari sighed patiently. "You will do no such thing."

"I can't go back to my old life just like that! I've given too much! You think I'm a normal human being now? I may not be one of you, but I've changed, and I don't think I can ever go back. I need you—I need—that sound in my head. Either you give me the location, or no death. Those are my terms."

"You've gone completely insane," Ricari said. He sounded impressed.

"Those are my terms!" I shouted.

He looked around us uncertainly, herding me into a side street. "Will you be quiet?" he hissed.

"Those are my terms. Accept one or the other."

"Who do you think you are?"

"I'm the only one who will help you!"

"I can get anyone to help me, my dear. All I have to do is invade their minds and tell them to cut off my head—"

"But that's suicide. God won't like that much, will he?"

"I could—" Ricari vainly grasped at straws. "I could go into the police department and show myself. They'd make short work of me."

"They'd shoot you. Won't work too well."

"Ariane! Will you shut up!"

"Make me," I replied, a thrill of disobedience running through me. He did not know I had his scalpel, palmed after our fraternal bath, in the pocket of my coat.

He grabbed my shoulders, intending perhaps to pick me up and set me down somewhere else, but I reached up and slashed the backs of his fingers with the blade. He let go, howling with pain. I ran the scalpel handle-deep into his cheek, intending to drink the blood as it poured from his lips. I wanted all the blood I had given him back. I wanted to taste it. For days I had been conjecturing about its flavor—salty? Honeylike? Something altogether different? A dark bubble pursed at his mouth and burst, forced by his startled breath.

I did not reach his lips. He struck my right arm and the scalpel slashed his cheek open as it cut and fell away. With his right palm, he slapped me on the cheekbone, and with his left-hand claws he struck at me, tore open the front of the violet suit, the gray blouse I wore underneath, and the flesh covering my throat and collarbones. I couldn't even cry out. I stood and looked at the shreds, the blood pouring down to my waist. It had been such an efficient move, so graceful, so simple. I felt the cold air on my flesh, on the naked bone, and only then did I sense any pain. Everything split into brilliant stars of amber light.

I dimly heard him crying out my name, but I didn't see the ground rush up to get me. I felt only that I relaxed.

Book Two
Haemodynamics

Chapter Six

I dreamt I was on a mountain, going very fast down a mountainside covered with snow. I was tied up, gagged, my mouth stuffed with dry, shit-tasting cotton rags; and I was trying to scream. I twisted and turned on the toboggan I was lashed to, trying to open my eyes and loosen my bonds or stop the horrible, rapid, shaking slide. I couldn't do any of those things. I gave up and let everything go black, convinced that I was going to hit the bottom and be crushed into a pulpy mess. I was afraid of the pain.

I was ... darkness. Swift motions passing over me, voices; I couldn't hear what they were saying. It sounded like someone laughing, or having an asthma attack, one or the other. I was still in my body, I could tell that much; my feet flopped to each side heavily, and I tried to move them, but I was too tired. It hurt to breathe. "Am I dead?" I managed to say, my voice like rubber dragged over concrete.

Definitely laughing. "What'd she say?" A girl's voice.

"She said, 'Am I dead?' That, my little victim, is a matter of opinion." A man's voice, accompanied by the feel of moist cool fingers stroking my forehead. "Now, stop worrying over matters of existential philosophy, and go back to sleep. You're in your bed at home. Can't you smell it?"

I *could* smell it. The sweat from my head, the synthetic tang of cheap pillowcases, even the faintest hint of . . . John? No matter; I was suddenly too comfortable to resist anything, remember anything, and I had to do as I was told.

Then I was awake.

I rolled over and felt for my bedside table, my alarm clock, but my hand instead knocked over something that fell with a small plastic clatter to the floor. I opened my eyes and looked down at the floor—a plastic thermometer lay there, on an unfamiliar linoleum floor, a smooth pattern of brown dots and seams in squares. Not my room. Not my bed either. I lay on a narrow bed with one metal rail on the side, a hospital bed. There was not enough light for me to be in a hospital, even late at night; also missing were the busy hospital sounds, the humming of fluorescent lights, beepers, the quiet but distinct hurrying of nurses. I shrugged off layers of cheap flannel blankets and half sat up.

I was wearing a white T-shirt with the collar and sleeves cut out, the front of it dotted with brown droplets of dried blood. I touched my chest. It seemed whole. I was in no pain whatsoever anywhere. I peeked down the front of the T-shirt to see. There were four tiny pink seams that ran from the base of the throat down to where the tits became ribs, lines as fine as plastic surgery scars.

I was not alone in the room. A dark-haired young man slouched languidly in a folding chair across from me, maybe ten feet away, as if waiting for me to wake up. His skin shone eggshell-pale in the umbrous darkness of the room, bright in contrast with his dark clothes—a fishnet blouse and black, glistening, reptile-patterned jeans. He pushed black hair off his brow, leaned forward, and smiled at me. "Hello at last," he said.

"Where am I?" I asked. My voice was full of mucus, and I coughed and spat into a fold I made in the soft, old bedsheet.

"You're at my place," the man said. He had the same voice that had, long ago, commanded me to sleep in my own bed. "My name's Daniel. You're in Hollywood."

I sat very still and blinked at him. "Daniel?" I said. The one and only? The black-hearted demon of Berlin, this, a quiet-voiced, jaunty California Goth boy?

"You may have heard of me," he replied with a straight face.

"How did I get here?"

"You may ask yourself—well, how did I get here?" he quoted the Talking Heads, smiling at last. "In fact, you were sent. Do you remember?"

"Remember what?"

"You arrived here four days ago, in a San Francisco Yellow Cab. You were slashed and unconscious, bleeding very badly. You had a note stuck to your chest with your own blood. I've got it on me—do you want to see it? I think it explains a lot."

I nodded jerkily, and he reached into his pocket and withdrew a slip of paper. He stood up to give it to me. He had an exquisite form, bones and sleekness, grace sliding through every joint and each lean, smooth muscle. The skintight jeans creaked as he walked over to me and bent down to give me the note. Then he sat back down in his chair and watched me unfold it.

On grainy cream-brown paper, in black ballpoint, was written in an unbalanced, florid script:

A little present from me to you. You are welcome to her; she is just like you in so many ways. If I keep her, I'll kill her or I'll lose my mind. Always and ever your slave, O.V.R.

The note was crisp with old blood, dried a darker shade of brown than the paper. I folded it back up and set it down on the blankets in front of me. "Oh," I said. "Yeah, that explains a lot. . . ."

"You're all right now," said Daniel calmly. "Tell me your name."

"Ariane."

He grinned, and I saw his fangs glisten wetly in what light there was. He had rather long, ostentatious fangs, as if age wore them down to smoother stubs. "You look," he said, half laughing, "*so* pissed off."

"I don't know whether I'm dead or alive," I said. "It doesn't make any sense. It feels like this has all been a dream."

"Yeah," he agreed. "You are alive, though, I can vouch for that." He regarded me with bright eyes ringed with messy black pencil.

I touched my chest, checking to be sure a heart still beat underneath. "So he *did* know where you were all along," I murmured.

"Of course he did. Did he lie and say he didn't know?" He didn't wait for a response from me, snorting faintly. "Candy-ass. When it comes down to it, it's 'Let Daniel deal with it, let's send evil into evil,' blah-de-blah. I get so sick of that Catholic bullshit."

"I loved him," I said numbly.

"And he probably loved you. Or he still loves you. Did he ever try that dying thing on you?"

"What dying thing?"

"Oh, you know, climbs into a coffin, 'bury me in my best suit,' et cetera."

"He did want me to kill him," I admitted. "I was going to incinerate him."

Daniel made a face. "Yuck. Ever smelled a burning vampire? Stinks like shit." He was gazing at me with some concern. "You should be OK now. We fixed you right up. Do you feel all right? Does anything hurt?"

"I have to pee," I murmured.

"I don't doubt it. Bathroom's through there." He angled his head towards a half-closed door. "You can take a shower too, if you want. I'll have some clothes when you come out. I got it under control."

I got out of bed gingerly. If anything, I was simply tired, as if I'd been fasting or running marathons. The T-shirt slid aside indecently, exposing my bare ass and the dark crescent of my pubic hair, but he didn't look away or even pretend he hadn't seen. I pulled a blanket around myself and tiptoed across the chilly tiles to the bathroom.

I felt too fragile to shower, but I used a grainy hotel-issue washcloth to scrub my face, my pits, my cunt and ass (I remembered losing control of my bowels and my bladder as I looked down at the gaping wounds in my chest, as the blood sprang out in glorious spurts, lit by the amber streetlights). I washed my hair with a little bottle of shampoo (Pert Plus, yet more hotel pickings, from the Hollywood Hilton), pulled the T-shirt back over me, and came back into the room.

He was still there, and laid out on the bed was a sleeveless dress of warm-gray silk, brand-new cotton panties, and black silk socks. "Wow," I said, quietly impressed. "Silk socks." I looked at him, sitting there, smiling crookedly. "You gonna sit there while I dress?"

"Unless you insist. I've seen you naked before."

I sighed, and began to pull the clothes on with my back to him. The silk enclosed me warmly and I realized that I had been shaking, and now I had stopped. "So . . . where . . . exactly am I, besides Hollywood?"

"My headquarters, sort of." Up till this point, his accent had been a completely normal American one, a little crisper than usual; here a slight accent crept through. "I almost live here. I have my own place too. This is where you can usually find me. I have a cell phone too. I get calls at all hours." He looked around him. "You are in what we call the Rotting Hall, in the basement. That's why it's so cold in here. It's a nice evening outside—the sun's just going down. You hungry? I'm hungry."

"What do you mean?"

He shrugged. "I'm hungry," he repeated. "Do you want to go out to dinner?" He held out shoes to me— black elastic flats, size eight. "You like Greek? It's California Greek, but it's still all right, especially if you actually eat meat."

I put on the shoes. "You—eat?"

"Of course I do. Don't you?"

"Orfeo doesn't," I explained.

He looked away, rubbing his thick eyebrow with his forefinger. "Oh, yeah," he said with a faint grimace. "He's too special for that. *I* eat." He held out his hand and helped me stand up. We began to walk from the room.

"Do you shit?" I asked in a slightly embarrassed murmur.

"Yes, don't you? You are one strange kid."

Outside the room with the hospital bed was a long, dark, empty hall that smelled of cobwebs and soil. At the end of the hall were wooden stairs, and at the top of the stairs a doorless jamb yawned into a vast room.

It was the lobby, I supposed; huge and littered with

old dusty couches, broken end tables with lamps, crates, spatters of wax. A few candles were lit in a massive candelabra that stood bristling by a spiral staircase. It was nearly the only light in the room; the windows were covered with black plastic trash bags, boards, or haphazard squares of red felt. A little light struggled against the red felt, warming the color of the atmosphere. The air reeked sweetly of marijuana smoke, incense, and the sweet sticky smell of burned opium. "Smells, uh, good in here," I commented.

Daniel looked round and smiled at me. "I can get you that too, of course," he said. "As much as you want, whenever you want."

"Right now I need a cigarette."

"In your shape? Allow me to be maternal—no smoking until after you've eaten something. I don't want you puking in my car. I have some Nat Shermans. You're welcome to them after dinner."

I followed Daniel out. A glorious sky greeted us over the ragged brick tops of the buildings—furious orange and sleepy violet, streaks of an ineffable azure. The sun was gone, as if swallowed by the murky Los Angeles skyline, only beginning to light up for the night. There were only a couple of cars on the narrow street outside, no pedestrians, no discernible human activity. I took a look behind me at the building we'd just come out of. It looked deserted from outside—sagging and cracked like an old wedding cake, mottled with grafitti, the windows blocked off with dust. "My God," I said, "what happened to this place?"

"Northridge quake," he said. "Just enough to shift the ground under the foundation. It's mostly safe. The ceiling's only fallen in on about three rooms."

I was aghast. "This ought to be condemned," I said.

"It is," Daniel said with great pride and affection. "*Der Verfaulenhalle*. I have a friend in city planning who makes sure that no wrecking balls ruin my palace.

Well, I mean, look at it. It's about average for this neighborhood. There's plenty of money in L.A.—but none of it's here, that's for damn sure. It's easier to ignore than to fix up—there's plenty of space." He said this without a trace of irony. "For them, and for me."

Across the street was the back exit of a rock club—a young woman with big blond heavy-metal hair stood outside emptying the trash, and she looked up without emotion as we walked past. At this time of the evening, the parking lot was still largely deserted. On the far corner as the block ended, a huge black gas-guzzling monster Cadillac Coupe de Ville waited, gleaming, whitewall tires and tiny-spoked hubcaps shining purple in the dying light. "Please tell me that's not *your* car," I said, smiling helplessly. This was getting better by the minute.

"What's the matter with my car? I think she's beautiful." Daniel brandished a ring of keys and unlocked the driver's side.

"I bet you have a name for your car, don't you," I said.

"Dolores," Daniel said, climbing in.

I shook my head.

He unlocked and opened the door. "Get in, already."

The interior was even better—red glitter vinyl upholstery, bucket seats, a rearview-mirror mobile made up of rosaries, Playboy garters, Mardi Gras beads, and what looked like a dismembered Barbie. I laughed until I felt the healed rips in my chest start to stretch. I leaned back and tried to catch my breath, wiping my eyes. Daniel was smiling at me. "What? You think I'm a big goober, don't you?" he said.

I shook my head. "I just didn't expect you to be like this," I said. "I expected . . . you know, Klaus Kinski. Some kind of baby-chomping monster." I fell silent and he started the car, smoothly peeling out of the parking lot and joining the artery of traffic. He turned the stereo on, quietly playing some harsh industrial music I'd never heard before. "I didn't. . . . Daniel, tell me why I'm alive right now."

"*I* saved you," Daniel said, eyes on the road. His eyes were narrow, heavily shaded with thick sparkling eyelashes, a brilliant dark green color like liqueur. "You were bleeding all over the place, in the back of that cab. You were wearing some awful lavender suit and it was completely black, dripping. The cabbie up front was dead—brain fried, bleeding out his eyes. Good thing too. Your fare came to nine hundred bucks."

"He drove me all the way here?"

"It's not like he had a choice. Once somebody as old as Ricari puts that mojo on your ass, you do it even after you're brain-dead. I wish I knew how he did it."

"I can't believe he let me live," I marveled. "I was pretty sure I died. How did you save me?"

"Fluids," he said. "We brought you inside, and we gave you some plasma, and then I kissed your wounds. I sweated into you. I masturbated, and smeared you with my semen." He darted me a sly, unsmiling glance. "By the end of the night you were starting to heal up. They put you on an IV with glucose and saline, just to keep you up till you regained consciousness. In the meantime I kept you asleep with my mind, so you'd heal faster. Worked out all right, don't you think?"

"You jerked off on me?"

"No, I jerked off, then I caught it in my hand, then I put it on you. Why?"

I didn't have an immediate reply. I looked at him for a while. Then I looked at the strip malls and palms and costume shops of Hollywood Boulevard streaking past. "I guess I should thank you," I murmured.

"I can jerk off on you if you want," Daniel said. He caught me staring at him again. "Just kidding," he amended. "Tell me about Ricari. How is the old son of a bitch?"

"Pious," I said. "Confusing."

"Repressed? He hasn't changed. I bet he's worse now."

"I can't believe he sent me away like that," I said.

"Hmm, I can't either. Anybody with good sense would have just killed you instead of going through all the trouble to hail a taxi, do a Jedi Mind Trick on some poor cab driver, and write me a nice note explaining his reasoning. He must really like you." He pulled the tape out of the stereo and replaced it with one that sounded almost identical. "He damn well didn't leave me a note when he ran away from me."

"He had nothing nice to say about you," I said. "He said, for one thing, that you were no great beauty."

"I'm not," Daniel said. His features, each alone, were well-formed, even classic, but put together they did not quite form a coherent whole. He had a long, large-nostrilled, noble nose, cheekbones for days, narrow almond-shaped eyes, and a wide, pointed, wicked mouth painted blood red. He was a perfect incubus. All he needed were horns and a lion's tail.

"I think you're OK-looking," I commented.

Daniel's jaw dropped with wounded vanity. "Oh, geez, come now, you will smother me with praise. Stop it this instant. You're OK-looking too, honey, especially now that we've gotten the puke out of your hair."

"Thank you for stimulating my appetite."

"Go on and tell me I'm beautiful," he said. "It's OK. My ego can't get any bigger than it already is." He glanced over at me and continued driving without looking where he was going. He was still going twenty miles over the speed limit, changing lanes like a man determined to win the Indy 500. "Would it help if I told you that you were a knockout even covered in blood and puke and all I could think about was how much I really wanted to—"

"Daniel, could you maybe *please* look at the road?" I said through my teeth.

At length we arrived at a typical Cali restaurant with big ferns outside and little ones inside. I felt like my belly had been left somewhere back there, eight or nine lane changes ago. Daniel, in his fishnet shirt and alligator vinyl jeans, stalked in like a supermodel and worked the place. Everyone stared at him, with dislike or lust or simple incomprehension, and by extension, at me too. I wanted to throw a tablecloth over my face. What a change from Ricari, who slipped into places so quietly that waiters were startled to see him! Daniel eventually stopped prancing back and forth as if looking for more beautiful people, and we got settled into a booth in the back of the restaurant.

"Are you crazy?" I whispered.

"What?" Daniel guzzled water from his drinking glass, licking his red lips.

"You just don't care, do you?"

"I like to give people something to look at," he said, running his fingers through his shock of thick, spiky, jet-black hair, hanging uncut down to the nape of his neck.

"But what if they guess . . . ?" I darted my eyes around the room, my heart hammering in my chest. I could feel it against the scars too, from inside.

"Guess? Oh, please!" Daniel shook his head patiently. "No one'll guess. This is Los Angeles. I look less undead than half the producers' wives in town. Look." He stretched out his hands to me. His fingers were not as exaggeratedly long as Ricari's, but they were bright and bony and tipped with long, slightly curved fingernails, painted with black lacquer. The effect was extremely freaky. "Does this look human to you? No, it doesn't. But people don't care one way or the other. They wouldn't care if Jesus Christ himself came staggering through that door, nor Satan neither. Half the kids in Burbank have fangs. Dental porcelain. Looks just like the real thing." To demonstrate, he touched the tip of his tongue to one shining ivory spike.

"How do I know you're the real thing?" I asked as a matter of course.

He smiled at me, and instantly I felt the seat and the floor and the earth drop out from under me. I was falling at a thousand miles per hour without moving at all, without the jade coins of Daniel's eyes ever leaving mine. I would have thrown up, had there been anything in my stomach; as it was, I let out a little scream and gripped the table with my arms.

In another second everything was normal again. I almost began to cry in relief. "What the fuck was that?" I moaned.

"Very simple. I just fiddled with the part of your inner ear that handles your feeling of falling. Vertigo. A child could do it."

"That's bullshit!"

"So am I real?" Daniel pressed, his smile like that of a wicked child giving Indian burns.

"Yeah, yeah, OK. I believe you." My heart had barely had a chance to stop galloping after the experience of driving there.

He pouted, suddenly contrite. "I'm sorry," he said. He picked up my hand and kissed it, then got up and slid into the other side of the booth with me and put his arms around me for a while. His body was very warm and firm, his touch on my damp hair gentle, and I lay my ear against his chest. I heard his heart beating quite solidly, distinctly. I hadn't known until then that vampires had hearts.

A waitress finally came, sparing me any more dramas, and Daniel ordered food and hot tea for both of us. When she was gone, he asked, "Should I go back to the other side?"

"No," I said.

He kept holding me, cheek pressed against my hair. "Why are you so warm? Why does your heart beat so loud?"

"Because," he said, "I am genuine. I do not deny myself anything."

"You mean you're a killer."

"I take what I want," he restated.

"You gonna kill me?" I looked up at him. It must have been seductive, and I didn't even mean it that way, but I looked up at him through my curly lashes like he was some kind of Superman who had just saved me. Kind of disgusting, now that I think about it.

"That's up to you," he said. "I like you. I don't want you to die. I saved your life. I want you to stay with me for a while."

The food came.

"Your heart's still beating so hard," he murmured against my temple. "I don't think that's fear happening now." I pushed him away then, and cleared enough space between us so that we were no longer touching. He smiled down into his vinyl lap disturbingly.

We ate. God, it was weird watching the vampire eat people food; he ate mostly with his fingers, except for the soup, continually licking bits from between his fangs and his first set of molars. "Do you have to floss?" I asked curiously.

"No," he said. "My teeth don't decay. I sometimes floss, just for the hell of it. I can't imagine why so few people do it regularly. I think it's a blast. I mean, who ever came up with this concept, dragging a little thread between your teeth? He must have been one crazy son of a bitch."

The food both strengthened me and made me sleepy. "Can I go back to bed?" I asked in a small voice, lean-

117

ing against Daniel as he played with spilled salt on the table.

"Why?"

"I'm tired," I said.

"Well, you don't want to go back to that wretched infirmary. That's just for folks who need it."

"Do you get a lot of those?"

"Nature of the beast, I'm afraid. Sometimes I go a little too far."

"So, what, do you have this little tribe of medical gnomes at your beck and call to fix up people you've 'gone too far' with?"

He laughed faintly. "Not exactly," he said, not volunteering more. "You're very welcome to stay at my apartment, in my bed. It's nice, I have a groovy wave generator across from it, it's very hypnotic. I won't disturb you. I must go ranging afield tonight anyway."

"Yeah, I think that'll be fine." I was fading already.

He paid the sizable tab, and half carried me back to the black Coupe de Ville. He even changed the tape—he ditched the industrial for the soothing nonsense of the Cocteau Twins. "You have good taste in music for a ninety-year-old guy," I murmured.

"Some people are simply born in the wrong era. I am lucky to have lived long enough to get to some music I can stand. I wasn't very impressed by music I didn't make myself until I saw the Doors at the Whisky in 1968. I thought I was going to lose it." He seemed deeply amused by my comment. "A hip ninety-year-old. I never thought of it that way before. I'm a pretty happenin' senior citizen. Maybe I'll move to Palm Springs."

His apartment complex was built in a horseshoe shape, of lovely old red brick, with a marble fountain in the center. At eleven o'clock, it was completely quiet except for the faint tones of someone playing a piano. "Ah—Mozart," Daniel ascertained, "that crazy fat Austrian bastard. Will I never escape him?" He unlocked the door of number three, and led me in.

Inside was dark except for the wave generator, a transparent Lucite rectangle with some viscous blue fluid inside, slowly forming tides and then waves against itself, rocking back and forth ever so gently. It was completely stultifying, and Daniel had to tap me to get my attention. "Ariane, darling, get in bed."

I sat on the edge of a black-flannel covered futon, and stared up at him. He was changing his shirt. The clean lines of his shoulder blades became complex further down the back, and the six faint swells of his belly shone out for a brief second before a black polyester cowboy shirt covered them. "You're welcome to anything," Daniel said, tucking the shirt into the waistband of his wacky jeans. "If you need me, pick up the phone and press one, star. That'll ring me. If you get hungry, there might be something to eat in the fridge, and there's some pepper vodka and some lime juice and tonic in there, and there's cable, and you can call phone sex or psychics all night if you want, I never pay my phone bills anyway . . . you OK?"

"Thank you," I said, my throat feeling slightly tight.

I saw his eyes moisten slightly. "That's all right," he said. "You need me."

I crawled under the cover, wriggling out of my dress and socks. I heard him leave and close the door. The piano played on softly, coordinating with the blue waves as I fell asleep.

I slept; I dreamt; of what, I've forgotten now. I half woke, then went back to sleep, sliding myself out of my cotton panties, rubbing my pubic fur against the sleekness of the flannel. The temperature was perfect— the bed was just slightly cooler than my body, the pillow hard under my chin, chilly like spring rain.

I know everyone has had moments like this, where

you are overtaken completely by the sensuality of a comfortable bed and an erotic dream; you diffuse, your sensuality fills the room, every sensation of comfort is taken as sexual stimulation. I was all wound up—I wanted to come, but for some reason it was not quite possible. I needed help. I thought to myself, *I should wake up and masturbate*.

When I woke up it seemed that I already was—a hand was stroking my cunt in exactly the way I do it when I don't want to get off right away, but want to prolong the pleasure for as long as I have time. But both my hands were under my chin. A warm sleek smooth body was pressed against my side and I felt lips caressing my neck, my cheeks. I turned over and embraced the body, pulling it tighter to me. The hand squeezed me, and I felt a claw poke gently against my anus. I held up my own lips to kiss, and they were kissed.

I felt for identifying genitals. A penis; thick and full, mostly hard, rooted in very dense, smooth hair. I heard a faint hiss in my ear, and a whisper of a chuckle. "Careful." And more kisses against my mouth. The mouth tasted sweet and salty at once, quite pure, clean. A sharp point pricked my tongue and almost brought me out of my fog, but it didn't quite. Salt became the dominant flavor in our mouths.

The hand below paused in stroking me, and instead spread the lips apart. I heard the moist smacking and it aroused me further. I had a firm hold on the cock now, bringing it near. Just before it brushed against my belly, I opened my eyes.

Daniel lay against me, half on top, his skin slightly imperfect this close; he had open pores on his forehead, a trace of a scar coming down out of the hairline. His eyes were focused on my face, the pupils clicking open and closed, like the sphincter of a camera shutter. "I heard you dreaming," he said. "I thought you might have some need of me."

I kept my eyes fixed on him as together we helped his cock find its purchase inside me. I felt like I was being stabbed slowly—the pain was sharp at first, then slackening. His face transformed with pleasure. Gone was the cynic's slight smile, the brightness of the observing eyes; now he was all one purpose. I rocked upward until we were completely joined. He paused with his back arched, poised for a second; then all at once, he had gathered himself and thrust in again.

I was wracked with orgasms almost immediately. He didn't stop fucking me; rather he kept a hand down with a fingertip pressed tightly against my clitoris, trapping its retreat, making it face one defeat after another. He understood the female orgasm probably better than anyone I've ever known—that it's not simply a function of the cunt and cervix, nor a purely clitoral event; the entire system ought be be involved. After a few minutes our thighs were bathed in liquid.

He let me be for a while, and concentrated on the work. He didn't seem to be working to any particular goal; he was like a man taking a class for the fun of it, rather than for credit. I could not have come any more if I wanted to. I was content to hang onto his sleek back, admiring his nubile form, his delicacy, his tendency to fuck to four corners inside me. I didn't doubt that he had made Ricari violently jealous.

We stopped for a moment so I could have a bathroom break; then we resumed again, tangled in the sheets. We giggled and wrestled, and he pulled me on top of him, the covers over us. Dizzy in the stuffy hot air, I protested, but he murmured, "Sunlight coming through the blinds," arching his hips in a drowsy, but professional, motion.

After a few lifetimes I groaned, "Don't you ever fucking come?"

"When I want to."

I lay back against him, wondering how I was ever going to walk again. His cock was still stiff as a poker, curved up against his belly, covered in a pinkish sheen. We had fucked till I bled. When I showed him, he held me down and licked at my wounded cunt the way an animal licks at a sore spot. At some point determined by him, he stopped and pronounced, "All better. Your turn."

Without complaint I bent over his penis. Oh, Daniel's penis, what a work of art, it belongs in the Louvre, in the Guggenheim of genitalia; thick and longish, just on the verge of being too big, with a prow-shaped tip poking through the delicate veil of foreskin. His skin was so translucent that his erection was dark violet, like berry stains—and the taste—like a strange vegetable, raw, the juice from a broken stalk. Daniel seemed to drift into a contemplative reverie, and I almost thought he was bored, but when I began to slow down, he seized my head and forced it back down.

At once he drew in his breath tightly, and gave out a throaty, clear, sharp cry. His issue flooded my mouth in a great copious stream that dribbled out of my lips and splashed on his lean white perfect thighs. "Swallow," he commanded. I shut my eyes and swallowed what I had caught—a big mouthful, the flavor of dry white wine, the texture of last night's avoglemono soup.

It burnt slightly in my stomach.

I lay beside Daniel, who had his eyes closed. I glanced at a red-numbered digital clock—it read 2:45 P.M. "I don't think that was fair," I murmured against the skin of his inner arm.

"No? But you were dreaming about me."

"I don't remember dreaming about you."

"Your pussy was wet. You were in my bed. And you were as tight as a virgin—when was your last time?"

"Months ago. But that doesn't give you the right."

"What gives me the right," he said, opening his eyes, "is that you grabbed my johnson, you sucked me off, you wanted me. Naughty child."

"You're pure evil," I said, tracing the halo of long dark fine hairs that ringed his areolas, the only hair on his chest. He kissed my hair and trailed his claws gently across my thighs.

"Ariane, will you consent to start falling in love with me, so I don't feel like so much of an idiot for being in love with you?"

"What the hell are you in love with me for? All we did was screw." But I blushed violently.

Daniel kissed me. "I love the taste of my cum in your mouth. Has nothing to do with screwing. That was inevitable. There is more. I can talk to you. You don't take me seriously. Plus, we've both been through Ricari University. And there's more besides that. You have such perfect breasts, did you know that? And a perfect round belly. And a perfect ass . . . you have the kind of body that I like . . . a Theda Bara body. A surrealist body."

"Jesus Christ, Daniel."

"Tell me you'll stay with me. Please?"

"Is there a Denny's around here anywhere? I really want some french fries." I began wiggling away from him, into the comparative coolness of the air.

He gave a patient sigh. "We're going to buy you some clothes first. Then we can go to Denny's in West Hollywood." He slid out of bed and stood there in the semidarkness, gloriously nude, stinking of me, hair tousled.

"When? Now? But you can't go out in the sun."

"Yes, I can. I've got long sleeves, sunscreen, and a hat. I needn't be outside for long—I know where we're getting your clothes. I hope you like black. I hate just about every other color."

I shrugged. "You're paying."

We didn't bother to wash at all. I sat in my dress and my pool of drying honey and watched him pull on a long-sleeved black shirt, black Levi's, fine leather gloves, and a black ten-gallon hat. When he was done I stood up and kissed him ravenously on the mouth.

It was a bright hot clear day, but Daniel, behind his Jackie O shades and gloves, didn't seem to mind. He drove like a demon back through Hollywood, blasting Snoop Doggy Dogg from the car stereo, and fondling my bare pale thigh.

Sometime after we started driving, but before we reached our destination, I felt a change seep into me, slowly but growing more rapid, like a drug, or a glass of liquor after dinner. I thought of my old clothes— the gray fisherman's sweaters, the hiking boots, my favorite pair of blue jeans that I wore until the crotch needed patching—and I didn't miss them at all. I didn't miss my apartment, or my students, or my dead rats. They seemed like old TV shows that I used to never miss when I was a kid, but that I forgot as I grew up. I tried to picture John's face, or his body, his belly, or his penis—and I couldn't get more than an impression. He was gone. All of it was gone. And I felt light, slightly dazed, happy in a European way. I stared at Daniel until we reached a stoplight. Then he looked over at me and picked up my hand and sucked one of my fingertips into his mouth. "Will you stay here with me?" he said.

I said nothing. I smiled, stroking the velvet texture of his tongue with my pinky.

He turned back to the road and smiled to himself.

So he bought me clothes at some pretentious Gothic chamber of a basement boutique—five pairs of black jeans, some T-shirts, some short uncomplicated dresses, chunky black Doc Martens shoes—and then zipped off to Denny's in the orange afternoon sunlight.

We sat in a booth at the back where the sun didn't reach, and immediately began to grope.

You must understand that I never felt like this before. I was deeply in love with John when I first met him, but what went on between us was rarified, mainly verbal sparring, understanding, and sex that was comforting and delicious; we never had a time when we couldn't keep our hands off each other, when sex was continually threatening to jump out of the woodwork. Some will disapprove of such public excesses. Honestly, we weren't trying to gross out the other patrons of Denny's #45312 (or at least, I wasn't), those hapless travelers and Grand Slam diners who stared at us with naked distaste. There was simply an ectoplasm oozing out of Daniel, creeping over and enfolding me, tormenting me into making love with him in public. It didn't help that he kept up a running narrative of obscenities in my brain, which I shall not try to replicate. It doesn't sound half so nice coming from me.

The barely-of-age waiter came over and glared at us. "Are you, like, ready to order?" he snipped.

Daniel turned his smoky eyes on the boy, and I saw the waiter wilt, a sweat visibly breaking out on his forehead. Daniel's lust was fucking contagious. Daniel gave the yellow uniform a frank appraisal, then said, "Nothing for me. The lady will have French fries with ranch. And coffee."

"Are you ever going to let me order?" I whispered to Daniel.

"Should I?"

I answered him by locating his nipple through his shirt and biting it.

"You clean up real nice, baby."

The waiter lurched off to the kitchen, crippled by a sudden boner, and I sat back and regarded my lover Daniel with a smile. He eased his hand up my skirt a few inches further. "I'll be honest with you," he said softly. "When you swallowed, I enslaved you."

"What?" I asked, laughing.

"It's a few steps away from my blood," he said. "You're mine now. I can talk to your mind. I can talk to your body. You won't want to leave me. You can, if you want, but you won't want to. It's the only infallible love potion I can think of."

"You serious?" The smile melted from my face.

He nodded.

"That's why I feel like this?"

"It'll wear off. But you are closer to me now, for a while, than you could be otherwise. I don't know how it works. Something, probably, on the cellular level. My cum . . . burns, doesn't it?"

"Yes. In my stomach."

He licked a curl of my hair. "I noticed it with Ricari."

"You—?"

"Oh, well, of course. He didn't know. I didn't either. I just wanted to go down on him. I was terribly, terribly attached to him—I had his semen all through my body, in my mouth, up my ass, everywhere, his sweat, his tears. Every drop of his body I tasted held me to him more and more."

"I can't . . . imagine . . . Ricari fucking anyone up the ass . . ."

Daniel laughed. "Hmmmm," he said, raising his eyebrows. "I wasn't the first. Usually he was a taker, from what he told me. He hustled quite a bit in those back streets of Paris, did you know that?"

"I thought he mainly went with women."

"He wasn't that picky."

I shivered. Daniel stroked the gooseflesh on my arm until the fine brown hairs lay smooth again, kissed my hand where the green veins stood up, fat and nervous. "Orfeo and I . . . used to fuck . . . for hours, like you and I did. We did nothing else for days. I would run afield, and bring home young men for him to kill and feed upon, and then we'd make love with their staring bodies propped up in the corner. Sometimes they'd die right when we were climaxing. I loved it."

"How many people do you kill a week?"

"I don't know. On average?" He stretched along the booth. "Three?"

"Three people a week?"

"That's an average. Some weeks I don't kill anybody. Some weeks I kill twenty."

"Did you kill someone last night?"

"Only myself," he said, touching his hand to his chin poetically. He chewed gently on the back of my hand. "Eat your fries, my darling. I want to have you in the car during sunset."

He did too; in the parking lot of the Rotting Hall, while the sky went through its daily convulsions of scarlet and puce, he raised and lowered me like a flag on a pole, holding my hair out of my face so that he could watch me. Heavy-metal people passed within inches of the car without seeing us writhing around back there. "I'm going to come inside you," Daniel told me, half starting up, jamming himself so tightly inside me that I felt something nearly give way.

"No," I pleaded.

"You can't stop me. It won't hurt you." His fangs glinted at me. "I can't get you pregnant, I can't carry disease. I am safe sex."

"I don't wanna become any more obsessed with you than I already am!"

"I need you! You're in love with me! Admit it."

"Fuck you." I gasped. "Oh, my God."

"Come on," he said. "Come with me. Come on."

"No," I said, but I already was.

Chapter Seven

Another glorious terrible evening had ended on the mattress in Daniel's office on the top floor; I could feel the contours of Daniel's penis inside me as if my cunt were a sheet of metal hammered into shape. I had fallen asleep at dawn, exhausted, in the middle of a sweaty fuck, Daniel whispering *Deutschen* exhortations of love into my ear. I slept hard, too tired to dream.

Awakening many hours later, I lay on my side blinking at the cracks of sunlight creeping through the shrouds of garbage bags that covered the windows. The tape we'd been listening to all night still ran—David Bowie's *Hunky Dory* and some Nico thing on the other side; "Oh! You Pretty Things" was playing as I awakened. All was vague brownish polygons. My back was cold as ice. I snuggled closer to Daniel behind me, trying to gain warmth from the phlogiston of his body, but that was where the cold was coming from. I felt like my back was to a cold tile floor.

I rolled over, rubbing my eyes. "Dan?" I whispered.

A corpse lay there where Daniel had been; it had Daniel's hair, the black shiny shocks of it lying across the mattress cover, and Daniel's bone structure, the long Adam's apple, and the jutting Teuton cheekbones. But the eyes were sunken, the lips dark and lifeless, the luminous white skin gone gray-blue. His hands were curled into mummy fists, like the feet of a dead bird.

My scream echoed three full times. Before the last died down I was in the far corner of the room, a single droplet of nervous urine streaking down my leg like quicksilver. I couldn't get far enough away. And to think that I could still feel the sweet displacement of that cock inside me, still feel his hot shaky breath on my ear!

A boy came tumbling out of the bathroom, half zipped up, and ran over to me. I stared at him. "What's the matter?" he asked me quizzically, squatting down and regarding me like a curious bird. I couldn't say anything for a long time. The boy had very white skin, but a mortal white, with pink fingers and bare toes, and a slightly rounded childish belly; his head was shaved, but for a blond and black forelock that fluttered in the slight breeze coming from the garbage bags on the windows.

"Daniel," I managed to get out, and pointed.

The boy looked over at the grimy mattress on the other side of the room, half covered with clothes and black sheets, and then back at me. "What's the matter?" he asked again. "Haven't you ever seen him sleep before?"

"Sleep?"

He helped me stand up, putting his arms around me to steady me. I was buck naked, but I didn't even care. He led me slowly back over to the mattress, and had me kneel down beside it. The boy put out his hand to the blue shrunken body, and touched the shoulder. The impression of his finger stayed there. I felt nauseated. "He's fine," said the boy. "You've never seen him sleep. You never saw your other vampire sleep?"

I was beginning to breathe again. "No," I said. "He wouldn't let me."

The boy made a sound of understanding. "If he were dead for real, there wouldn't be anything left except bones—maybe not even that."

We looked at each other.

"You wanna shower?" he asked shyly. "I brought you some towels."

"Yeah," I said. "Thanks."

I somnambulated to the bathroom, and took a shower. The tiles in there were white and clean, but the grout between the tiles was black and shiny, with God only knows what. I soaped myself for twenty minutes, silently thanking Ricari for those small, ruthless mercies.

I toweled off with more stolen hotel towels, and put on a pair of new black jeans and a plain black T-shirt that the boy had kindly set on the tiles while I was in the shower. He was outside sitting in a folding chair when I got out, reading a comic book with one leg crossed over his lap. He was a beautiful morsel of a young boy—handsome legs, narrow girl-shoulders, a smooth flexible torso with a tattoo of a question mark on the belly and a crescent moon on the right shoulder. Both of his marzipan-perfect rosy nipples were pierced laterally with delicate steel barbells. He smiled at me. "Feeling better?"

"I don't think I ever want a shock like that again."

"Dan loves to shock people," said the boy. Politely he closed his comic book. "It'll be sundown soon, and he'll be waking up. I think we have plans for the night. Do you want to come downstairs with me and smoke some kind buds? I have some French bread and chocolate."

I followed the boy down the winding staircase. The formerly deserted building was now host to probably a dozen young kids, mostly dressed in black, from punky tatters and safety pins to elegant black lace gowns and silver buckles. They smiled at me as we went past, as if they knew all about it. I blushed my head off. They all knew. Had they all gone through waking up next to the graying horror and having their screams echo through the broken bricks? I felt like a royal idiot.

The boy led me to a smallish room three floors down, strewn with couch cushions, tapes, comic books, stubs of votive candles. He left the door open. "Do you have a cigarette?" I asked wanly.

"Of course." He had a crushed packet of black Sobranies, one of which he lit for me. He took a swallow from a plastic container of pinkish liquid, and busily began to pack a tiny purple plastic bong. "I'm sorry. Don't feel bad. They all look like that when they sleep. Or at least, Daniel does."

"Who are those people?"

"Them? They're just Dan's kids. You know. They follow him around. They hang out here. A lot of them saw Daniel's shows, and came here to find him. A lot of them, he picked up off the streets and brought here so he could take care of them, you know, have fun with them. Most of them ran away from home, like me." He handed me the bong.

I took a short, soothing hit. "What's your name?" I said, exhaling slowly.

"Lovely," he said. "Well, duh, of course that's not my real name. My real name sucks. The first thing Daniel said when he saw me was, 'Oooh, lovely,' so I decided that would be my name from now on."

"Do you know my name?"

131

"Sure," he said. "Ariane. Daniel told us a long time ago."

"What were you doing upstairs?"

He paused while the smoke worked its way around his lungs, then blew it all out with a mighty cough. He shook his head. "Daniel called for me," he said. "He wanted me to watch over you both. I've been there since about noon, just chillin', listening to Bowie and reading comics. I do it all the time."

I refused a second bong hit. "How long have you been here?" I asked.

"About two years now."

I smoked my cigarette, watching the tiny flames licking up the sides of the smooth black paper. "And how old are you?"

"Eighteen."

"You Daniel's lover?"

He nodded slowly. "Yep," he said. "Most us of are, or have been, at some point."

"And you all know . . . ?"

"That he's a vamp? Well, yeah, of course, why else would we be here? I mean, Daniel's hot, and he's talented and great, but there's one reason mainly why most people stay. Some people come around just to find out if it's all true, then they drift off. But a lot of kids stick around. He's *real,* you know. It means a lot to us."

"How'd you find out about . . . uh . . ."

"Your other vampire?" He smiled at me over the rim of the bong. "Daniel told some of us. His most important folks—me, Chloe, Mimsy, those of us who were there when we found you. Chloe was the one who actually did a lot of the fixing up. She used to be a nurse, I guess. We gave you plasma. I should say, I gave you plasma."

"What do you mean?"

"We've got the same blood type," he said. "She set

us up on some tubes, and I dripped all this blood into you. Then I passed out. I missed the big ritual—Daniel's big laying on of hands and all that. I've never seen him so into saving someone's life before. But he showed us all that note that was stuck to you, and said, 'You know who wrote this? It was that bastard who changed me over. He's too chickenshit to do it again, so he sends 'em to me, like fruit baskets.' I'll never forget it for a million years. I could have puked laughing. So what was he like? Was he really horrible?"

"I don't know," I sighed. The dope was soaking into me finally, making my body throb. My body missed Daniel, all asleep and dead upstairs. "I was totally in love with Ricari. I would have done absolutely anything for him—but he didn't want me to do anything for him. Except kill him. Which I didn't do. Which I should have done."

"Wait a minute. Wait a minute. What?"

"He wanted me to kill him," I said. "He couldn't do it himself, because it was a sin."

"No way!"

"And I couldn't do it either, because I loved him too much and I wanted him to take me away or something. All he wanted me to do was stuff him in the oven and walk away. But I fucking couldn't. I didn't want to face life without him." I crushed out my cigarette into an overflowing brass tray.

Lovely was completely absorbed, his pot-reddened eyes wide and awed. "Was he really, really beautiful?"

"Really, really beautiful."

"More beautiful than Dan?"

"In a way. He's a tiny little eighteenth-century guy."

"Blue eyes?"

"Gray. Brown hair. Really amazing skin."

"Oh, wow, he sounds cute." The boy stretched out on the cushions. "I kind of like my men a little more macho. Daniel's just about perfect. He has the *savory* body."

"I don't know if I want to hear about Daniel's body," I mumbled.

He laughed. "Tough. I talk about it all the time. I am so, *so* into Daniel, you have no clue. I seriously love him so much more than life itself. I don't even want to be like him. It would be wrong. I just want to be with him until the end. Listen, I have it all planned out, and Daniel even said yes." He rolled over and grabbed my ankle. "So, we're going to make out in a big bed all hung with black satin, like in an old movie. He's going to fuck me really hard. Then he's going to bite my artery and drain me dry in one big swallow. That's how I want to die, and Daniel said yes. Isn't he the greatest?"

"And when are you planning this blessed event?"

"On my twenty-first birthday."

"Oh, Lovely, don't you want to get a little older than that?"

"Fuck, no!"

He punctuated this with another bong hit and a fit of coughing that left him prostrate on the cushions, giggling faintly.

I fingered the French bread and chocolate and began to nibble tiny bites from it. At some point a very small girl in a black corset and floor-length skirt came in and asked for a bong hit; she was followed by another girl, and then a boy, and another girl. They crouched on the couch cushions smoking, introducing themselves. I was a little too stoned to remember any of their names, but they offered me drinks from flasks of hot tea, wine, whiskey, and water; they shared their berries and cigarettes. I asked them their ages; sixteen, sixteen, nineteen, seventeen. The boy had clear piercing pale blue eyes and hair colored black with shoe polish; he began massaging Lovely's bare, dirty-bottomed feet. One of the girls braided my hair, cooing in admiration of its color.

At last Lovely sat up and looked at a clock. "Shit," he said, "sundown."

Everyone scrambled up and ran up the stairs as quietly as possible. Not just us, but kids from every corner, galloping up the stairs two at a time, making little macabre haunted-house noises, giggling, spilling fragrant drops of wine.

We all gathered round the mattress where Daniel slept on. They made a place for me at the front. For a long time he looked as wretched as ever; then, as suddenly and as slowly as the sun begins to rise, his flesh began to come to life.

The gray shaded back to white, then to a healthy pale cream. His nipples pinkened and became erect, his lips flushed with color. Everyone was silent except for taped David Bowie, moaning, "It's War-*hole*, War-*hole* . . . as in 'holes.' "

Daniel took a great breath; and stirred. He scratched his face. He scratched the top of his head, and his balls. Some of the girls giggled faintly.

He rolled over and opened his eyes, and smiled like a pampered king.

"Morning, Daniel," Lovely said, his voice thick with adoration.

The liqueur eyes scanned us. Then he reached out and grabbed the tiny corseted girl from Lovely's room, dragging her into bed with him. He pulled the covers over them and a giggling and shrieking ensued.

I turned away, a wave of jealousy rising up so fast it made me dizzy. How could this have happened? What did I care? The girl made desperate noises of pain, culminating in a hollow "Owwwww!" that rose up like smoke. Lovely put his warm naked arms around me and hugged me very tightly; if he hadn't, I would have gotten up then and left that place and never returned.

Daniel sprang up from the bed, wrapping a sheet around him like a big black toga. The girl lay motionless on the mattress, her eyes rolled up in her head and one wrist trailing red streaks across the cheap fabric of the cover. "Get out, all of you!" Daniel shouted majestically, and without a word of protest, that was what everyone did. Everyone except Lovely and myself.

"What have you done?" I demanded of Daniel.

"Nothing, Ariane, keep your panties on." He rolled back his head, smiling and licking his very red lips. "She'll be fine in a few hours. Go on, you too. Lovely, take her outside, would you?"

I went down the stairs with Lovely.

"I don't get it," I said.

"He does it almost every day," Lovely explained, drinking from his plastic container. He handed it to me and I had a sip—gallon chablis. "Everyone wants to be it. He grabs you, gives you a little fondle, then he goes CHOMP! Sometimes you get more than a little fondle—I've sat there for hours while he fucks someone's brains out. But the bite's always part of it. It's Daniel's breakfast. He can't get going without it."

"That looked kind of serious," I said, glancing over my shoulder. "Does he ever . . ."

"Go too far? Sometimes. Part of the game. You never know." Lovely shrugged and smiled. "He doesn't kill any of us except rarely, and usually because they've asked him in advance. But he can't be told. Sometimes a kid will beg him and beg him to be taken and killed, and Daniel won't do it unless he feels like it. Usually, though, when someone comes to him and wants it ended, Daniel does what they want him to do."

"That's so fucked up."

"Isn't it great?"

"Is this what I'm to become?" I said out loud bitterly. "I just hang around, hoping he picks me to go with his bacon and eggs?"

Lovely stared at me with his eyebrows up—well, his eyebrow muscles anyway—his eyebrows were shaven clean off. "Do you really think that?"

I shook my head in mute fury.

"Girl, everybody gets jealous like that. You don't have to worry. He loves you. You're special to him—you've seen his sire. You've been with him. He loves you, Ariane, I mean it. Daniel may be a slut, but he doesn't say he's in love when he's not."

"When did he tell you he was in love?" I snapped.

"Night before last." Lovely blushed. "When you were asleep in his apartment. We went out hunting together in Venice Beach, and he told me, 'Lovely, I am completely nuts about this girl, and I don't know if she even cares.' "

"Hunting? Together?"

"I'll tell you about it later," he said. "What's important for you to think about now is that you're important to him. Has he bitten you yet?"

I thought about it. "No," I said.

"He would have killed you a long time ago. And he hasn't even bitten you. Maybe he should, then he'd know what you're thinking."

I began to laugh despite myself. "You're a real vampire expert by now, aren't you?"

"I damn well ought to be." He put his arm around me and led me away. "Come on."

That evening I had dinner with the others at a dim Middle Eastern restaurant in Hollywood, the kind of place where the guests are supposed to lounge on embroidered cushions and the only utensil allowed is pita bread; the lights are terribly dim, and young actors who have yet to be discovered languish in the shadows.

The food had already been set on the table when

Lovely and I arrived and sat down. A young woman with a cloud of dark hair and an oval, cameo-stone white face poured my cup full of red wine with mysterious shreds floating in it. "Good evening, Ariane," she said with a formal pleasantness. "I hope you don't mind, I've taken the liberty of infusing the wine with psilocybin mushrooms. It's not very strong, but the flavor is wonderful. My name is Chloe." She indicated, with one delicate white hand, a lanky gentleman with a spikier, blacker version of Daniel's hair and fishnet tights, relaxing back against the cushions, nibbling from a handful of black olives. "This is Mimsy, he's my lover; this"—she nodded to a shining platinum-blond femme in blue velvet and white lace—"is Nora, and I see you've already met Lovely. It's our honor and pleasure to meet you. We're Daniel's cabinet, so to speak." Chloe smiled as I took a cautious sip of the poisoned wine. It was pleasantly bitter, like unsweetened chocolate. "You could say that I am Daniel's right hand. Lovely is his left. Nora is sight and sound."

"I'm his butt," Mimsy said.

There were giggles. "We haven't found a body part for Mims yet," Nora said modestly. Her voice was surprisingly gravelly, coming from that fairylike body.

"I'm Daniel's fist," Mimsy said, quite serious.

"The executive branch," I said, selecting some food.

"In a way. We're not really a government. We're just the ones who take care of things."

"We're the only ones with responsibilities," said Nora. "Although I don't usually think of 'Lovely' and 'responsibility' at the same time." She smirked at Lovely nastily, and Lovely pursed his lips and looked at the ceiling.

Chloe rested again, leaning her head against Mimsy's chest. "I've been with him the longest. Seven years ago I was in nursing school, wondering why I wanted to kill myself every ten minutes. I had a friend, well, not really a friend, this guy I knew, who was a designer, and one day I went to his studio to see if he had anything interesting going on. And that's when I met Daniel." She paused to drink her wine cup dry. "He wasn't really doing anything at the time—just hanging out in gay bars all the time, picking up guys. He had picked up this friend of mine, came home with him. By the end of the evening he had gone home with me."

"Seven years?" I said. "So that makes you, what . . . ?"

"Twenty-seven," she replied with a smile.

"I'm glad there's somebody here older than me," I said.

Mimsy laughed. "I'm twenty-five, so don't worry too much. But we're about it. Nora here just turned twenty-two."

"Not like it matters," Nora said quickly. "I've still been setting Dan up for three years."

"How do you mean, 'setting up'?"

"I'm his manager," said Nora.

There was a faint bluster of protest from everyone else.

"Like, she knows all these people," Lovely explained, pausing to swallow, "so, like, she sets up club dates like the one we're going to tonight. And, like, making sure people don't figure out too much . . ."

"I'm the screen," Nora said. "The makeup. I show him, but only in a way that's safe. Daniel's a little reckless sometimes. I don't want him making any disastrous mistakes and ruining all our lives. I want him to be famous, but not too famous, y'know?"

"What are we going to tonight?" I asked, sipping my wine somewhat more cautiously. Not too strong, my ass—already I felt the telltale edge of excitement and nausea from the mushrooms, the hallucinogen ushered in by warmth, hunger, and wine. I began to nervously pick at my cucumbers.

"You'll see," Chloe said with a smile.

I relaxed upon the cushions.

At one point in the evening Chloe and Nora followed me to the bathroom, where they not-too-covertly fed me tiny methedrine pills; when I returned, Mimsy gave me marijuana chocolate truffles. Lovely was gone, and I hadn't even noticed when he left. I stared at my comrades helplessly through a wavering technicolor curtain, trying to express to them that I probably shouldn't be getting this fucked up, but I couldn't really speak. They were taking good care of me, though—giving me lots of cold water to drink, making sure I got something to eat and that I didn't mistakenly drink more of the wine.

Later Chloe helped me out of the restaurant into Nora's car (it smelled of patchouli and book mold), and we drove somewhere, listening to David Bowie's *Low* on the car stereo. Chloe sat in back with me, petting my hands and seeming to listen to me intently, though I wasn't sure if I was talking out loud or merely thinking a hundred miles an hour. I didn't feel too bad, all things considering—the wine had barely made me drunk, the mushrooms were good and not too nauseating, the speed was clean and pure, and the dope wore the glass-sharp edges off everything. The world shot by in a liquid concoction of amber and red lights. Nora and Mimsy seemed to be arguing, but I couldn't understand a word and decided that it had nothing to do with me.

By the time we arrived at the club, I had begun to sober slightly. It was a very pretty nightclub, most of the interior walls made up of square glass bricks, glowing purplish with black lights. A bar stretched along the wall to the right as one came in, the liquor bottles glittering in the uneasy rhythm of red light ropes; to the left was a partial wall, half solid black, the other half glass. Directly in front was a dance floor or stage, slightly raised, and currently set up with a wicked tangle of electronic instruments and drums.

"Want a drink?" Chloe asked me, leaning in close to my ear.

"Yeah," I said, suddenly thirsty from the speed. "I need a gin and orange juice. Can I have a cigarette?"

She gave me one of her Turkish ovals, lit it for me, and then walked away to the bar. The club was not crowded, and I wasn't so high that I didn't feel silly just standing there in the middle of the floor, so I meandered along to the wall of glass bricks, intending to run my fingers across them to make sure they weren't really ice.

Perhaps a dozen people were loitering along the wall, dressed in varying stages of severe black and vinyl, smoking bright sticks of smoking chalk. I thought to myself that in this light they all looked like vampires.

I saw Daniel then, leaning up against the wall where it became solid and black, his head thrown back and eyes closed; his arms were stiffly down at his sides. When a person moved aside to shift her weight, I saw Lovely as well, on his knees in front of Daniel, his head slowly weaving up and down. Daniel's hands gripped the suede sides of the boy's head so intensely that the veins stood out, the tendons like the skeleton of an umbrella.

I felt suddenly very sick, and it took me a moment to realize that I was angry, I was jealous, I was wounded. I felt like throwing up; I wanted to become sober again, to leave there and get back to something safe, something that made sense. But there was nothing to go to anymore. Nothing would ever make sense again. I wrung my hands, wrapped my arms around myself, digging my fingers into my ribs.

Daniel opened his eyes and looked straight into me. He smiled, slowly, knowingly, and he said to me, *Yes, I know. But look. See here. See this boy. He is giving me head. He is giving you head. I am giving you head. You are mine always and he is mine always and I am yours always. This pleasure shall never be mine alone, as long as you stay with me and trust me.*

And he was right. I held out my hand to the glass bricks to steady myself. Lovely was really giving it his all; his nude back muscles working intently to keep himself upright or from falling against Daniel with fatigue. A hot eroticism swelled inside me.

Chloe arrived with my drink. "What's the matter? Oh." She turned me away from them, blushing brightly against her white moon face. Her eyes were marked out in the face with smudges of black powder, the same makeup statement that Lovely himself employed, but in a more understated manner. "Jesus, he's always doing shit like that in public. It's so childish. Don't let it bug you."

"Are you Daniel's sex slave too?" I blurted out.

She laughed. "Mn-mn," she said, shaking her head slowly. "Oh, no. That's all in the past, long, long past. I was, for a long while. It's much more . . . filial now." She tugged at her hair. "He's kind of like a crazy uncle. Anyway, I'm with Mimsy, he's plenty."

"And Mimsy . . . ?"

"He and Daniel never were. Mimsy's straight, if you can believe that. What Mimsy feels is loyalty." Chloe put her arm around me. "C'mon, let's go sit down. How do you feel?"

We sat in stiff chairs to the right of the stage, and I assured her that I was quite all right. She lit me another cigarette and we talked lightly about medicine. I spilled to her about my schooling, my ambitions, my experiments, and she listened quietly, looking up at me once in a while to say, "Yes, I know what you mean." At some point Nora joined us at our little table with a tall flute of champagne. She was brittle with speed, her jaws clenched in a tight little smile. She jarred Chloe's and my trippy repose, and I fell silent after a few minutes.

But then the show began and I forgot all about drug incompatibilities.

So this was what Daniel did: He and six or seven (I was too gone to count accurately) other people came out onto the "stage." The others, including Mimsy, were dressed in black jeans, exercise tanks, rubber shorts, ripped tights; an athletic and dangerous crew, male and female. Daniel himself wore a tight maroon velvet suit with no shirt under it, his livid clavicles shining under the black light. I changed my mind about the people looking like vampires under a black light; only a vampire could look that way, the skin glowing a brilliant blue like a gas flame, the color of the eyes clearly discernible through the light distortion. Daniel calmly gathered up a microphone and began to sing.

The songs were a kind of liquid flowing, accented with clangs from the woman playing a heap of metal parts mounted on cinder blocks; Daniel himself manipulated a tape machine, playing back recorded loops of industrial sounds—rumblings, drones, samples from old films—and sang. Daniel's voice was guttural and melodic by turns, a deep register without much range; he sang in German. I had the sensation that I wasn't so much watching a band as an impromptu collage. Mimsy played guitar, sparely, only adding an accent to the music now and again, sort of as an additional percussion instrument, like the car parts.

At length Lovely came and sat on the floor at my feet. Absently I petted the soft blond suede of his head and he rested his head against my knees.

The audience sucked it up; most of them eschewed the tables and chairs and huddled close to the stage, watching Daniel's every move. As he moved across the stage to play another tape loop, the heads of the audience waved with him, like spectators at a tennis match. I found it deeply amusing, and largely watched the crowd for most of the songs. They were an even admixture of the L.A. intelligentsia and hopeful-looking Gothic teenagers, certainly far too young to be of drinking age, the whites of their eyes gleaming like jelly. The entire body of the Rotting Hall seemed to be in attendance, including Daniel's breakfast of earlier that day, her formerly crushed wrist held, bandaged, close to her heart.

The band paused for a while, switching instruments. Daniel set down his tape machine, after turning on a low throbbing growl, which I recognized as a fetal heartbeat. "All right," he said into his mike, winding the cord round and round his hand, "this will be our last song tonight, and anybody who knows me knows this song, and a few of you who don't know me know this song too. It's a David Bowie song, *of course*." He gestured wearily, and there was a smattering of understanding and indulgent laughter from the audience. "From the Ziggy Stardust album, and it's called 'Rock and Roll Suicide.' It's really a quite cheerful song."

The band began to lurch through a much slower and grainier version of the famous tune, Daniel slowing and lowering his voice to a nearly subsonic level. The girl who had been banging on the car parts, and a young man who had previously been manning some sort of synth console, began to dance with one another with an agile, athletic grace. I realized with a start that they must be brother and sister, two robust but delicate Asians, nearly identical in their black cutoffs and their elegant, spidery movements.

David Bowie, in his Ziggy phase, would drag out the last verse of "Rock and Roll Suicide" for ever and ever, getting more and more melodramatic and hysterical while the androgen-maddened crowd went into frenzies. The only real lyrics of this outro are "Give me your hands, 'cos you're wonderful." Ziggy's backup band, the Spiders, would continue this litany while Ziggy took the opportunity to shovel on the drama.

Daniel's band chimed in with this at the appropriate time, and for a while Daniel sang along with them. His voice trailed off, though, while their chanting continued, and I looked up from studying the fine sparkle of light on Lovely's scalp to find Daniel staring straight at me. There could be no mistake—we weren't so far from the stage that I couldn't tell exactly where his eyes were trained. He unbuttoned the red velvet blazer, leaned in to the microphone on its stand, and began to talk across the gulf to me.

"I hope you'll forgive me for everything I've done. You see I can't help myself." He reached into a pocket for something, brought it out, unfolded it. The stage lights glinted painfully off the polished edge of a straight razor. The crowd between us let out a faint moan.

"When I speak of love, I don't mean the ordinary thing. No such thing for me. What I need, what I feel, is far deeper, far more consuming, than anything these tiny minds can command. Only you and I have the possibility." He took a great deep breath against the mike, and the sound went sighing through the club, echoing and echoing. He held up the razor. "I want to climb inside you . . . climb inside you, love, and wrap your skin around me like a blanket. Slither around in your blood. Inside you I feel warm, I feel . . . immortal. Invincible."

He drew the razor across the sleek smooth skin of his belly. The audience reacted with shock—not as much as a straight crowd would have given, but they had clearly not been expecting this. One fellow said

"Whoa!" over the susurrus. The blood flowed down over Daniel's belly, black in the fluorescents, and down to the low-slung waist of the velvet trousers. "I want you to climb inside of me," Daniel said to me, cutting again. For a split second I saw the pink edge of flesh curl over; then the waterfall of blood rushed out anew.

The Asian twins danced on heedless; the band continued to play.

Daniel was sweating, sighing, a thick erection bulging in the velvet, and we all watched as the blood flow slackened, slowed, the blood dried on Daniel's belly, the heavy cuts smoothed themselves over. "Yes," Daniel whispered, "yes, I want you."

I could smell my own cunt wettening by then.

The band finished the last chorus on the major chord. Daniel idly flicked away the dried crust of blood from his stomach, revealing the smooth wholeness underneath. He turned back to the audience and smiled. "Thanks, good night," he said.

The crowd went wild, deafening me with their screams and whistles and applause. Lovely turned round and looked at me with surprise. "That was cool," he murmured.

"Does he always do that?" I said when I could find my voice.

"Nope," said Nora. Her normally bloodless cheeks were pink. "He'd better not do it too much, but that . . . really worked. We could be onto something here."

Chloe said, "C'mon, Ariane, we should get out of here."

Nora dropped us off at Chloe's apartment, across the street from the Rotting Hall, and we went up on the roof for a while, smoking and being quiet. I was almost completely sober by now, but there was no way I was going to be able to sleep. Chloe and Mimsy stayed with me for a while, but they got tired and decided to go to bed; I remained outside, my lungs raw, my brain a smoking wreck.

The eastern sky had begun to turn salmon pink as I stared at it, hypnotized, and Daniel came slowly up onto the roof by way of the fire escape. He was back in black stretch jeans and a white Jim Morrison T-shirt, and he sat easily beside me. I didn't say anything.

"Did you like it?" he asked shyly.

"I can't tell if it was for me or not," I said.

"Do you want to come back to my place and get naked?"

I shook my head and laughed. "Yeah," I said. "Sure."

In the darkness of his apartment, as the sun was coming up, he undressed me, kissed my body gently, almost chastely, then slipped his cock into me and we fucked. It was all so gentle. In the middle, as I was almost ready to come, he bit my neck, puncturing it easily with his sharp upper teeth. I felt the orgasm build abruptly within me. Then my spasms pumped the blood steadily into his mouth, and a sweet, umbrous darkness came.

Chapter Eight

Chloe and I had gone to Denny's for an afternoon breakfast of hash browns, apple sauce, orange juice, coffee, and cigarettes. We must have looked like sisters; Chloe voluptuously plump in a lacy dress and me more butch in jeans and a T-shirt, both of us with wild damp straggles of curly hair and makeup-less night-bleached skin. She was telling me her repertoire of sick jokes, which was vast, and had me snorting orange juice into my nasal passages.

At once Lovely burst into the Denny's, his forelock flyaway, and threw himself at my feet next to the table. "Oh, Ariane!" he wailed. "I'm so so sorry, please don't hate me, I hope you don't hate me."

Looking around the restaurant at the amused gazes of the other patrons, I pulled him off the floor and made room for him beside me on the yellow vinyl. "Ummm . . . of course I don't hate you," I mumbled. "Why would I hate you?"

148

He clung to me, burying his face in my shoulder. "I'm just such a slut! I should respect you!"

Chloe smiled and lit another Turkish oval; I realized that Lovely must have been referring to last night's public blow job at the club. I gave the boy a reassuring squeeze. "No, don't even worry about it," I said, shaking my head and stirring my coffee. "You should hate me. I'm horning in on your boyfriend."

Lovely wiped his nose and began picking at the hash browns with his slim fingers. "No, he's totally not my boyfriend," he said. "I could never hate you. You're so cool."

I must have been blushing something awful; Chloe was all but grinning by now. Lovely didn't allow me to go on apologizing, but drew a little crumpled black plastic bag out of his baggy back pocket. "I stole this for you, to make it up to you," he said, holding it out at arm's length. I took the little parcel from him and unwrapped it; it was a gorgeous silver pocket watch on a chain, etched with a picture of a rat's skull, open in a furious-looking snarl.

I was aghast. "Oh, Lovely, you shouldn't have."

"I know, but I saw it, and I thought about you immediately. Do you like it?"

"Where did you get it?'

He shrugged and smiled a wicked child's smile. "Nowhere," he said.

Chloe leaned over to look. "Lovely's got what you call talent," she explained. "He could steal a warhead from the Pentagon. He'd just stuff it down those idiotic big shorts of his."

"Shut up, bitch," Lovely said playfully. "Can I bum a cigarette?" He lit up and looked around him at the Denny's, now held in thrall by our dark little table. "Where is our lord and master anyway?"

"He's fucking Nora," I said tiredly. I played with the watch, flicking the delicate exoskeleton open to look at the face, already set to the right time. "He dismissed it as an 'unpleasant obligation.' You know, what a hardship."

"I can't *stand* Nora," Lovely said. "She's so holier-than-thou. One of these days I'm just gonna snatch her bald!" He suffered a little paroxysm of hatred, then composed himself and went back to picking at my plate. "I guess we'll just have to amuse ourselves. Sooooo, tell us about your other vampire. I'm dying to know. Chloe is too, she's just too polite to bug you about it."

Chloe shrugged her agreement.

I poured the last glass of orange juice out of the force-pressed glass carafe. "I don't know," I said. "What is there to tell? What do you want to know?"

"Well, does he have a court like Daniel? How does he score his feeds?"

I paused while the waiter—the same pissy young boy from last time—came over and asked Lovely if he wanted anything, brought Chloe and me more coffee, rolled his eyes at the lot of us. "I don't know," I began. "He doesn't really drink blood all that often."

"Huh? How does he live?"

"I guess he takes just enough to keep him alive," I said. "I gather it's not very much. He's pretty old."

"That's weird," Lovely said. "That's like eating just enough to keep you from starving to death."

"Not that weird," Chloe replied. "Nora does it. She thinks eating is boring. She hates everything."

"You guys don't like Nora much, do you?" I said, trying to disguise the fact that I didn't either. The look on her face had been just insufferable when Daniel had announced to us all at "breakfast" that he was going to spend the rest of the daylight hours tickling her ivories.

"I used to like her fine," Chloe explained, running her hand nervously through her hair. "But she's been getting on my tits. She's so into money and rank and class and 'the industry.' She thinks she's making all of Daniel's money and managing it, when she has no fucking clue how much money Daniel's worth. You think he'd tell her? She'd embezzle the hell out of it, buy herself a mountain of crystal meth, and put him on MTV. Shit, she'd *buy* MTV."

"Does Daniel know this?" I asked.

Chloe nodded sagely. "Daniel knows everything," she said. "She wouldn't have the guts. She's just as pussy-whipped—or should I say cock-whipped?—as anybody else. I can't say I blame her—I've been there." Everyone at the table nodded in agreement. "So tell us more about your other vampire," Chloe said.

"I don't know. All we ever did was hang around in his hotel room and talk about nineteenth-century Europe. He took me out to dinner a lot and spent money on me and trashed my apartment. You guys would probably find him really boring."

"I don't know. He sounds kind of cool. Like a really genteel sugar daddy." Lovely got misty-eyed.

"I don't want a sugar daddy, though," I mumbled. "I just wanted to be in love with him, I think. I think I wanted a normal boring relationship with fucking and sweet talk and all that lame bullshit. I don't think he knows how to do anything like that anymore, if he ever did. I don't really want to talk about it anymore. He really, really hurt me."

"I'll say," Chloe said. "I stitched you up. But that's OK. If you don't want to talk about it, we don't talk about it, right, Lovely?"

Lovely frowned and sighed, but conceded.

That evening I ended up haunting the streets with Lovely. We got made up in zombie finery—he wore the jewelry that looked like silver bones piercing his nipples and his black eye smudge filled the entire space between brow and cheekbone—and hung around on the sidewalk outside a Goth club in Los Angeles. It was twenty-one-and-over and he had been thrown out of the place repeatedly for buying liquor with a fake ID, he said, but he was drawn there again and again, especially on Friday nights when he was without Daniel; hanging around on the sidewalk outside was better than going inside most clubs.

Certainly, the sidewalk was a raging scene—women dressed entirely in shiny black vinyl leading half-naked men around on leashes, more big crimped hair, purple lipstick, and skull buckles than you could shake a stick at, and always the swelling din of the music coming from inside. We weren't alone in the rejects pile either; a couple of other tatty young punks slouched in their personal corners, drinking alcohol from 7-Eleven Big Gulp cups, greeting friends they knew as they went inside.

Lovely and I shared a flask of amaretto and dope-laden cigarettes. "So where the hell did you come from?" I asked him.

"Precisely," he replied. "From hell."

"Whereabouts in hell?"

"Oklahoma," he said. "Norman, Oklahoma."

"No kidding!"

"I only wish I were," he said. He handed me the flask and eyed a strapping young man with a sheer, moth-eaten black skirt and bare torso. In my opinion, he didn't hold a candle to Lovely himself, but there's no accounting for taste. "I spent fifteen years there. There's just nothing there—just gray grass, as far as the eye can see. And Norman's not so bad as far as Oklahoma goes. My grandparents lived in Tulsa and they sent me *there* every summer—and I thought I was going to go nuts. I remember I spent one whole summer locked in my room, jerking off all day, then going outside at night and catching bugs and killing them. I think I was twelve that year."

"Ever thought of reading books?"

He smiled at me knowingly. "I did that plenty," he said. "I forgot to mention the book reading. I read *while* I was jerking off. I got sick of reading the books I had—I must have read them ten dozen times apiece. I read a whole lot of Michael Moorcock."

"Oh, child, that explains everything."

"Doesn't it? Doesn't it just? By the time I was fourteen I used to hustle my ass in Tulsa in the summer, just for something to do. I let anybody pick me up. It's a wonder I didn't get myself fucking killed doing that—more than I care to remember, some redneck bastard would pick me up hitchhiking, then beat the hell out of me and tell me to read the Bible or something else retarded. But you'd be surprised—a lot of the time I'd be peeing my pants going, 'This shitheel's about to blast me with his shotgun,' and they'd buy me a hamburger and then just take me to bed and suck my dick as nice as you please. Go on home to Bessie Lou and say, 'Aw, honey, I was just shootin' some pool over at the Dew Drop Inn.' " It was striking to see the urbane and bubble-headed Lovely putting on his homegrown heartland accent, much rougher and drier than my swampy polyglot Southern one. He was looking off into the distance at the punks across the street, who had grown sick of sitting still and had begun to half dance, half fight.

"How'd you get to L.A.?"

He smiled slowly. "I robbed the student council," he said. "They'd just had a bake sale and dog wash to buy more Sunday school books for the church across the street from the high school. Got myself a cool eighty bucks. Stole the rest from my dad's wallet while he was sleepin'. I got my faggy ass on a Greyhound and came out here."

"And then what?"

"Then I fucking hustled, obviously. Hustled my

faggy, skinny, white, podunk ass." He took a deep drag on his cigarette and showed no signs of letting go. "I slept on the street for a month or two, mostly in the stairwells out back of buildings. Then I was kind of successful. I didn't get beat up too often. I guess men liked how I looked—I had sort of long blond hair then, you know, big brown eyes, looked kind of like I was straight, T-shirt and jeans. I knew a lot of really nice men who paid me OK money to sit on their cocks. No hardship, as far as I'm concerned. I'll climb on top of a hard cock any minute, even now. All I ask is that they wipe their ass every now and then, and don't think I look cuter with some of my teeth missing." He smiled at me to demonstrate, and I saw that one of his lower canine teeth was gone, and the other teeth had valiantly tried to fill the space.

I moved over to him and hugged him as hard as I could. He kissed my hair, then nudged me away for another mouthful of amaretto. "No, see, it's fine now, I'm with Dan now. I don't regret it. I don't regret anything."

"And how'd you hook up with Daniel?"

"He was a trick, of course." He grinned. "He called my pimp, who apparently had done Dan wrong sometime in the past—maybe it was just the fact that he was a pimp. Daniel fucking hates pimps more than anything. He loves hookers—he thinks hookers are great—but if they don't get all their money, Daniel goes on the warpath. He's wasted more pimps . . . But anyway, my old man brought me over to some party or something, and I had cut my hair like this for the first time that day, and my pimp was *so mad,* he was ready to sell me to Shanghai or some shit; but there was this party in Beverly Hills, and my old man brought me in, and brought me up to Daniel—I remember Daniel was sitting there like a prince in a big red velvet chair, in a proper Umberto suit and white shirt and tie, but with his lips painted the same color red as the chair. So my old man goes, 'Well, I'm sorry, he cut his hair, like, two hours ago, and it was either this or bring you a skinhead,' and Daniel goes, 'No, no, that's fine . . . quite all right . . . lovely, really. Lovely.' " Lovely imitated Daniel's voice perfectly; he must have been practicing it for years. "So, like, Daniel and I go off into another room, and he asks me if I really want to, and I'm like 'Uh, *yeah*,' and he goes, 'I have something I want to show you,' and he bares his fangs at me. I was like, 'Cool, nice fangs, dude, that's so *Love at First Bite*,' but then he starts taking off his clothes, and I can see how fucking white he is—he's like snow. Snowy white. And he, like, reaches out to me and tweaks my tit, this was before I had them pierced, and he tweaks my nip with his fingernails, and I'm like, 'Whoa, shit, that ain't fake.' But I never panicked or anything. He was nice. He kissed me just a little. He kind of bit my lip and tasted my blood just a little bit, and I was ready by then to do fucking anything the man said. He, like, asked me how old I was, and how long I'd been hustling for that guy, and then he was like, 'Watch this, little one.' And I followed him into the other room where my old man and some other, like, coke-dealer guys were sitting around smoking cigars and talking and shit. And . . . Daniel just *goes to fucking town*." Lovely held out his hands in parallel planes. "He fucking killed those dudes so fast, I didn't know what was going on until the last guy fell. Daniel just like . . . he like . . . I think he crushed their hearts and slit their throats. All he has to do to crush a guy's heart is punch him in the chest and his breastbone just goes *whooom*. Instant death. Guy doesn't feel a thing except he can't breathe so good. And there I was just standing there and watching this one guy's neck just kind of pouring blood all down the front of his yellow silk suit, looking at Daniel all startled, but he's, like, already dead. And Daniel just kneels down and drinks the blood coming out. He fills his hands with it and drinks it like he's drinking water out of a river. My pimp is sitting there with his chest caved in like somebody hit it with a sledgehammer. Four men, just like that. When he was done drinking the blood he came over to me and said, 'Get undressed, I'm going to fuck you, and I don't want to ruin your clothes.' "

I sat there stunned for a long time, my cigarette burning away to a long ash between my fingers. "And you did?" I said at last.

"Damn straight I did. Best fuck I'd ever had too. We got all sticky with the blood and he licked it off me. Then we took a shower, and he left a hundred-dollar tip, and we left." Lovely threw up his hands. "Mental, isn't it?"

"And you were sixteen years old."

"Almost."

"Lovely, you're a cold-blooded motherfucker."

He smiled modestly. "More or less," he said. "Fuck this, my ass is getting stiff. Let's go get some coffee and pie."

I was walking around Hollywood at night alone.

It was a hot night—not temperate but hot—the fire hydrants had been running all day and a sick sweaty heat rose off the streets. I had caught a bus back to Vine, and I could have called Chloe from a pay phone and had her come pick me up, but I just didn't feel like it. After Lovely's and my journey to get coffee and pie, I had left him back at the club again, hustling his lithe young body at the death-rock boys going inside. I was deathly worried about him, but he assured me that everything was all right and that he could defend himself if it came to that.

The lights of the sex clubs glittered luridly off the black skin of the street. The road was full of taxis and

Mercedeses, driving past too fast, with the legs and arms of starlets and debutantes hanging out; it was Saturday night in the first weekend of May. Occasionally a man would say something lewd to me, but catching my blank-eyed stare, he would gather that I was not for hire, and didn't bother me any further.

I took out my new pocket watch and looked at it. The skull of the rat yawned at me, painted orange and red with the neon brush. It was almost three in the morning. I didn't think I'd ever sleep. And where would I sleep when I did? I found my thoughts straying back to Ricari and the smell of the candles burning in Suite 900, the mellow softness of his mouth brushing against my breasts. I didn't understand how he could profess to love me the way he did, then send me away to an unfamiliar place to a creature who might have killed me as soon as looked at me. My love for him and my hate for him twined around each other like the trunks of braided fig trees, growing together to form a single system.

A couple of biggish men in badly fitting suits stood in front of me. I tried to get around them, but they blocked my passage, smiling like they were playing a game. I shook my head at them. "I'm trying to get someplace," I informed them impatiently.

"You can get someplace with me," said one of them. They both laughed.

"Christ." I turned round to look for someone to distract them with, but there was nobody near enough for me to say anything to. I started walking for the intersection, hoping to get traffic between me and them, but they followed me, muttering to each other. I walked faster, trying to keep myself calm. Finally I reached the curb and stopped there, looking back and forth in panic.

"Hey, mulatto, get in the car," someone called.

"Fuck *off* already," I said over my shoulder, walking faster.

"Is that any way to talk to a senior citizen?"

I finally gave it a glance. A Coupe de Ville (Dolores), gleaming in all her seventeen-foot glossy black glory, Daniel grinning fiendishly in sunglasses and fishnet blouse at the wheel.

I looked back at the suited thugs. They were stopped in the middle of the road, their eyes rolling in confusion as their arms reached out for each other. Groaning with disgust, they squished their sweaty faces together in a deep tongue kiss. Without being able to help myself, I started to laugh. "Don't call me mulatto," I shouted to Daniel in the car. "I'm technically a quadroon, asshole." One of the men gagged, but his hand went down the other's pants anyway. Daniel's eyes gleamed and he smiled a bitchy, satisfied smile.

"Get in the fucking car. Are you crazy walking around out here dressed like that?"

I opened the door and got in. In the intersection, the men broke apart and promptly began punching each other and cursing. Whistling, Daniel turned onto Sunset and put his foot to the floor, dodging slower cars, missing by whispers. "Dressed like what?" I managed to mumble.

"Like Lisa Bonet in *Angel Heart*. Where did you get that dress? Seems familiar somehow."

"Chloe's."

"Ah. Back when she wore something other than black. Long ago."

We drove through the city sprawl, listening to a mix tape Daniel had found in a bedroom of some young hippie chick upon whom he'd slaked his thirst some ten years ago. There was a lot of the Doors, a lot of Syd Barrett, some Lou Reed, Joni Mitchell. He said that it made him feel like crying, but he simply steered his way through the heat-wave streets, looking straight ahead.

We went through a typical L.A. fast-food drive-in, got burgers and fries and alien fried-dough desserts, tall skinny plastic cups of Dr Pepper and Mountain Dew mixed together. Daniel parked in the parking lot, and together we unwrapped our treasures and ate them in big, half-disgusted bites.

"What were you like as a child?" Daniel asked. "Did you eat a lot of fast food?"

I shook my head and smiled. "Only sometimes. New Orleans wasn't fast-food paradise back then—the worst we ever did was buckets of chicken." I sat still for a second and let him dab mayonnaise off my chin with a stiff napkin. "I mean, why go out when you can get gumbo at home?"

"I've never had gumbo," he confessed, smiling.

"Oh, Daniel, you've never lived." The whole night was still now, as if Daniel had stopped Los Angeles in its tracks; perhaps he had. I figured he was capable of just about anything. "It's an interesting place to grow up."

"Is it really filled with dead things?" he asked naively.

I laughed. "No more than Berlin, no doubt. Unless you count the rotting kudzu. I mean, it is ancient, comparatively; there's lots of places, old churches and orphanages and houses, that are just empty, just waiting to be squatted in. I think Louisiana is allergic to tearing anything down."

"Let's go," he decided.

"Huh?"

"Why don't we get out of this suntanned hell and go to New Orleans? Stay there for a hundred, two hundred years? D'you think anyone would notice?"

I didn't reply. I wasn't quite sure what he was getting at, and my brain was only just starting to work itself out of the smoky knots of the early part of the evening. I didn't want to talk about it if I couldn't trust what I heard or said.

"Tell me," Daniel said, taking me into his arms and

resting my back against his chest, "what do you want more than anything else in the whole world?"

Again I didn't reply. I just shook my head and smiled. He could see into my head anytime he wanted to, gather up the secrets like ripe berries. I just wanted to be close to him and feel the half-warm half-cool weight of his body. He turned my face gently towards his. "Ariane," he said insistently. "Tell the truth. You're not dealing with Ricari anymore. I'm not going to get mad if you tell me what's real."

"I want to understand him," I said.

"From within."

"I . . . want to know . . ."

"What it's like to be like me or he? To live for a very long time, see everything change, fall in love again and again, forgive yourself every sin?"

"A little," I admitted.

"I will make it happen," he said. When he felt me tense, just slightly, he added, "When you're ready. If you're ready." He broke away from me, lighthearted, and started the car again. "But first I want you to become yourself again. A scientist."

The caffeine was sobering me up. "I am a scientist," I said reflexively.

"What makes you a scientist?"

"I observe, identify, describe, experiment, investigate, and theorize."

"Your junior high school science club motto." He was right. "Yeah, whatever. But what does science *mean* to you? What do you study? What makes you a born scientist, the way that, say, I am a true artist?" He tossed his hair and examined himself in the rearview mirror, straightening his smeared red lipstick.

"I don't know," I said irritably.

"Exactly. Exactly the answer I was looking for. If you spouted any more dictionary definitions, I was gonna smack you. You don't even know what it is that draws you to the sciences. It's a part of you. Something you can't escape. That will be instrumental in preparing you for your life as a vampire."

"I never said I wanted to be—"

"You don't have to say it," he said, cutting me off. He turned the key in the ignition. He drove in silence for a while, then eased the stereo back on and Tim Buckley's voice rose up ghostlike from the speakers on the doors.

I've got this strange feelin' deep down in my heart;
I can't tell what it is, but it won't let go;
It happens every time I give you more than what I have.

"You're breathing and walking and dancing and talking desire. You're like a horny twelve-year-old girl. You're not fooling anybody."

"It's just because you have it all," I sighed.

"We do have it all. We're angels without morals. Isn't that great?"

I kissed his ear. "What did I do to deserve you? You're like Charlie Manson with looks and charm."

"That's the nicest thing anyone's ever said to me," he said.

Daniel put me to bed in the alcove of the Hall with great tenderness, unhooking the difficult fastenings of my dress, massaging my feet, and pulling a light blanket over me. He kissed my forehead, leaving faint smears of fast-food residue on my skin. I reached up and embraced him tightly before I would let him leave, and he stood in the doorway and blew me a kiss before he was gone.

In the early morning Lovely slid into bed beside me, put his arms around me, and kissed the back of my neck. "I had such a good fuck tonight," he whispered. I smiled against the pillow. Together we resettled, and I went back to sleep.

Chapter Nine

Some mornings I just couldn't sleep.

I found some lined loose-leaf paper on a table in Daniel's office and scribbled on it with a bright pink ballpoint pen, chewing off bloody hangnails.

performed microhematocrit on D. B.'s left thumb. it was difficult to employ the capillary tube— though skin is soft and easily penetrated, blood does not readily flow

blood is deep red in color—hypoxic almost

really thick buffy coat, plasma transparent, colorless

RBC infinitesimally small—platelet size. impossible to tell configuration of RBCs without stronger microscope. shitty Radio Shack product. best Lovely could get without having to raid supply stores—might send him to one anyway. RBC count abnormally high, crowding into a solid layer with barely any plasma trace after centrifuge at 1500g—may try again at 1000g or even less. much fibrinogen/prothrombin? might have some relation to healing ability

insane hematocrit—just insane—it hardly makes any sense

Basically it looks like vampire blood isn't really "super" natural, it's "un" natural. Many of its properties are beyond my ability to study given the limitations of the research materials. Need scanning microscope, MRI, lumbar puncture, marrow biopsy, more human blood to study effects

I'm turning into Dr. Moreau.

In between having his thumbs stuck, Daniel did a lot of interviews, phone calls, schmoozing. Nora was almost always at his side during these, trying to give instructions to Daniel as to what he should and shouldn't say. Sometimes he said what she wanted, and other times he said whatever he felt like, no matter if it was foolhardy, obscene, or just plain incomprehensible. During one of the last of these, Nora threw up her hands and started yelling at Daniel, cursing him for being so difficult and for ruining so many things for her. Daniel watched her rail calmly, then stood up and held out his hand to the woman doing the interview. "Thanks, that'll be all," he said to her. "Just make up stuff you didn't get. OK? See you at Billy's on Tuesday, my love to Eileen." He gently nudged her toward the door of his apartment, closing the door behind him.

Nora had picked up a cheap brass figurine of a Venus and thrown it onto the bed petulantly; and Daniel turned from the door and had her underneath him faster than she could react. He closed his hand around her throat. "Remember what I am?" he hissed into her face. "Remember what I can do to you? You're not my zookeeper. I'm not a trick pony you can ride onto the society pages. Fuck society and fuck your conventions."

"I'm sorry," Nora panted. I sat frozen on the floor next to the television, Lovely stretched out asleep on the Moroccan rug.

"Our professional relationship is at an end," said Daniel.

"I'm sorry—I won't do it anymore—"

"I'm so bored with you," said Daniel, and let her go. He walked into the kitchen and poured himself a glass of bright blue soda nonchalantly, standing at the window drinking it and humming. Nora picked herself up, her eyes brimming with tears, and stared at me, horrified that I'd seen what happened.

"You're next, you know," she whispered, her breath coming in shudders. She let the tears fall, streaking her white face powder, and shakily gathered her things together in her black alligator briefcase. She closed the door behind her without a sound.

I got up and sat on the bed, pushing my hair from my face.

"Don't listen to what she says," came Daniel's drawl from the kitchen. "You're not next for anything. She's the one who's next. We'll see how she enjoys being used for a little while."

Lovely and Mimsy and I lay around on the cushions smoking pot.

It was a typical day—or should I say night—at the Rotting Hall; Daniel had ordered Indian take out for us, and we made short work of the tandoori and hot, fresh nan. Lovely and I watched *The Bride of Dracula* on the snowy black-and-white TV set. Mimsy and Daniel had previously been sitting in chairs, playing David Bowie songs on two fine old classical guitars. Daniel was an excellent guitarist, blinding in his speed and skill, but he broke strings. At last he gave up, laughing, shook Mimsy's hand, and kissed Lovely and me. "I must run. Night's falling . . . I have things to do."

Slowly, with clumsy fingers, I began to roll a cigarette. Lovely had stolen me a black leather tobacco pouch, half full of expensive Virginia shred, bright gold in color and smooth on the lungs. "What's your real name, Mimsy?" I asked. "Lovely won't tell me his."

"I don't even know Lovely's name," Mimsy replied, stretching all six feet and four inches across the cushions. The younger, more disrespectful kids called him "Plastic Man." "My name's Jason Thomas. Thrilling, isn't it?"

"Did you come out of the boonies too?"

"Naw, man, I'm from San Diego." Since he had come for his visit straight out of bed, his hair wasn't spiked today, and it flopped around his ears in black wings. His face was as sharp and animated as a bird's—not the bitterness of a crow, but the common prettiness of a blackbird or a starling. I had grown to adore his face. "I came up here to play in an industrial band one summer while I was in college. By the time I got up here, the band had broken up, but I met Chloe and Daniel, and I just said, 'Fuck that, I'm staying here.' " He rubbed my shoulder gently. "What did you do before you met Ricari?"

"Who, me? Well, I was a scientist. I went to NCIT and was a teaching assistant there. I was trying to get my doctorate." I shrugged. "Pretty fuckin' boring."

"Did you have a boyfriend before that?" Lovely asked.

I glanced at him, but he was blissfully zoning out, staring at the snow on the TV. "I did," I said.

"Did you break up?"

"Well . . . not exactly . . . I guess you could say I left him for Orfeo . . . or he left me . . . or something. It's kind of complicated."

"I understand," Mimsy said. "We all gave something up for this. I gave up school, I gave up my band back home. Chloe gave up nursing school. I just think it's worth it. This to me is like a religion—this is my cloister, or whatever. But this is what I believe in, more than anything else. I never thought I could be so happy in my life."

It was many hours since Daniel had left. Eventually we three went up onto the roof of the Hall, along with some of the other kids, and brought Daniel's boom box along so that we could listen to music. The sky was a dark stain, with no stars visible behind the smog and the glare of the Hollywood streetlights; the moon was a wan blob, almost ashamed to show its homespun face to the city of angels. We listened to Galaxie 500, long, looping songs of painful addiction, desire, regret. I cuddled up in Lovely's arms as tightly as I could, trying to drive away the chill from the desert air, from being high.

The moon touched the edge of the apartment building across the way, where Chloe and Mimsy lived; and Chloe came up onto the surface of our roof and sat down with us, drawing her skirted knees up to her chin. She was pale, and when I touched her shoulder to offer her a pipe hit, I could feel that she was shaking.

"What's the matter?" I whispered.

"Nora," Chloe said softly to me.

"What about her?" I could tell by the set stillness of Lovely's and Mimsy's back that they were listening intently, without looking like they were.

Chloe looked up at me, shaking her head. Her lips, without lipstick, held their dark stain, the full lower lip chapped from biting. "She and Daniel went to the desert," she said, and that was all.

"Oh, well," Lovely said heavily.

"What does that mean?" I whispered.

Mimsy and Lovely both shrugged. I looked at Chloe,

but she also just shook her head and wouldn't say any more, and she looked away to the moon, which had now sunk partially below the edge of the building.

We never saw Nora again.

When I asked Daniel about it two safe weeks later, he stretched beside me and yawned. "Oh, that," he said. "Well, she had begun to grate on my nerves, and the nerves of everyone around me, and so I asked her to tell me what she wanted next. I told her all her alternatives. She was a fuckin' speed freak, and she was totally unhappy. She's always been totally unhappy. She chose a drive to the desert."

"Is that your convenient euphemism for killing someone?" My Southern upbringing stood me well here; my voice never rose above a bedroom softness.

Daniel responded well to it. He shifted me around so that I was resting on the plane of his body, my elbows dangling down his ribs and my breasts pressed against his belly. He opened his legs and my knees fell down between his thighs, and he closed the thighs, trapping me gently. "I can kill someone anytime I want," he said. "Anywhere. The desert is simply more spiritual."

"And was this her choice? To die?"

"Eventually," he said, smiling.

"Did you drain her?" I said, growing aroused despite myself. His body leached a kind of decadent warmth into me; I was always aware that this heat that came from him was the burning bodies of human beings. But his skin was like the finest velvet, his nipples always hard and ready to be pinched, bitten, suckled. His penis rose sluggishly, thickly, against me.

"We made love, out in the open. Once she felt her pleasure, and had time to enjoy the feeling, I broke her neck. I slit her neck the long way. Drank the blood as it poured out in streams. I fucked her again as she died." He raised his eyebrows innocently at me. "She'd told me to."

"And?"

"I buried her in the sand, in her blue velvet gown. It was very beautiful."

His cock was very hard now, straining against my navel, as if trying to fuck me abdominally. With his hands he fondled my buttocks, separating them, stroking in the dampness down the hollow. When I didn't say anything, he pulled me up, slid me until his cock was bent under me, pulsing unevenly against my cunt and my anus. Finally I said drowsily, "I can't fuck you again."

"The hell you can't. Didn't you like the way I sang last night? Cavorted around like Valentino on LSD?"

"You waved your dick at the audience."

"They've seen dicks before."

I began to laugh. "My decadent angel," he murmured, reaching over for the carved earthenware pot of solidified olive oil and smearing a handful of it, instantly melting, onto his penis, "you've become so very much like me, in all the best ways." With a modicum of slithering and adjusting, he mounted me, like a butterfly on a display case, onto his cock, spearing with a terrible ease into my ass. I stopped about halfway, my toes curling with the effort. "Just bear down. Yes. That way. We used to fuck this way, Orfeo Ricari and I. He would climb on top of me and he'd have that look on his face—yes, that look exactly. Yes. It's almost as if I have him back. Did you ever have that urge? That . . . overwhelming urge to fuck Orfeo Ricari right in that . . . sweet little ass of his?"

"You're killing me."

"Did you or did you not?"

"Of course I did," I said through gritted teeth.

He was smiling as calmly as a Buddha. "Had enough? Girls have no stamina."

"Just . . . too much."

The sensation of him sliding backward out of me was in fact so intensely pleasurable that I came, and he made an executive decision not to stop, but to keep slipping with great care into and out of me until my orgasm had spun itself out. When he had finally stopped, I rolled over and curled up on my side. Daniel laid his chin against the curve of my side. "You know what you look like?" he asked. He took one hand from under my chin and bent it back so that I could touch his cock; it was thick, slimy, throbbing. "You look like you're thinking that if you experience this much pleasure, you have to balance it with pain somehow. Am I right?"

I didn't say anything.

He moved my floppy arm back and forth to stroke himself off. "I can see it in your face. Catholic guilt. Karmic guilt. It's kind of the same."

"Daniel, I'm not a fucking Catholic. I'm not Ricari." I yanked my arm back. "Fucking *me* is not fucking *him*." But the thought of that slight whip of a young man, painfully caught on this insatiable member, made my knees turn to water.

"Don't get coy with me. I know. I can see it. OK, so you're not a Catholic. You're a scientist. A rationalist. Cause and effect—pleasure begets pain. Right?" He hissed suddenly in my ear. "Well, bloodylocks, I'm here to tell you that you don't have to be bound by a rational means at all. No need to find cause and effect at all. Pleasure without guilt! Without fear! There is no meaning in any of this—just a bundle of neurons firing at random. Random configurations of cells. Tell me if I've lost you in there somewhere."

"Necrophiliac," I mumbled into my arm. "Buggerer."

Daniel chuckled in surprise and delight. "Well, I've never buggered a dead body before. I suppose there's a first time for everything." Daniel playfully bit me, with his incisors only; and he turned me over to face him. In the semidarkness of nightfall, he glowed like fine paper. "Ariane! Don't go into a mood. Should I have asked first?"

I laughed at him sitting up concerned, his still-hard cock standing at attention between his hipbones, and I pulled him over on top of me and guided him into my wet cunt. I locked my legs tightly around his waist. He gasped, even more surprised and very pleased, shuddering as I rammed against him as hard as I could. I ground out through gritted teeth, drowning out the earnest strains of Mozart coming from outside, *"You monster . . . you fucking monster . . ."*

Lovely gave me a back rub later that night.

We were at Chloe's; she and Mimsy were out doing something entirely unrelated to vampires. She claimed it was good for their relationship. Lovely and I were watching the very, very, very late movie—*Foxes,* starring the young Jodie Foster, about a group of rebellious, overmature teenagers in L.A. in 1980. "I've seen this on late-night TV about a hundred times," I said, sighing as Lovely rubbed cold aloe vera into the bruises on my ass. "I love this flick. I would be up all night studying for a final or a paper, and *Foxes* would always come on. I love the scene where they go to see KISS."

"KISS are cool," Lovely said. "I always went as one of the members of KISS for Halloween every year—the only time of year I could wear makeup and not get beaten up for it."

He dug a little too hard and I hissed breath between my teeth. "Ouchie."

"Sorry, darling. More wine?"

"You can have the rest."

His hands paused on me while he sucked away the last few centimeters on the bottle. "You have to get over being scared by Daniel," Lovely said.

"I'm not scared of Daniel. It's myself that scares me."

"Don't scare yourself either. Just flow with it."

"No pun intended." I smiled to myself. "Honey, that feels so, so good. If I could give you a medal and some cash prizes, I would." I was, in fact, aroused by the touch of his small, perfect, youthful hands, so innocent of claws, skillful at massage.

Lovely laughed quietly. "I'll tell you something," he said. "I'll tell you about how Daniel and I hunt."

They did it once or twice a week. Daniel and Lovely's little social outing. Lovely always came back from these sessions quiet, sometimes rather bruised and bitten-over, always freshly showered and fragrant with the smell of Dr. Bronner's almond-scented soap. He would slide into the alcove, cover up, and go to sleep without his usual "Hello, darling."

"I'll tell you about the last time we went out," Lovely said, returning to his work, this time on my lumbar curve, where the muscles were spasming, shortened by Daniel's brutal, goaded thrusts. "We went to a leather bar in Santa Monica. The real hardcore deal—slings, sub-dom, handcuffs on the bar, all that kind of tired shit. I'm not that impressed, but I guessed Daniel had something in mind, so I kept my mouth shut. And we were all tricked out as master and slave that night too; he had me in the collar and leash, and he was wearing that black suit of his. He bought me a girlie drink and he started scanning the place.

"Eventually he poked me and whispered in my ear. 'See that leatherman over there,' he said to me. I looked—guy looked like the leatherman in the Village People, I shit you not. He had a big handlebar mustache, leather cap, bondage top, chaps, motorcycle boots—I was soooo over that type by the time I was, like, fifteen. But Daniel seemed really amused by him. He said to me, 'Why'n't you go over there and tell him I said that I told you to go suck his cock.' So I was like, uh, OK, and I go over to the leatherman, really

171

obviously sent over by Daniel. And I go, just like he said, 'My lover really wants to see me suck your cock. Can I?' And the guy thinks for a minute that I'm bullshitting him, but then he's like, 'OK!' I mean, this is the kind of hardcore bar where some guys were over in another corner, fucking on the pool table. I mean, the light over it was broken, but still.

"So the guy, like, shakes out his dick, and I go down on him, right?"

"Lovely, Lovely, wait a minute, hang on here. You just start whaling on this skanky leatherman without knowing jack shit about him?"

Lovely arched his eyebrow, confused. "Well, yeah, of course," he said.

"Whatever. Go on."

"I mean, he didn't look too grungy, he tasted like dick, you know. I'm like, it's a cock, I'll suck it if I feel like it. The guy's obviously impressed by my technique—I give the best head in the world, I'm proud to announce. Finally, after a while, Daniel comes over and says, 'What do you think of my little friend?' And the leatherman's like, 'Jesus fucking Christ.' And Daniel's all like, something like, 'You wanna . . . get out of here? I can get us a room.' Or something like that . . . and the leatherman just like can't believe his fucking luck. So, like, Daniel gives him the address of some no-tell motel, and we leave, and we tell him to meet us there in an hour, and bring some rubbers. Daniel's not stupid. Leathermen are often pretty stupid, but Daniel never is. He just won't be seen leaving somewhere with one of his kills. He'd rather kill them in public than leave with them and have them turn up dead later.

"So we go to this hotel room, and Daniel does me up pretty good, gives me some poppers and some more drinks, and he tastes some of my blood so he can get a little convincingly fucked up, and we fool around for a while and see if the leatherman comes or not. Sometimes this trick works, sometimes it doesn't—a lot of the time the guy freaks and doesn't show up. That's fine too. Daniel and I just have a high old time with the dirty movies and the free ice.

"But this leatherman, this Village Person, he shows up! And he brings the condoms too! What a guy. And Daniel tells him the score; he wants the leatherman to suck me off, then he wants him to fuck me while I suck Daniel . . . one of these complicated things. He's like, Sure . . . So leatherman sucks my cock, which is interesting because I never get sucked, I'm always doing it myself; and Daniel's kind of slowly undressing, touching himself. He's really coming across as wasted. I'm impressed. So I come, no big deal, and then we start the whole circus; the leatherman and his big fat cock fucking me on the edge of the bed, and Daniel kneeling in front of me while I suck him. This goes on and on . . . it's kind of cool . . . I'm wrecked on the poppers and the rubber feels pretty good all stretchy inside me . . . and I'm, like, I don't want this leatherman coming inside me anyway.

"So Daniel comes in my mouth, and the leatherman still isn't done—the rubber probably—and Daniel creeps off the bed and circles back around the leatherman, caressing him a little bit, maybe teasing him that Daniel's going to fuck him next. And suddenly I hear this *'rip!'* and 'argh!' and then this hot, sticky splash on my back. I look over my shoulder—and Daniel's ripped his throat wide open and is sucking out the blood. The leatherman is dying, and he's still inside me, and I can feel him coming and pissing and thrashing . . . and I just kind of slide across the bed away from him. Daniel's an efficient drinker—I don't know if you've ever seen him kill—but he wastes as little as possible. I've seen him drink what must have been fifteen, sixteen pints a night. He just sticks onto the wound, drinking and drinking, way faster than either of us could. It's like he's just absorbing it. And he looks so good when he's done—he looks just like he must have when he was alive, so pink, so soft around the edges. We almost always make love afterwards." Lovely paused to light a cigarette, which hung suspended at the corner of his rosebud mouth. "This time we didn't, we were both really spent. We just took our shower in the motel room bathroom, washed up with Dr. Bronner's 'cos it kills the smell of blood the best without being obvious about it, got in the car, and went to Denny's for coffee and pie. That was last Tuesday."

"And you do this once a week," I said.

"*I* do it with him once a week. He does it on his own practically every single day."

I shook my head. "It's a wonder there are any leathermen left in Los Angeles," I muttered.

"Well, you know, it's not always leathermen. He kills anybody. Cabbies, bums, pimps, housewives, Rottweilers, ushers at the movie theater . . . They all taste good to him. There's billions of people in the world and, like, a hundred million in L.A. alone. I don't think he's going to hurt the population much." Lovely briskly slapped my behind. "Turn over, I'm gonna do your thighs. Back feel better?"

"Much." I stared at the glitter ceiling. "You know, he killed Nora."

"I knew he was going to," Lovely said.

"Aren't you afraid you'll displease him one of these days and he'll kill you?"

"Nope," Lovely said calmly. "He's promised me. Two and a half more years, and he's going to make sure I die exactly the way I want to die. How many people ever get to choose that? Nobody really. And it's not like suicide; I'm not doing it because I'm unhappy. It's just the best way to die I could ever conceive of. That's an incredible luxury."

"I'm still afraid he's going to kill me one of these days," I said in a small voice.

"Ariane, Ariane, sweetie darling, has Daniel ever even gotten angry at you?"

I had to admit that he hadn't.

"All he does is adore you. Jesus, he's never going to kill you unless you fucking beg him to do it—and probably not even then. You don't understand how lonely Daniel gets. He's really, really old. He has to surround himself with people, but he doesn't make connections of lasting depth. Not to him! To him fifteen years is a casual acquaintance. I think he's wanting to make another, to keep him company for good." Lovely's eyes were huge and earnest. "He wants a lover and a confidante and an ally and an equal. Girl, you are so dense!"

"Why would he want me?" I mumbled.

"I don't know," Lovely said, his voice halting with honesty. "I think he wants me too, but I don't want to go. I don't even want to turn twenty-five, let alone three hundred and fifty."

I turned over onto my side again to think, feeling my slightly sore bowels tug and move inside me. Remembering Daniel's violation made my whole body throb gently, my nipples hard against Chloe's terry-cloth robe. Lovely gave up the massage and curled up beside me, occasionally flicking at his cigarette. Should I even dare to want such a thing? Did I dare to eat this particular peach? I had thought that Ricari had cured me of the urge to immortality, but the idea again swelled inside me. To be with Daniel forever . . . to stop feeling like his inferior and truly understand him, understand Ricari's immense pain . . . how wonderful could that be? I didn't bother to see the end of *Foxes,* where Cherie Currie gets into the car wreck and dies in the hospital; I already knew how the movie ended. Lovely stayed up, though, watching the screen with his eyes wide.

Chapter Ten

Subjects D. B. (*hemophagius*) and A. D. (*sapiens*)

D. B. Blood pressure: (before feeding) 40/30 (after feeding) 200/160

A. D. Blood pressure: 120/82

20mg sapiens blood added to 20mg *hemophagius* blood. Blood mixture increases in temperature to 43°C, darkens in color. Volume decreases almost immediately (≤ 0.1 sec) to a final total of 21 mg.

Observation of this process under microscope (that shitty Radio Shack thing turned up to maximum, which is about 500x) shows the vampire thrombocytes becoming phagocytic, which I've never heard of happening. It's as though the vampire blood cells eat the human blood cells. They gobble them up and produce more microcytic RBCs, releasing a tremendous amount of energy in the process. I have a feeling ATP is involved here, and I don't know where that comes from—experience, I guess. It generally all comes down to ATP, especially since "becoming a vampire by blood exchange" doesn't quite seem to explain how it works. Ugh, I've got to get some sleep.

I watched Daniel taking photographs of all the children who lived at the Rotting Hall. Photo-studio-style, he draped some broken furniture with a dark cloth, posed each subject, and snapped a few shots while Rodan, a new friend he'd picked up cruising, adjusted an umbrella lamp slightly. Lovely posed simply and demurely, wearing nothing but a strip of black cloth wound around his groin; Chloe leaned forward in a classic fifties cleavage shot; the Asian twins, Joey and Blue, entwined intimately together. "What's all this for?" I asked, leaning against the wall.

Daniel paused to put on a new album. "I'm making a photo book," he said. "You're next, Ariane. Jump up on there and sit still."

"Me? But I don't want my picture taken. I look like shit."

"Nonsense. Cooperate." He gestured at me with one set of lacquered claws. "Just a few minutes. I'm really almost done with the photography. Then I'm going to treat the pictures and do the layout. I'm on a deadline."

So I sat down and consented to being photographed. "A deadline?" I said, blinking just after the flash.

"I have a gallery all ready to show my pictures, if I can finish them by next week. Nora set it up months ago and I forgot all about it. I always overextend myself. Mimsy! Mimsy, get in here, I need a picture of you, and then I'm done." Daniel adjusted the lamp himself. "I'll show you something in a minute, Ariane."

Once he had rewound all his film, dismantled the lamp, and paid Rodan a hundred bucks, Daniel led me up into his office. He opened his desk drawer and leafed through a pile of 8x10 black and white prints. At last he found one and put it in front of me, under the light.

It was shot inside a car, a body sprawled in the backseat, spattered and soaked with something dark like black glossy paint. I held up the picture, recognizing the mane of spiraling, flyaway hair. "That's me," I said.

"That is the moment when I fell in love with you," Daniel murmured, kissing the lobe of my skull behind the ear. "You were so beautiful, so vulnerable. Stinking of blood. You were so lost inside, so confused, not angry at all, just . . . you needed me."

"And you're gonna publish that?"

He nodded. "I think it's a beautiful photo."

It was. "No," I said frustrated. "You do not have my permission. What other kind of—of *pictures* do you have in there? Maybe your last picture of Nora?"

Daniel smiled crookedly. "I wish I'd thought of that. Sweetheart, come on. I'll treat the picture so that—so that it's nicer. Really. Please let me, it's just an obscure little gallery, you'll be a star. Please. Please do it for me."

I sighed. "You don't have my permission," I said, "but I bet you're going to do it anyway."

"I promise it won't be horrible. I swear. It's art."

Daniel played his last performance in the glass-brick club the week after my twenty-fifth birthday; he played a whole lot of very loud industrial noise, and ended the set by tying a razor blade to a piece of fishing line, swallowing it, singing a verse or two while the blood ran out the corners of his mouth, and then amid the horrified screams of everyone present (including myself), proceeding to yank the razor blade back out of his esophagus, spattering the front row with fine crimson specks. Needless to say, he was not asked back for another show.

The next week, after he had been made rather famous in the L.A. underground press for this little sideshow, his exhibition of photographs opened at the Graber Gallery in Hollywood, and he invited any and all members of the press. He and his band, and a few other kids, sat around on pure-white couches and chairs, wearing pure-white clothing. Everyone else had their faces painted mime-white. Daniel did not, of course, and his face was slightly less white, in contrast, and he painted his lips his customary crimson red. Photographers crowded around the group, and the art press knelt at Daniel's feet asking him questions. I hung at the back with Chloe, both of us conspicuous in our black, eating sandwiches and drinking the complimentary champagne.

The questions drilled through the clattering of camera shutters. Daniel held court like a slightly dissipated, elegant duke. "So was your performance at the Gibbet real?" "I don't know, what do you think?" "Are you a real vampire?" "Yes." "What do you say to your critics who say you're just a dilettante, calling on all the most popular artistic movements of the twentieth century?" "I say, for heaven's sake, get a life, art isn't made to be criticized. Read some fucking Dali." "Where were you born?" "Outer space."

The photos were beautiful and bizarre. He had cut and pasted different parts of the photos together, as well as making collages with cardboard tampon boxes, broken red glass, and newspaper clippings about murders and accidents. Some of the photos he left intact; the one of Lovely sitting in a stiff, formal pose in his wee loincloth, and the simple pose of me in the Rotting Hall, somewhat slouched, cigarette burning between my fingers. I looked like a tough, cynical bitch having a pensive moment; like a sophisticated high school dropout. "That's a great picture," Chloe said to me, startling me.

"I don't like photos," I said, rubbing the goose pimples off my arms. "I don't like this spectacle. Doesn't seem . . . safe, somehow . . ."

She put her warm arm around me and led me away. "It's gonna be OK. You worry too much."

The week after, Daniel sprawled in his office at the Rotting Hall, surrounded by L.A. art papers from the most marginal zines to the glossy professionals, extremely pleased with himself, talking on the phone. I lay on his bed running over my test results, craving my lab facilities back at the Loony Geek Farm. I never thought I'd miss that place; fortunately, the homesickness came in slow waves that were easily muddled.

He hung up the phone at last, pouring another glass of Orangina soda. "Well, I was right," he said to me. "I'm not an exile. Do you have Ricari's mailing address? I'd love to send him a copy of these rags and see what he thinks."

"He's probably still at the Saskatchewan Hotel in North Beach," I murmured, then turned on my side to look at him. "What do you mean, you're not an exile?"

"Well, I told the print press that I'm a real vampire, but I just talked to the Revikoffs, and they don't seem to mind at all."

"Who are the Revikoffs?"

"Old friends. Emphasis on old. They'd like to meet you, in fact. They're very interested in your scientific experiments."

"Others? Really? You mentioned my work to them?"

"Of course. The Revikoffs make me look like the uninhibited teenager that I really am. Alex was made in the late nineteenth century, and Risa about thirty years behind him." Daniel picked up his favorite magazine, a cyberpunkish ultra-glossy crowded with balloonish fonts, and fingered the photographs of himself, relaxing majestically in his white linen suit. "Part of your gradual immersion. I find the transition isn't so painful if you're eased into the lifestyle, get a couple of friends who know where you're at, you know. Lovely's already met Sam Rifkin, who's an old queer who spent most of his formative years in Morocco . . . they got along great."

"I don't think Lovely wants to be a vampire, Dan," I said slowly.

"Nonsense. He'll do as I say. He'll change his mind once he's there." He cocked an eyebrow at me. "Don't tell me you're chickening out."

"I never chicken out," I retorted. "I may decide not to, but I don't—"

"Ah, don't get peeved, sweetheart. I was only teasing." He dropped his glossy print narcissus and curled up next to me on the mattress. "You still love this disgusting old degenerate?" he asked softly, curling his finger around my ear.

"Like I can help it. Can't live without you." I kissed him to let him know that I meant it.

"Getting anywhere on the antibody problem? Or the strength problem?"

"Not too much—I'm not that big on biophysics. I can only guess its something in the resilience and toughness of the bones and tendons involved . . . you've basically got the strength of an insect, proportionally."

"God, I love it when you talk dirty to me. Call me an insect again!"

I let him know that he was not immune to tickling. He was particularly susceptible, in fact—sometimes his shrieking and thrashing accidentally left bruises on me. "Don't complain. You'll inherit the earth, you locust."

"A plague of me upon the land. Ha!" He jumped up. "Do you want to go visit the Revikoffs? Risa said they'd be home tonight. I'm sure they wouldn't mind a couple of visitors. You'll absolutely have to take off that T-shirt and jeans, though, honey. They're pretty conservative."

"What do they want, a diamond tiara and evening gown?" I griped.

"Part of the reason why I like them is that they wouldn't mind if you did show up dressed like that. I miss that kind of thing. Come on, put on that gray dress I first brought you."

Washed, with makeup, and clad in gray, I accompanied Daniel into the verdant hills of Brentwood (stopping first for a Taco Bell run), winding around the complicated roads without a single stoplight. "I feel like I'm being taken to the secret rendezvous," I said. "There's no way I could find my way back here."

"That's deliberate, I'm sure," Daniel said, tossing his taco wrappers into the back seat. "The Revikoffs like their privacy. I don't know why they don't just move to Montana or Arkansas or something, where nobody would think to look for them."

"Is there a reason why they're so . . ." I was going to say *paranoid,* but amended it to "Secretive?"

He knew what I meant anyway. His smooth rice-paper face crimped in a smirk. "You know, the usual list of crimes . . . murdering heads of state, embezzling millions from the Soviet government . . . nothing major."

"Where'd you get your money, Daniel?"

Of all the obnoxious questions I asked him every day, I had never yet asked this. He was quiet for a moment, eyes trained carefully on the road, his fingers uneasily flexing on the leather-wrapped steering wheel, and at last he answered me. "Well, technically, I'm still alive. I had put a bit of money in the bank just after Ricari transformed me—his advice. Not very much money, mind you, not much more than any burgher might put away to build an indoor toilet for his summer house. It's still there, quite safe and happy; I transferred it to Switzerland just before the war, and it's weathered many political storms there, letting the gnomes toss a few more deutschemarks on it now and again. The interest alone is punching seven figures." He yawned. "And some of it I stole from Ricari."

"Daniel."

"Well, he was giving it to me for so long I felt entitled to it. Call it paternity. He'll never miss it, the stingy bastard, he's worth God knows what, under twenty different names, probably. And some of it I acquired through charm . . . or through what you might call public service."

"Your little side business as a pimp exterminator?"

"They carry huge sums of cash upon their person. Thank me, sweetheart; that's where your French fry money comes from, huh? You know I'm a scoundrel." He'd just seen *Empire Strikes Back* again recently, and he'd taken a shine to that word. "Get used to it. Naughty deeds come easily; you're not exactly part of the moral majority yourself."

"I wasn't passing judgment."

"Sure, baby," he said. "Hey, we're here."

In the moonlight a white-painted wrought-iron gate gleamed like struts of bone. Unlike half the movie/TV/sports stars who lived in this area of Los Angeles, the house itself wasn't hidden up a winding drive beyond the gate; a white and dark Tudor was plainly visible up a short, wide gravel drive. Daniel leaned out the car door and punched a code into a lighted security grid, and the gate swung open slowly and in perfect silence. Indeed, in Brentwood all was silence except for the humming of Dolores's overblown engine and the discreet anarchy of *Diamond Dogs* on the car stereo.

We ditched the car in the driveway, and I followed the skipping Daniel to the front door. A slight young Latino girl, dressed in a white dress and whiter apron, peeked her head out the door. She blinked at us without saying anything. "We're here to visit Alex and Risa," Daniel said. "They're expecting us."

The girl didn't seem to be inclined to believe him and didn't budge, but a low masculine voice came out of the house as if carried on the wind. "Carmen, he's all right. Let them in."

She bowed her head and silently let us pass.

The house was a vivid contrast to the charming but chaotic squalor of *Verfaulenhalle*; equally Gothic in its way, the foyer was a short hall of walnut lined with small sitting-room paintings of nobility and white votive candles fluttering in the breeze we let in. The front room was dark, curtained, vast, elegant; white jacquard settees, hardwood floor lined with a dark blue runner, a huge showcase filled with tiny, expensive things that glittered faintly in the candlelight. I nervously took Daniel's hand. It gave me no comfort; his fingers curled around mine, unusually icy and skeletal. "Hey, Alex," he called out into the nothingness. The girl had vanished silently behind us as we'd come through the door.

"I'm in the kitchen, Daniel. I expected you'd want a drink."

There were no lights on in the kitchen either. A smallish, slender figure clinked glasses, leaning easily against the polished counter. "Vodka all right?"

Daniel laughed. "As long as you don't mind if I offer you *hefeweizen* when you come to visit me next, Alexander."

"You know I don't drink, Daniel."

"This is Ariane," Daniel said, offering me up.

"Pleased to meet you," I murmured, stifling the urge to curtsy. "I hope you don't think I'm too forward, but would you mind a little light, so I don't feel like I'm facing the Great Unknown?"

"Ah, but you are, my darling." Obligingly he flicked

a tiny switch, and a blue-tinted night-light lit up at the outlet beside the sink. Alexander Revikoff was perhaps a bit taller than I, dressed simply and expensively; his hairline and the slight crow's feet around his eyes placed him at about forty. He was not particularly handsome, but the cast of his features gave his face a kind of wistful gravity. "A Southerner. Let me guess. Georgia?"

"New Orleans," I said.

"Forgive me. I'm terrible at accent identification, frankly." He handed Daniel a cut-glass tumbler of colorless fluid. "Do you drink vodka?" he asked me.

"Among other things."

Daniel and Revikoff traded a smile. "Yes," Revikoff said.

"You're talking about me," I suspected.

The Russian's smile was trained on me. "Yes," he admitted. "Forgive me. Not really talking, Daniel and I are not that close. There was merely a feeling of pride, and a reply of approval. I think you'll be fine."

I took my shot of vodka. It was bitingly cold, syrupy; it tasted faintly of grass clippings. "Polish, isn't it?" I guessed. "Zobrovka?"

"Not that brand, but made in the same way, with *zobrovka* herbs." The Russian vampire placed his hand on my shoulder. Interestingly, his claws were clipped short, blunt, just to the tip of the pale-pink vein in the center. The claws were layered keratin, about a millimeter thick. It looked uncomfortable. "You'll do. Come downstairs, meet Risa. She's a little more stimulating than I." He guided me to the back staircase, Daniel following behind us with the vodka bottle in hand. "In the end I am simply a boring old man. I always have been. Risa is the light between us."

Downstairs was an extensive game room with billiards, swords of all kinds, pistols hung in show racks; Risa was playing darts by candlelight, tossing bull's-eye after neat bull's-eye. She was taller than Alex, round-shouldered, skin a luminous white, hair very close-cropped with a stylish messiness. She looked up and bellowed with pleasure at the sight of Daniel, and he picked her up and kissed her and swung her around, not letting go of the vodka bottle. "My angel!" she cried. "How good of you to come! Please, give me a taste of that vodka, it took me a whole afternoon to find it."

Alex Revikoff retained me in the stairwell. "Her name is Elisabeta," he explained to me, running his fingers along the wood grain in the walls. "She's thirty. Or she would be. Or she was." His pale, glass-ornament-blue eyes watched Risa and Daniel pawing and kissing and chattering to each other. "She adores Daniel. We met him when he first came to Los Angeles in 1957. He came for the beatniks. Risa also adored the Beats, and they ended up in the same filthy cafes together listening to infernal bongo music and worse poetry."

"Did they have an affair?" I guessed.

"I wouldn't say an affair. Affairs are for soap operas. Adultery is for the Bible. She brought Daniel home to stay with us as her lover."

"Weren't you upset?"

"I was confused. My wife, who I adored, was bright again after fifteen, twenty years of unhappiness. We traveled the world trying to find a place that would make her happy. She liked Hollywood films, so we moved to Hollywood in the end. But she was so melancholy all the time. This life was a terrible weight upon her, the knowledge of what she'd done, what she had endured so that we could be together. I cannot express . . . I cannot imagine . . . how it must be, to follow the one you love into death. She never said to me that she thought she'd made a mistake—how could she? But she was simply quietly miserable for years.

Then she met Daniel." Revikoff patted my shoulder gently with his unsettling hand. "Suddenly she was alive again, the way she was before I changed her. She was full of light and love, not just for Daniel and her beatniks, but for me. Daniel wasn't serious about her. She knew that. She didn't mind."

"That Daniel," I said. "He's like a shot in the ass."

"Pardon?"

"Just an expression."

He frowned, and then smiled at me. His expressions were so very strange—they reminded me of Ricari, and at first I had thought it was simply Old World charm. Then it became clear that this man hardly ever drank blood. His skin reacted, not fluidly like a human's, or like Daniel's ordinarily, but suddenly, friendly lines appearing on his forehead instantly. His smiles were mechanical. As gentle as he was, I didn't want him touching me anymore, and I excused myself and joined Daniel and Risa downstairs at the red couches next to the billiards table.

"Here's our little sister." Daniel made room for me next to him on the couch, topping off my shot glass with vodka. "Risa, this is Ariane; Ariane, Risa. I was just remarking to Risa how much their names have changed since I knew them. Alex used to be Sascha, and you used to be Beata. I'm glad he's not Sascha anymore, he's much more mellow now. Right, Alex?"

"Mellow is not an adjective that should be applied to people," Alex said, coming slowly down the stairs. He sat on the second-to-last stair and stayed there.

"Do you play darts?" Risa asked me.

"Not too well," I admitted.

"How about archery? I have targets set up in the back. I love archery—anything involving targets!" She had a great big smile and very long, polished white fangs. "I'm an excellent shot. I always have been. Any-

one else for moonlight archery practice?" She jumped
up off the couch. "Anyone?"

"Go on, Ariane," Daniel said.

"Uh . . ."

"You'll be all right, I promise," Daniel said.

"And I should believe *you?*" But I let Risa drag me
up from my seat, and take me to the back room where
the bows were kept, chattering at me all the time.

The back property was vast and probably where all
the worth was; a great lawn rolled out and became a
hill topped with thick groves of cypress. Risa walked
with big boyish strides, her long sleek legs flashing
from under fluttering printed shorts. "I used to hunt
rabbits with a bow and arrow in Russia," she said to
me. "It was my favorite sport. I am lucky that I was
neither of noble blood nor of common; I was not always working, and it didn't matter whether or not I
was ladylike."

"No?" I said. "There wasn't much of a middle class
back then."

"There is no middle class in Russia and there never
has been. Russia is feudal. It doesn't matter who runs
it; there are always lords and vassals. I suppose I was
close to being middle class; my father was a military
adviser on the staff of the czar. My mother was a minor
titled lady, died in childbirth with me. My brothers
raised me." The targets beckoned from down the field,
and she began busily stepping on the bows to bend and
string them.

"How'd you get out during the war?" I asked quietly.

She strung my bow for me and handed me some
chalk for my hands. "Alex," she said, shrugging. "He
transformed me just before the Bolsheviks were going
to come for me; they'd already gotten my father and
brothers long before that. Then Sascha and I . . ." She
blew out her breath in a little burst. "We killed our
way out, essentially. We let nothing and no one stand

in our way—friends, allies, total strangers. We hid for a long time in Australia, of all places." She notched an arrow, squinted, and in a beautiful simplicity and economy of movement, let an arrow fly into the center circle of the target seventy yards away. "We went everywhere—England, Ireland, Egypt, Brazil. . . . I don't remember where. I had begun watching movies to work on my English, and I got addicted to them, of course. I fancied that Sascha and I were like Nick and Nora Charles from the *Thin Man* movies—just substitute blood for cocktails, huh? Do you want to take a shot?"

Obligingly I attempted, and my arrow landed fletch-up in the grass. She patted me reassuringly on the back and shot again, scoring the arrow next to her first one. "So I dragged him here and here we've stayed—well, we moved from Hollywood to Beverly Hills to Malibu to Brentwood. We try to get away from modern culture—when we want it, we go to it, we don't want it coming to us. We're rather old-fashioned, in case you hadn't noticed. Daniel notwithstanding. He's just fun. Outrageous. I adore him."

"What do you think of Daniel's little advertising campaign?" I asked. This arrow of mine actually hit the target, sticking just in the outside rim.

Risa shrugged. "I don't care. No one really believes him—and if they do, no one will believe *them*. Alex gets a little uncomfortable, but I can usually talk him down. As long as Daniel's not going on any talk shows giving out our name and addresses. I'm sure there are still factions in the world who wouldn't mind getting their hands on Alex and me. We killed a lot of people."

"I think the vodka's negatively affecting my aim." It was certainly negatively affecting my ability to sublimate my accent. I flopped down into the grass and poured myself another, giving up my target practice to watch Risa nock and fire arrow after arrow into the bristling center of the target. She was the very picture of the Dianic maiden, white legs gleaming in moonlight. "Too bad vampires can't be in the Olympics," she said.

"Will my aim improve once I'm made?" I asked.

"No, not really." She smiled at me, then strode forward to retrieve her arrows from the target.

i just watched D. B. kill a man—he was so fast my eye couldn't follow. The man was just a middle-aged fast-food employee walking home outside the Rotting Hall. Daniel went from the lobby out onto the street and grabbed the man and dragged him back to the lobby, breaking his neck as he went. Then he crouched over the limp body and sucked blood out of the back of the man's neck. There was a lot of blood left over—D. didn't even really need the blood, he was just in a playful mood, and most of the blood just ran down his chest. Everyone watched. Kids too young to be watching this kind of thing. They were as transfixed as I was. It had no more emotional importance to me than a nature show on TV. D. invited some of the kids forward to lick the blood from his chest, and quite a few of them complied—one of them being Chloe and one of them being Lovely. They love the sight and they love the taste.

Later Daniel stubbed his toe and he screeched and cried in pain like a child.

I don't know if I'll ever understand this, even with a scanning tunneling microscope and all the immunoelectrophoresis in the world. I really don't know if I'll ever understand. But I've got to try.

Chapter Eleven

On the Tuesday after our visit to the Revikoffs, Daniel
got the notion in his head that he and I and Lovely
should go to the Ready Room. Lovely and I both protested; the Ready Room was a dreadful combination of
Hollywood starlets and Hollywood predators, and their
drinks were scary. Daniel insisted, however, and when
Daniel insisted, we knew it was better to give in rather
than deal with one of his tantrums. We did refuse to
dress up, though, and compared to the Italian/Japanese/
Calvin Klein–wearing crowd inside the bar, Lovely and
I looked like beatnik students. Daniel wore his black
suit and tie; he looked like a beautiful hit man.

"Glen Livet," Daniel barked at the waitress.

"Absolut and tonic," I sighed.

"A big glass of your cheapest, shittiest wine," said
Lovely.

Daniel wrapped his fingers around my hand, brushing my palm with his claws. "Okay, kids," he said,

"we're going to have a big party. To celebrate the new birth of two beautiful young vampires."

Lovely's face immediately went very pale; he hadn't been sleeping well lately. "I hate parties," he said weakly.

"I hate parties too," I added.

Daniel frowned. "You've been going to the wrong parties. Lovely, you're a bald-faced liar; you're a veritable party whore. You crash high school proms. This will be the party of the season. Beautiful boys, gorgeous women, and I'll invite people other than you two as well." He chucked Lovely under the chin. The waitress brought our liquor, and Lovely downed half his glass of mysterious blush in one swallow.

"I'm too old for parties," he mumbled.

Daniel smiled a fangy smile. The waitress gave him a second glance; then her eyes glazed over and she wandered in a daze back to the kitchen. "You're not too old for parties," he said. "You'll never be too old for parties." Getting no response, he blew out his breath between his lips. "Look, I've only ever made two children before in my life. It was over thirty years ago and they're both dead. Allow me my indulgences, why don't you?"

"Dead, huh?" I sipped. Heavy on the vodka—too heavy. "What happened to 'em?"

"Oh . . . them . . ." Daniel gazed into his scotch pensively. "The first one didn't work; I didn't know what I was doing, and she didn't get enough blood. She starved to death before the sun came up . . . not pretty . . . Jameson suffered from melancholy, and he allowed himself to be caught by a bunch of Anton Le Vay-type Satanists, who worshipped him for a few days and then left him to die in the sun. Hell of a scandal. He lasted all of three weeks."

"And you're going to try it again?" I asked, arching my brow.

"You two are of a different caliber. Laura was a stupid accident, and I know how to avoid that problem, don't worry about that. Jameson was just a depressed pretty-boy who amused me; I thought I could change him. I don't want to change either of you; I want you to stay the same. Like I did. Besides, you two have each other. Now, both of you drink up, and cheer up. It's decided. We're having a party."

Most of the kids at the Rotting Hall were crazy about the idea anyway. Daniel proceeded to rent out a whole floor in the Chateau Marmont, and invite not only all the other local vampires he knew, but a whole bunch of famous, rich, sexy, or otherwise desirable Los Angeles mortals. He spent hours on the cell phone shouting at caterers and liquorers; the stress seemed to make him glow.

Lovely and I spent many days huddled in the alcove, watching horror films with the sound turned off, drinking cheap champagne, and worrying. "I don't know," Lovely whispered to me, fondling recently shoplifted Depeche Mode tapes. "I really don't know."

"Just tell him no, Lovely."

"Well, I don't know. Maybe I do want to be a vampire. I mean, look at me." He spread his arms wide, showing off his torso, which was so translucently pale that I could trace the blue veins across his ribs. "I can't figure out whether or not I've been lying to myself all this time."

"He's brainwashing you."

"You know, Riane, I don't think I'll mind this whole thing, so long as you're there. You totally make everything better." He was wasted and emotional, but I still felt the truth in it. "Promise me you won't ditch me."

"Lovely, I'll follow you anywhere." I kissed him on his dry lips. "I dunno . . . I see myself getting sick of the Daniel scene in . . . oh, twenty years or so . . ."

"Merely an eyeblink!" He flung out his arm and let it drop into his lap.

I contemplatively rubbed the tattoo on his belly. When he drank champagne, the black scar swelled and I could feel the question mark thick against my fingers. His stomach sucked in, struggling to hold in a massive hit from the bong, but the smoke was stronger than he was; it exploded outward, clouding the alcove, and he coughed until I thought he might be sick. I hugged him roughly and we lay there, listening to the strains of Ryuichi Sakamoto coming from the duct-taped tape player.

Our reverie was shattered by the banshee hooting of Daniel and the clatter of his boots on the stairs, right overhead of us. "Where are my babies?" he yelled. We were his babies now. He flung open the door and stared down at us.

"How darling! My *liebchens*." Daniel cocked his head and smiled like a demented housewife. "Stoned."

I eyed him. "Stoned," I agreed.

"Come on, get up, you can cuddle all day. We have to go to the salon and be fitted for your party clothes." Daniel grabbed my wrist and pulled me half up.

"I wanna go naked," Lovely managed to say.

"You can. You can tear off the clothes if you want. But please be fitted for them, please wear them to the party. It's a status thing! Jeez, you *are* still in L.A." I stood up so that Daniel wouldn't tear my arm out of the socket in his enthusiasm. "See? Ariane's cooperating."

"We're just getting stoned now while we still can," I explained.

"As long as there are stoners, you can be stoned. Come *on*."

That whole evening in the stuffy fitting salon, standing there while bored French girls measured my plump breasts and frowned at my legs, I stared at Lovely, trying to send him telepathic signals to tell Daniel the truth before it was too late. But Lovely did no such thing. He smiled at the caresses of the tailors, he shone under Daniel's attention. Poor boy! He was so afraid that Daniel wouldn't love him anymore. The worst part was that *I* wasn't sure that Daniel would keep loving him if Lovely said no. I wanted what he had to give, but I wasn't sure if it was worth the price of his companionship.

I wanted Lovely with me too. I had my selfish reasons. I wanted someone who I could just hang out with, be comfortable around, a friend, to spend my piece of eternity with. I didn't want to spend a hundred years with Daniel and his insanity. Daniel was a godlike lover, but he was exhausting; I didn't want to be exhausted in the twenty-second century. Each time we made love, he drained me of some of my essence of self, sometimes figuratively, sometimes literally. I didn't even have scars to keep track of his wounds.

Poor Daniel. He couldn't pick up on anything that I tried to transmit to Lovely. He was spinning around like a fairy godmother picking out the glass slippers for his prince and princess. Afterward he took us out for shakes and grilled shrimp at Killer Shrimp, and held Lovely on his lap in full view of everyone, rocking him and crooning lullabies in his car. Daniel leaned over and kissed me and said, "Thank you, Ariane, thank you for being in my life." I could only wipe the tears off my face and whisper back, *Thank you, Daniel*.

The color scheme of the party was red and black.

The rich people showed up first, knowing a good snack opportunity when they saw one; the sexy came next, and then the famous. From the pool down below, Lovely and I watched them come in, each being greeted and air-kissed by Daniel as they arrived. We were sipping Singapore slings and watching the starlets and starlettes splashing around in the hippest pool in town. "He's amazing, I have to admit," Lovely said.

I thought Lovely was amazing this evening. Daniel had managed to get him into black silk drawstring pants, black cobweb lace blouse, and Italian jacket; Lovely had managed to remain barefoot, but Daniel had insisted on sterling-silver toe rings and henna designs on hands and feet. Lovely's forelock, now blond, black, and red, snaked artfully behind his left ear, which, upgraded, bore six-gauge surgical steel hoops. "He just knows how to schmooze," I replied, pushing aside my black paper drink umbrella. The Marmont certainly had admirable style.

"I guess we should go inside sometime," Lovely said. "I think I hear Daniel calling us."

Laboriously we staggered up off the deck chairs. I was less burdened under expensive fabrics; Daniel had managed to get me into a red velvet dress with red metallic jewels around the straps. I had never worn red in my life, and I felt like a walking stoplight.

We witnessed chaos as soon as we reached our floor of suites. The kids from the Rotting Hall were racing about, leaping on the furniture, squealing. They were all in their finest clothes, which wasn't really saying very much compared to the Givenchy and the Bill Blass and all the rest surrounding them; but they seemed to be having a great time. The rich were pretty obvious, even though they had tried to dress down for a "casual party"; they often had trophy wives in tow. Most of the famous had fled early on. Famous people usually have no stomach for parties; they'd rather go home and go to bed. The sexy seemed also to be enjoying themselves; how could they not, with the suave Mimsy taking care of every need of the ladies and Chloe paying just enough attention to the men so that they knew what was up?

Daniel hadn't told anyone about the real purpose of

the party except the vampires. They were the most obvious of all, mostly by their very subtlety. Alex and Risa occupied a balcony, Risa talking and sipping red wine, and Alex drinking in her every word. I saw others whom I didn't recognize, but the low subconscious hum of their presence thickened the atmosphere like steam.

Daniel seized me by the arm as soon as I came in. "Ariane. You must come meet Sammy. He's been dying to meet you." While walking me to another suite, he kissed my exposed shoulder. "Oh, God, you look beautiful."

"I look like a cherry tomato."

"I want to bite into you."

"You can't, I'll squirt," I said.

He looked up from nuzzling my throat. "Ah, Sammy, there you are."

In a suite, almost alone, a beautiful man was talking to Genevieve, a delicate teenage girl from the Rotting Hall, cupping her tiny hands in his huge ones. He looked up. "Daniel! Finally."

Alex and Risa were not particularly vampiric-looking vampires. Samuel Rifkin was different. He was as tall as Daniel, if not slightly taller, powerfully built, with a beautiful dark tan skin, black eyes, and black hair that ran in sheets to the small of his back. He'd eschewed the color scheme tonight, preferring shades of brown. "I was getting sick of waiting for you," he stated in an arcane, crisp British accent. "I was starting to think this was another of your Dadaist hoaxes."

"No hoax this time. This is Ariane."

"The intended." Rifkin kissed my hand. He was cold as tile, his hands huge, segmented, possessed of inch-long claws polished to a high sheen. "Good to meet you."

"This is all very amusing," I said, thinking of nothing else to say.

"Samuel's very old," Daniel said to me, still gripping my arm in his hand. "What year were you born again?"

"Ordinarily I'd refuse such a gauche request. But for you," Rifkin said to me, "I'll ignore his boorishness. I was born in 1872, in Calcutta. My father was an officer in the East India Company. My mother did the washing-up."

"How . . . Kipling," I said.

"I don't know," Rifkin replied, amused. "I've never kippled."

Daniel convulsed with silent laughter.

"You've met Lovely?" I asked. It took me a full minute to realize that he scared me. I deeply regretted that drunken crack about Kipling, but he seemed to take it well. He smiled at my query.

"A few times. A charming young boy. Daniel is deeply enamored of him."

"He's my best friend," I said impulsively. God, I wanted another drink and a cigarette. "Excuse me, I have to go have a cigarette, Lovely's got them."

I escaped, feeling their eyes boring holes in my bare back. In the hall some kids, Rotting children and un-discovered young actors, were sitting cross-legged, playing rock-scissors-paper for quick whiffs of crystal meth. I found Lovely in the middle suite, where the food was, stoned and picking sadly through the remains of the catering plates. "Do you have my tobacco?" I grunted at him.

"Huh? Oh. Oh, fuck." He rubbed his forehead. "I lost it."

"Lovely . . . !"

"I'm sorry. Have Daniel send out for some smokes."

"I got some tobacco," said a voice behind us.

It was a fourth vampire. This one had been very young when he was made; younger than Lovely even; green-eyed and blond with the faint shadows of freck-les on his face. "Come on out to the balcony."

We followed him there. He rolled three cigarettes with lightning speed and lit them for us with an army zippo. "I'm Leland," he explained. His handshake was warm. "Y'all are Daniel's friends, right?"

"Right," I said. "Where are you from?"

"Virginia."

His tobacco was excellent—tasted faintly of whiskey and honey. Lovely shed his jacket and unbuttoned his shirt. I leaned against the balcony rail, looking out at the black L.A. night sky; were there never any stars there? Had they been outlawed? "What are you doing in Hollywood?" I asked Leland.

"I dunno. I was bored. I ended up here."

"Do you know Daniel well?" Lovely stretched his shoulders.

"Hell, he stalked me." The young vampire laughed. He had buck teeth, and it looked humorous with his short fangs. "I finally gave up and said, 'Yeah, you figured it out.' We get along."

"Get along," Lovely repeated, and chuckled. "Three Southerners here. I'm from Oklahoma."

"Shit, boy, you ain't no Southerner. You a redneck," said Leland.

"Hey, we had a Gremlin up on blocks in the front yard, gimme a break," Lovely mumbled, taking the bait. I smiled at them and smoked.

Leland stared out at the swimming pool. In repose his young face was mundane and powerful. He looked like a green soldier, ripe for the scythe of war, on the cover of a *Life* magazine. "I ain't stayin' long," he said. "I think I'm leavin' this week. I'm going to Amsterdam."

"Take us with you," Lovely said.

"No way. I need to keep a low profile. I like Daniel, and I know them Russians, but I don't feel like knowin' nobody. I feel like disappearin'. That's what I wanna do. I wanna be someplace where nobody knows me."

"Can you speak Dutch?" I asked.

"I can now." He smiled. "I been learnin'."

We stayed out on the balcony for a long time, smoking until he left, and Lovely and I reluctantly returned to the party. Risa wanted me to sit with her on the couch, so I did. She looked dangerously cute in a red Chinese dress and tennis shoes. "You look so sad," she said, stroking my arm with her hot fingers. Her nails were painted red as well.

"I am," I said. "A lot of things make me sad."

"Like what, dear?"

"Like . . . That boy. I don't know how old he is but he's a vampire and all he wants to do is disappear. Like the fact that I was in love with someone, and we were even talking about getting married, and now I'll never see him again, and I'm sad that I made the choice to never see him again, but you know, I still love him. I still love Ricari. I love Daniel. Jesus, and why isn't there anything left to eat?"

Risa got up momentarily, and returned with a glass of red wine and three sandwiches—salmon, mushroom, and cucumber. She patted my shoulder. "It's all right," she said. "You'll get used to it. Soon you'll begin to treasure the fact that you never fall out of love with people. It will become precious to you, like a string of pearls . . . each one of them individual and special."

I ate the sandwiches.

Lovely was asleep on one of the couches with Genevieve stroking the velvety suede of his shaved head. His breathing was even and calm. His black lipstick was hopelessly smudged and he'd lost his toe rings.

"Did you ever know Ricari?" I asked Risa.

"No. I've never met him. We were never in the same place at the same time. He seems interesting. I think Alex would like him."

"I can't believe he's the oldest vampire I've ever known," I said.

"There are older ones," Risa said, smiling. "You've met them."

"Who?"

Risa smiled in the general direction of the balcony.

"*Leland?* He's just a kid."

"He's from Virginia, isn't he? Virginia was a colony once, wasn't it?"

I shook my head, and shook my head again. "I can't believe it."

"Strange. We are strange creatures." Risa gently nudged me with her tennis shoe. "Go wake your friend. He's sleeping through all the best parts."

Eventually I was popped into a taxi back to the Rotting Hall, and I stumbled up the creaking steps to the alcove. My dress and expensive lingerie came off and I collapsed onto the cushions and pulled the blankets, fragrant with old pot smoke, over me.

I slept for a while. Then I felt Lovely join me on the cushions. His lace shirt scratched me, and I mumbled for him to take it off. I fell back to sleep before I thought of it again.

Later I woke up again. There was something vaguely erotic happening. Lovely's skin against mine was damp and silky and fragrant and his fingers were stroking and squeezing my nipples with a sleepy lassitude. "Hmmm," I said at first. All right.

His sticky girlish fingers crawled down my belly; then one hand went back to the nipples and the other one crisped in my pubic hair. "What are you doing?" I asked groggily.

"Touching," Lovely said.

I let him. I wanted to go back to sleep, but what he was doing fought the impulse to sleep. I opened my legs slightly, and his fingers squished into my folds, damp with oily sweat. "Lovely," I admonished.

"What?"

"What are you *doing?*"

"Touching your pussy," he replied.

I giggled despite myself. "Why?"

"I want to know what it feels like."

He moved his hand behind me and slipped the hand in sideways, rubbing the side of his hand along the slit, opening it. I felt tiny gushes of wetness come out of me. Christ—his girlish little fingers—I rolled over and bit his collarbone gently. In reply, he slipped three fingers into my cunt.

"Oh—Jesus!" I kept my eyes closed, but I sought out his nipples with my fingers. The barbells in his tits were hot to the touch. He took one of my hands and put it on his penis. He was hard as stone. It was so odd—I hadn't felt a human body in so long—it was different, certainly. Lovely's body was soft and delicate and his skin lacked the perfect velvety texture of Daniel's. I removed his fingers from my cunt, and he wiped them inexpertly across my belly. He made me finger myself, and smear the wetness across the head of his cock.

I opened my eyes then. He was very awake, watching me, eye makeup smudged in his eye pits, his pupils dilated in his intensity. "Lovely?" I asked. "But . . . you don't like girls."

"I do too," he protested in a whisper. "I like you."

He grabbed my cunt and poked the first two fingers inside again. I was a dripping mess. "I'm so confused." I laughed.

"Come on, we're halfway there. Do you wanna get fucked?"

I didn't reply anything verbally; his fingers inside me digging insistently, adding more fingers, killed off any protest I could possibly come up with. He lay half on top of me, grinding his penis against my thigh, my haunch, the plump part of my hip. "Pussy is so cool," he murmured. "So weird . . . from an another planet . . ."

I grabbed his cock to try to wrest some control back, but he was used to rough handling and it only made him bite me. We began to wrestle. Giggling happened. We kissed. His mouth tasted like poetry—funky and strange and slightly sour and slightly sweet. I sucked at the nipple barbells, and he made sounds like cats in heat.

He rolled on a Trojan and we commenced battering the pillows. I began to laugh almost immediately, and didn't stop. He fucked completely differently from Daniel; compared to Daniel's deep slow manly thrusts—very German—Lovely fucked like a jackrabbit. Speed was everything. Friction and heat built up between us immediately; then we lubricated it with sweat and my slime, and then the friction burnt that away. I rolled him over at last, impatient with his ministrations, and did the rest myself. Lovely had an orgasm within ten seconds of me jumping on top, and he obligingly finished me with his tongue and his fingers. It didn't take much.

It was evening. We lay there together for a long time, listening to classical music radio and licking each other's genitals gently. His injuries weren't too bad, but he made much of my bruises and swelling. "I'm sorry," he said, in between cat-licks. "I'm used to butts."

"I'm surprised you didn't go for my ass, frankly."

"No way. I haven't had sex with a girl since high school. She wasn't nearly as good as you are."

"I don't want to hear about it," I said. He had a barbell through his penis as well—I hadn't noticed it before. Slimmer than the piercings in his tits, the tiny silver globes rode suspended on the grainy-smooth pink meat of his glans. It was fun to lick around them. "Did this hurt?"

"Only while she was piercing it."

"How can you fuck with this thing?"

"Can't fuck without it, honey."

I relaxed back onto the cushions, and Lovely drew the coverlet back over me. He pulled it half over himself too, leaving ankles and feet sticking out. He kept on doing what he was doing, and I decided to try to get back to sleep.

"Oh, how darling."

Daniel loomed over us, gleaming in head-to-toe black vinyl, his presence sending out heavy vibes like waves of heat. He looked like a futuristic assassin. Lovely scrambled half up, drawing the covers up to his chin and blushing bright pink.

"D-D-Daniel . . ." he stammered.

"I can explain," I said.

Daniel smiled tightly. He was upset; I could feel it. His vibrations made my temples tremble. "No, it's all right," Daniel said. "Really. I think it's cute. My little children engaged in incest."

"Daniel," I begged, "oh, please, please be reasonable."

"Honest," Daniel said. "Really. It's fine. I'm not angry. I'm startled. I really never thought about it. I thought you didn't like girls, Lovely."

"I don't," Lovely said. "I like Ariane."

Daniel knelt, crawled into the alcove, shut the door behind him. He creaked. Gently he put out his hand and touched my tangled hair, his expression changing from the brittle and fake-pleasant to the introspective. Lovely curled up in Daniel's vinyl lap. "Is it really OK?" Lovely said. "I mean, it probably won't happen again."

"It's fine," said Daniel. He stroked the boy's bare back, claws clacking together. "It's fine. I really do think it's cute actually. You looked like you were caught eating Santa's cookies." Daniel laughed to himself. "Did you like your party?"

204

"It wasn't our party, Daniel," I cut in. "It was your party."

"Did you like *my* party?" Daniel amended.

"When's the big day?" Lovely murmured. He was perfectly sober for once, and his usually beatific face was drawn, older with worry. I should have said something then, and perhaps . . . But I didn't. I lay there and let Daniel's stroking and heartbeat lull me, hypnotize me.

Daniel chuckled. "I thought I'd surprise you," he said. "Like having a baby. You know when it's about time, but you never know really. What is this you're listening to—bloody Mozart again!"

"It's only the radio," I said.

"Do we have to hang out with the other vampires after we're . . . ?" Lovely asked.

"No, you don't have to hang out with anybody. That's the nice thing. You never have to deal with anyone you don't want to ever again. If you don't like them, leave, or feed on them, even better. You will have enough strength to handle anything. You'll never be afraid to do anything ever again. You don't even need money, though I would recommend it. Without money you end up like that sad fuck Leland, who roamed around in the backwoods for a hundred years wearing deerskin or something retarded like that. He doesn't think about money. He's going to Europe finally and he's going to be poor there. But I don't want that to happen to you. In fact, I've put some money away in Switzerland for the two of you. After you're made, do whatever you want with it."

"How much money?" I couldn't help asking.

His eyes sparkled. He was glowing faintly, and I figured out why he'd come down to the alcove; we'd missed the breakfast ritual. "You'll have to find out, won't you? Little birthday present. Keep the wolves away from your door."

Out of habit Lovely's hand strayed to Daniel's vinyl crotch. Daniel kissed the boy's arm. "Don't worry, precious," he said to Lovely softly. "Don't worry about a thing."

Chloe and I had dinner later at the Denny's. She was quiet and tired. I took her hand and massaged it gently. "What's on your mind?" I asked her.

She half-shrugged. "I'm . . . I dunno. It's nothing." She smiled at me unconvincingly. "Just PMS-induced superstition."

"Like what? Maybe if you tell me—"

"No, no, no. It's dumb. I've got enough psychology to know when talking about your fears is really counterproductive."

"Do you know something I don't?"

"Now, don't get suspicious, Ariane." She dipped a breaded cheese stick into a tureen of sauce. We'd gone all out on the sleazy food—burgers, salad with Thousand Island, cheese sticks, Dr Pepper; later we'd have Key lime pie. It was an antidote to the fussy sandwiches, crudité, and eighteen-year-old wine from last night. "We gotta stick together if we're gonna prevail. One of the many things I learned from Daniel—stick together. Support each other."

"I hope you're paying for dinner then."

"Hey, we support each *other,* honey. And you ate all my salad." She poked at the remains of the burger on her plate. "So . . . you and Lovely . . ."

I blushed. "News travels fast."

"Small community. Plus it was obvious. Everyone frankly thought you guys had been at it all along. Why now?"

"I dunno. He started it. Totally took me by surprise." I signaled for the fourth refill of my Dr Pepper; bitchy waiter was there tonight, and he usually had to be threatened by his manager before he'd come over and serve us. "It was weird. I guess it's not going to happen again. Daniel busting in really fucked Lovely up; he's all freaked out now. Jesus, I hope this all wasn't a huge mistake. I usually don't have sex so . . . casually."

"It wasn't at all. It's totally natural to sleep with your brother, even if he's not really your brother. Why do you think there's so many plays about it?"

"Not to mention *Star Wars*."

"Not to mention. You're his best friend in the world, including Daniel. He idolizes you. Besides, that childish hustler shit can't last forever; maybe he's a fag, but that doesn't mean he can't be in love with you, emotionally, physically . . ."

"Stop it, you're sounding like a Harlequin Romance novel."

Chloe laughed, her signature snort. "I can't help it. I think it's really cool. Shame it won't happen again."

"Yeah . . . he's a regular fuck machine."

"Get *out* of here!"

We escaped the Denny's at last, met up with Mimsy, saw an old movie starring Tyrone Power and Rita Hayworth, and settled in a club, drinking. Both Chloe and Mimsy had seemed tense earlier in the evening, not with each other, but more alongside each other, as though each had the same concerns that went unsaid, even between them. After a few martinis, they began to relax, laughing almost too much, as if to assure themselves that their fears were groundless. I was glad to be with them, and my worry about their worry slowly faded away.

When I went to bed, Lovely wasn't there. I couldn't sleep without him. I wandered upstairs to Daniel's office and found Daniel there, watching the Late, Late Movie, motionless on his side on the mattress. "Daniel," I said, "I can't sleep."

"Come here, love."

207

I curled up in his arms. His body was pleasantly cool. No bloodletting, no dead leathermen tonight then. "What's this movie?" On the screen, an overfed actress knelt by her bed and prayed, a menacing cross of light on the wall above her. Out of nowhere a terrifying silhouette appeared. I rolled toward Daniel to avoid looking at what came next.

"The Night of the Hunter," Daniel said. "One of my favorite movies. Robert Mitchum plays this psycho preacher who's actually after a stash of money, and he'll do anything to get it. He's a real bastard."

"Do you know where Lovely is?"

"Nope," Daniel murmured. "He probably went to meet the dope dealer. He'll be back by sunup, I bet. Go to sleep."

His heartbeat was a slow, heavy swishing in his chest, the sound of the ocean in a very narrow cave. It lulled me and I slept.

Chapter Twelve

Daniel awakened me with a kiss. I touched his lean cold arms and put up my knee to caress him. "Let me sleep," I complained.

"You must get up," Daniel said. "This is the day."

I opened my eyes and looked at him. He was up, dressed, his armpits fragrant with amber, but he hadn't yet fed. The sun was still breaking brightly through the cracks in the garbage bags on the windows.

"You have to go out now, enjoy your last day in the sunlight. Do mortal things."

My first sensation was panic. *I don't want to go today!* I thought, my heart galloping. Then, in another breath, the calm came over me. When I had my appendix out, the anesthesiologist came for me with his bright smile and his blue shower cap; at first I panicked so that I thought I would throw up, or claw his eyes out. Then I felt a calm acceptance of my immanent death, and it was the best thing I'd ever felt. I simply gave up, relaxed into the arms of fate, thought, *What good will it do me to fight? If I'm supposed to die now, let it come without fear.* I had felt more powerful than I ever had, after this many straight A's, after that many science prizes and prep school scholarships. I felt that I controlled my own destiny.

Of course, this was an erroneous notion.

I let Daniel get me up, I took a shower, I put on a T-shirt and jeans—it was Daniel's Andy Warhol shirt, black with a white halftone print of Warhol's melancholy face. I put on black Converse tennis shoes that Lovely had stolen from the mall. He had written on the white rubber toe-caps ARIANE and RULES! in green Sharpie marker. Daniel watched me with a smile on his face. "Go have fun," he said. "Come back when you're done."

"Where's Lovely?" I asked, braiding my hair.

Daniel shrugged, and I saw that he was tired, bloodless, annoyed. "I don't know. It's not his day, I guess. I'll find him, sometime today or tonight. Don't worry about him."

"I guess I'll go to the beach," I said doubtfully. I slipped the rat pocket watch into my back pocket.

"Whatever," Daniel said. "That's good. Get some sunshine. Enjoy the feel of it on your skin. Get sunburned if you want—it won't matter afterward. Get wasted. Just come on back here when you're done."

I walked down the stairs. It was early—around noon—everyone was still asleep in the Hall. A ghostly quiet followed me to the door, but balked at the street noise and the light outside. I went outside alone, leaving the silence behind me.

All day I walked and bused around. It was hot and bright and noisy, all brilliant color and tight blue sky. I found that I couldn't stand the light and the heat. I was no longer used to it. The sunshine gave me a terrible headache and burnt painfully on the delicate skin on my arms.

I didn't go to the beach; the idea of the glaring sand and the tanned and oily bodies filled me with nausea. I went to a second-hand bookstore and spent two hours reading old science-fiction paperbacks—Edgar Rice Burroughs, Roger Zelazny, Michael Moorcock. I never liked old sci-fi—John did, though, and his apartment was cluttered with flimsy paperbacks with muscular green women and fantastic planetscapes, the yellow pages falling out in clumps like a chemo patient's hair. Reading them was like seeing him again; touching the crumbly covers was like tracing the contours of his cheeks and jaw, taking off his glasses for a kiss.

I didn't buy any of the books.

Later I saw the year's summer blockbuster film, didn't take in any of it; sneaked out halfway through the climactic chase-and-explosion scene to masturbate in the bathroom. I was too distracted to come, and I finally hitched my jeans, flushed the empty toilet self-consciously, and returned to the theater only to catch the credits.

I had some tacos.

I was hoping I'd run into Lovely in Hollywood; perhaps he'd be hanging around Retail Slut panhandling, smoking a fat spliff in the parking lot of the Mc-Donald's, being romanced by a suave Latino orchestra cellist; but I didn't see him anywhere. I wished that he had a cellular phone that I could call and make sure he was all right. Most likely, I conjectured, he's just gone home with some silky gothic mister, and they were spending the day in bed feeding each other Cap'n Crunch and watching Bela Lugosi movies. I could see him—laughing, worrying, getting high, and then laughing again.

The sun was beginning to sink at last; it was past eight o'clock. I caught the bus to the stop a few blocks away from the Rotting Hall, and walked the last few blocks in a state of impatient agitation. *Never mind! I'm a failure as a human being! Get it over with!* The blond woman who worked at the heavy-metal club waved at me as I passed, and I waved back.

Inside there was more silence—a heavier one this time. Everyone was gone, I could feel it. A single candle, new and as thick around as my arm, burned with a flame straight and true; the light was still and even. Slowly now, I mounted the stairs.

Up in the office, Daniel was reading aloud from a wide book; he didn't look up at me as I came in, but continued reciting:

"Curly-locks, Curly-locks, wilt thou be mine?
Thou shalt not wash the dishes, nor yet feed the swine;
But sit on a cushion, and sew a fine seam
And feed upon strawberries, sugar, and cream."

I stood there.

"How was your day?" asked Daniel.

"Kind of a waste of time," I confessed.

"No, that's all right. I just wanted you to make a go of it. I didn't want you to feel cheated out of a day. Don't worry, it won't seem like a waste of time." He turned round and smiled at me. "Come here, don't be a stranger."

He settled me into his lap and kissed my cheek tenderly. I put my arms around him and embraced him tightly, sighing, butterflies in my stomach. "I love you," I whispered.

"Good." He smiled. "Come, let's get started."

I took off the tennis shoes and massaged my tired feet. "My neck's all stiff," I grumbled, then took the rat pocket watch from my pocket and gave it to him. "Here, hang onto this for me."

"Good idea. Here." He handed me a glass filled with a dark, cloudy liquid. I sniffed it. "It's wine," Daniel said. "With a sedative. It works faster in wine. Drink it."

I downed the glass. It was bitter and sour, but unmistakably wine with something in it—perhaps an opiate, which would explain the bitterness. He began to massage my feet for me. He had fed in the meantime, but not much; his flesh was supple, but white as ice, and his hands were only lukewarm on my hot feet. "What would you like to listen to?" he asked.

I laughed, faintly goofy from the draught of wine. "I dunno . . . that mix tape of yours with the Peter Gabriel and the Bowie instrumentals . . ."

"Actually, not a bad choice." He hopped up and slapped on a tape. "This will flip over automatically. How do you feel?"

"Kind of . . . buttery . . ."

He kissed my throat, then my mouth. He was flavorless. I clung to him anyway, seeking something indefinable in his cheeks and tongue. I tried to prick my tongue upon his fangs, but he drew his head away and regarded me without expression.

The music swelled and my skin, for a moment, began to crawl in time to the music. In another moment this sensation was gone.

He helped me into the bathroom. My legs didn't work very well. He pinched the skin of my arm, and I moved and said "Ouch," but I didn't really feel any pain—well, a pinch, that was all. Daniel took off his shirt. "Feel my heart," he said to me. I felt for it and felt nothing, then a slow, steady throb and retreat, throb and retreat.

"Is what you gave me going to kill me?" I mumbled thickly.

"It won't even put you to sleep right away." He laughed. "I need you awake for this. You're just feeling the rush. Chloe concocted this for this purpose specifically—it's a general anesthetic, but in a low dose . . .

or something. I was thinking about something else when she described it to me." He closed the door, but the stereo was right against the wall on the other side and I could hear the music just fine. I liked this tape because it had This Mortal Coil on it—at least that's how he described it—but to me it was the voice of the Cocteau Twins, hopelessly expressive, singing an old song I felt I should recognize but didn't. It had the feel of the supernatural about it. Daniel was stroking down my throat with the tip of one of his claws; it felt cold and dangerous. He pinched me again, and I barely registered the sensation.

Under the single fluorescent light his face was intent, too thoughtful to be demonic. He knelt at my feet and pulled out my arm and rested it on my lap, between us. "Where is Chloe?" I asked.

"She's at home," Daniel said.

"Can I talk to her?"

"No," he replied. He stroked the pale flesh of my forearm.

I closed my eyes, for I could feel that sensation; just nothing of his pinches and prods. I could still feel the gentleness.

Then I felt something very odd—a tearing, a slicing, and then hot and cold at the same time. I opened my eyes; with a scalpel, Daniel had opened up an incision three or four inches long, longways down my forearm. I felt the hot blood soak into my jeans. Very slowly, the pain sensation swelled up, but bumped its head against the glass ceiling of anesthetic. Nonetheless I cried out.

Daniel put his mouth to the wound and sucked swiftly, and then the pain seized me in its teeth and shook me viciously. I hurt too much for tears. His mouth slid around in the mash of blood and tendons, drawing it into himself with the steadiness of a nursing child. He was not wasteful—the only blood I had wasted was that from the initial cut, that blood running down my jean legs and coating my left foot in a sticky syrup. My body tried to pull away from Daniel, but he wouldn't let go, and my other arm was no good; it might as well have been filled with rags. I lay back and keened like a dying coyote.

I screamed until my throat ran dry. I didn't know you needed blood to scream. The room had dissolved into chips of white and dark, growing larger and darker by the millisecond. ". . . Oh Daniel . . ." I whispered. "I'm dying . . ."

"Soon," he agreed. His voice came from far away. "Now."

I felt that I had his permission to die. But he pushed something into my mouth that ran a cool-hot liquid down my throat. For a moment I thought he was feeding me water or wine so that I could continue screaming, and I thought, how compassionate! But this was thicker, saltier, sour, and bitter; semen? Why did it continue to flow? I choked and moved my face away.

"No! Damn it, drink it or you'll die, do you hear me? I know it's nasty! Keep drinking, you're almost there."

I wanted to refuse, wanting no more of this sickening elixir, but I hadn't the strength, and the stuff poured into my mouth, over my cheeks. I opened my eyes and found I could see quite clearly, if somewhat distortedly; Daniel held his wrist to my mouth, slit crossways with the same knife as he'd used to open me. My arm lay motionless, useless, but beading up with tiny grains of flesh as his drops of his blood fell into the wound. His blood was fresh and red, fat with mine. I felt its heat clearly now, and I swallowed and swallowed, feeling the fluid fill me, fill a strange and awful void.

Daniel pulled back from me and hit the far wall, stumbling. Now he was high on the anesthetic; his pupils in the green absinthe irises swollen. His arm left red swathes on the white tiles. I stared at him, then back at my arm. It felt like it was being burned with drops of candle wax. The swellings I took to be new flesh I saw were blisters; they grew, and under my gaze they burst, spilling drops of reddish pus along the skin.

Nausea began to rise in my belly.

Daniel stood up straight and staggered towards the door. "Christ, I'm sick," he mumbled in a blunted voice, and went out the door.

He left the light on.

I heard it lock from outside. The song playing on the tape—had been playing for the last six or seven minutes from the time that he'd cut me—was "Blackbird" by the Beatles; the tape seemed to be stuck. I slid onto the floor from the toilet seat. "Daniel?" I called out to him.

Book Three
The Circus Movement

Chapter Thirteen

First there was the nausea.

I thought it was brought on by the sight of those nubby tumors on the edges of my wound, and later as it continued, by their breaking and releasing their cargoes of reddish-yellow effluvia; then I realized that that couldn't be all of it. I felt like I'd eaten a combination of devilled ham and broken glass. I lay on my side on the floor tiles, holding my belly, wondering if I should try sticking my finger down my throat and vomiting.

I didn't need to bother. Even in my fetal position on the floor, I let loose a projectile stream of viscous, dark red goo—Daniel's blood, flooding my stomach. I sat up and opened the toilet lid belatedly, and another round came up. This time random bits were strewn through it, anonymous and pink. It could have been from my lunch. I hovered at the edge of the toilet, gripping my belly with fingers so tight, I knew I would leave ten bruises.

* * *

The tape stopped.

There could be no mistaking this time; the blood was bright red, not dark, and there were translucent shreds of flesh there—the lining of my stomach, the delicate orchid mucous membrane. I screamed, choking on it, feeling blood fill my nose.

At almost the same time I felt a great spasm grip my lower intestine, and I convulsed, filling my jeans with a thick, foul, heavy liquid substance. I untwisted myself long enough to unzip my jeans and kick them halfway down. More blood—darker this time, but undigested. I bled freely from the mouth, from the anus, from the urethra.

I screamed again, this time out of anger, and pounded the door with my bare foot. *"Daniel! What the fuck is happening! Daniel! What the fuck!"* I began to cry, but it was so bitterly painful to do so that I wanted to stop. My tear ducts were on fire. There was no reply. I hoisted myself up on the toilet and the shower rod, and looked at myself in the mirror. I wept tears of blood and salt water; my eyes were rheumy, yellowed, the irises gummy, the lids slack.

"Daniel! Let me out of here!"

Nothing.

I retched again, terribly. Red vomit stained my arms, my legs, blood squished between my toes. The anesthetic effect was gone—I felt the loss of my stomach lining, the lining of my colon, my villi, the fine skin between my throat and my nose, eaten away as if by acid or flame. My teeth suddenly filled my mouth like a spoonful of pearls; I couldn't spit, but had to let them drool from between my lips.

I scratched at my leg, itching from the coat of blood, but my nails felt funny—soft, bendable. I looked at my hands with what sight I had left. The fingernails were loose, falling out, leaving raw bleeding beds. I tore at my legs anyway with them; the skin was shedding itself in big sheets, first the dead skin, then the pink new skin underneath, and finally the pale fat, the muscle. I was losing me. All that I was came apart at the scams. I felt more surely than anything I'd ever felt that I was going to die, in this most horrible way, a fate I wouldn't have wished on my worst enemy, tens of billions of cells screaming out as they were torn from each other.

I thrashed around blindly for a long time. I felt the mirror break, my forearm thin-bone with it. No matter. My hair came out in fist-sized balls and stuck to the blood that had been my face, then was washed away clean by the blood. My body was dissolving. My eyes had finally run away from their homes, coursing down my face like melting pudding.

I swam in it.

And then, there was nothing. First no pain—a blissful cessation almost all at once—the death of the minor nerves, then the major ones in their turn. Then there was simply nothing.

I was thankful.

I woke up feeling cold.

At first I couldn't open my eyes; they were stuck together. Instinctively, like a newborn child, I scrubbed my fists against the lids and felt a strange crackle, as if my eyes were sealed shut with the finest cellophane.

My first sights were blurry, and mostly red, with a great pale form to my immediate right, where my head lay against the foot of the toilet. I blinked; tears squeezed out of new tear ducts and coated the eyeballs. I felt this with great wonder and pleasure. When I opened my eyes again, I saw with incredible clarity; again, mostly red, but this time made up of many distinct shades of red; rust red dried to a crackle on the side of white porcelain, black red of the clotted surface of the pool where I lay, vague pinkish shapes splattered against the broken tiles of the shower.

I sat up.

Then I realized I was a whole body, an entire corporeal form, a human form; two legs, a torso, breasts, collarbones, two arms with hands and fingers and fingernails. The fingernails were very short, barely covering the nail beds, but they were a very distinct silvery color with pink half-moons.

I felt my face. It crackled too. I was all red all over. For a while, I didn't understand why I was so red and crackly; then I touched the liquid in which I bathed. *Blood.* My first word, my first comprehension, the first thing I really understood.

I began to itch. I was tingling all over, especially in my armpits and between my legs. I lay there for quite some time rubbing the mound of my pubis, enjoying the pleasure I got from rubbing the itch, until I felt it grow strange. I looked at it. Hair was growing there; so fast that I could see it gradually lengthening, growing thicker and curly. It too was red, the red-brown of the dried blood on the sides of the toilet.

Scratching my head, I slowly stood up. Where the mirror had been, there was only a fragment of silvered glass; enough of it so that I could see myself; red and wild-looking, but quite whole. I touched my face, pulled down my eyelids so that I could see the clean pink undersides, opened my mouth to look at my teeth—new and white and straighter, the canine teeth pointed sharp. When I closed my mouth I bit myself, and tasted my own blood.

A sharp pain went through my spine. *Hungry.* I began to shake. I became sad, and cried; it felt plaintive to me, but it sounded dreadful; a primitive wordless howl. That made me angry. I had to get out and get something to eat, something to drink, something . . . something out there that I could smell . . .

Door.

Then no door. I bashed my fists against it, and the door came off its rickety hinges and collapsed into the outside. I hadn't meant to hit it that hard, but when I looked at the fallen door, the imprints of my fists stood out clearly, biting through the white paint into the wood itself.

I recognized the room and I smelled Daniel's smell on everything, but it told me nothing; he wasn't there. My anger grew. I would have shouted out his name, but I couldn't think of it; I couldn't think of anything.

Escaping, I walked slowly down the stairs, getting used to the feel of it. Everything was dark except one doorway where a dim yellow light shone out, clearly outlined on the graffitti-marked stairwell.

A young girl stuck her head out into the stairwell. "Hello?" she called softly.

In the next instant she was beneath me; I tried to tear open her throat, but my fingernails were still too short and soft, and I merely sunk my fingers through her neck until I was gripping the corrugated pipe of her larynx in my hand. She didn't even have time to scream; her eyes rolled in panic, then slid up under her eyelids. I ducked my head and took a handful of her fluids, supping it from my fingers. I bent over her and put my mouth over the huge wound.

Maybe a minute later, I sat back and took a breath. The girl was cold as a stone, blue, shrunken like a voodoo fetish. There was barely any blood to seep out of the slack artery that had so recently fed me. I recognized her face at last; it was the little girl who had been Daniel's breakfast all those afternoons ago. She was just barely fifteen; she had been miserable that Daniel's huge party had overshadowed her birthday so much that everyone forgot about her.

I thought I might puke, but already the blood that I had drunk was in my veins, refreshing my tired heart and feeding my brain. I could think now, recognize things, remember what had happened to me and what was happening now.

But already I wanted more. That was simply an appetizer; now that my body knew more than ever what it needed, I became a turmoil of sickness and nausea and pain and sensation. *This is no good,* I thought. *What if it's always like this? What if I always need more? This is going to be hell.*

I covered the body with a flowered cotton bedsheet, turning away from the dark stain that slowly rose up to dampen it, and ventured back into the hall. More lights? I sought more lights. More people who might help me. *I won't kill the next one,* I promised myself. *I can't kill my friends like this.*

I came upon Mimsy sleeping in Lovely's and my nook under the second-floor stairs. He looked like an angel, asleep; like Daniel. I bent down to kiss him, thought, *Maybe just a quick taste, something to get me to the next one. I won't hurt him.*

The taste of his skin was exquisite. I didn't even remember touching my tongue to the soft perfect fuzz of his cheek, the slightly roughened skin of his chin. I rested my nose against the yielding flesh of his neck. My teeth found their way to the visible pulse of his carotid and pressed it gently.

He never woke up. Perhaps if he had, he might have been able to stop me; or the shock of his eyes opening and a scream of protest from him might have reminded me of the time I'd spent gently absorbing the warm flow of blood from him to my mouth. But I never thought anything until the pulsing was long gone, and I realized that I had been sucking the blood from the artery because it was no longer coming to me of its own volition.

I sat back and wiped my mouth.

Mimsy was dead. His lips were the grayish violet

that had not yet come into fashion as a lipstick, his skin as colorless as Daniel's in sleep.

I sat there for a while and digested his blood. It wasn't quite the same as eating food; I could feel it immediately soaking through the lining of my stomach and racing through my veins. Mimsy looked peaceful, at least; he didn't have a gaping wound where a slender white throat used to be; the marks of my teeth were solidly outlined in his neck, just below the jaw. It was pretty obvious what had happened to him.

I felt a chill of rising anxiety. I had to get out of there. I found some of my clothes that were hidden away in the darkest corner—a dress and some underwear and a pair of shoes—and put them on over my stinking, peeling skin. My hair was a mass of clotted blood and my fingernails were sticky with it, but there was no time to think of tidiness. I needed to find Daniel.

As I was ducking to leave the alcove, I bumped against a warm, sweet-smelling form, scratchy with black lace. "Oh! Jesus, you scared me!" Chloe laughed and put her hand to her breasts. "I thought I saw Mi—Ariane?"

A thought leapt out of her head at me, almost visible—it shot between my eyes and into my head, voiceless but distinctly hers and not mine. *She's still alive, the mixture didn't take, Daniel and she's been changed, it didn't work, she's still alive.* "Ariane?" she said again, fearfully.

"What do you mean, I'm still alive?" I said, my voice a sickening hoarse croak. I sounded monstrous.

"I didn't say anything," she said.

"I thought—you *thought* it," I stuttered, "you thought it, I heard it, you—what didn't work?"

Chloe began backing away from me, shaking her head. I could smell her fear, feel it coursing through my skin. It galvanized me. I followed her, hemming her against the wall. "What, what are you talking about?" she said. "Please, Ariane, don't."

"What didn't work?" I demanded, putting one arm on either side of her. "What didn't work?"

She swallowed with difficulty. "I guess it's too late now," she said. "Don't kill me. You weren't supposed to survive the wine. I poisoned it—an overdose of the anesthetic. You were supposed to be dead in less than a minute. Before Daniel could give you his blood."

"Why?" I put one hand on her shoulder and squeezed it, for something to do with my restless hands. The joint collapsed under the pressure with a heavy dull pop. Chloe screamed and crumpled, but I caught her before she could fall to the floor. She was half hysterical with pain. "Why did you want to kill me?"

"I didn't want to lose him!"

"So you'd kill me instead? I thought you were my friend!"

"I am your friend!" She had bitten her tongue, and the blood trickled out the side of her mouth.

With a tenderness that sickened me as I did it, I bent my head and kissed the trickle away. Her tears filled my mouth with the blood. The combination was incredible; it made my heart sing. She cried more quietly now, in less pain.

Her blood spread thinly through my mouth, mostly just taste, but a few glimmers of her thoughts, too. That predominant sharp, sour flavor had to be adrenaline, and with it, the state-dependent memory of when she had been in so much pain before. A brilliant, sharp flash of Risa, on her knees in the middle of that funeral-home decor that was the Revikoff's parlor, sobbing heartbrokenly and not caring who saw her, even the naive and confused stranger Chloe, until Daniel turned Chloe away murmuring, "She just had to kill her only human friend. Don't worry, she'll get over it." And then Lovely, abruptly vomiting into his lap in a restaurant, pushing his plate away muttering under his breath, "There was shit everywhere. Pouring out a hole in his belly. Shit everywhere, there's nothing but shit everywhere." And then Daniel himself, holding Chloe and kissing her, telling her he'd never let her go, holding her tighter and tighter until Chloe couldn't breathe to scream, even as she felt her ribs snapping inside her body like so many popsicle sticks.

Chloe had stood vigil over my unconscious body in the Rotting Hall infirmary, telling herself that there was no way that both she and I could survive Daniel, that someday, probably sooner rather than later, one of us would be dead. "I didn't want to see you as unhappy as the others," she explained through sobs and hiccups. "I thought—I thought it would be kinder . . . "

"There's no point in lying to me now; you know that," I said gently, brushing her hair from her face. "You wanted me dead. And you were probably right to do what you did. I only wish it had worked. Now, where is Daniel?"

"I don't know . . . he's probably poisoned too . . . but it won't kill him. He'll never forgive me for this, though—he'll—"

"Well," I said, letting her rest on the floor, holding her useless arm, "you killed me, I killed Mimsy. He's dead. I drank him. I didn't mean to . . . I didn't want to . . . I'm so sorry . . ."

"Oh, God. Ariane. Do it," she pled. "I can't"—*can't live*—"not without Daniel. Not without Mimsy. Not without everything. Help me."

"I don't want to hurt you," I begged. "I don't want to hurt anyone."

"You won't be hurting anyone," she said, forcing a smile. "I'm going into shock—do it now while I can still appreciate it."

"Oh, Chloe," I sighed, and knelt beside her. In the

sixty seconds she had allotted for the end of my life, I left her limp, poetically slumped and white and drying against the wall. My hands left bloody streaks on the wood next to her head, and I tore myself away reluctantly from the fascinating glister of the patterns in the moisture.

I knew I wasn't going to be able to come back.

I began to walk to Daniel's apartment, then to run. Running was good. I could charge along so fast that people in cars couldn't see me, a dark specter blazing through the early evening gloom. I passed people walking on the street, listened with grim pleasure to their confusion.

But it made me tired, and soon the terrible hunger was consuming me again, eating me away from inside. I burnt blood like mammals burnt glucose. After a mile or so, I stopped, bent double in a parking lot, clutching my empty gut and retching. I thought furiously, *Daniel, help me, you fucker; you got me into this. Help me. Help me, somebody, anybody, I don't care*.

I stumbled on, weeping bitterly, stopping every few blocks or so to pant air that wouldn't help me, to double over, sick as a dog. At last I couldn't go on anymore; I sank down onto a bus bench, round so that you can't lie on it, and cried tears that burned.

A big car swept so close by me that I could taste the foul exhaust, and I cursed it for leaving me alone, for being able to sweep by without taking notice of the fact that I was dying so fast that I could feel it. I had drawn my knees to my chest, huddling in perfect balance on the top of the curve, when the car returned, doing thirty miles an hour in reverse, until it was stopped in front of me.

A pale face with dark hollows for eyes and a multicolored forelock peeked out the passenger side window. "Jesus, get the fuck into the car, Ariane!"

I almost couldn't unfold myself for long enough to

get up and take a closer look. It was my boy Lovely, his human scent almost overpowering me even at a distance. Still doubled over, I crept closer, opened the door, and fell inside.

"Jesus Christ," he said, driving away, foot to the floor. "It's happened, hasn't it."

"What has?" I said, in between moans of distress.

"I'll pull over in a minute," he replied. "You look like shit."

"I'm going to die," I told him, groaning, my head against the cold lock of the dashboard. "Everything's gone wrong . . . I . . . I killed Mimsy and Chloe."

"I know," he said, his lips drawn tight. "I was just there."

"Please don't hate me," I begged him, afraid to touch him for fear of killing him. "I didn't mean to do it. I was only going to have a little. I couldn't stop myself. And Chloe—"

"Never mind. I could never hate you," he said softly. He reached out for me and touched my shoulder. Immediately he snatched his hand back. "God, you're so cold! There's, like, this static charge on your skin—"

"It's my hair growing back . . . my muscles . . . it hurts so much."

"It's OK," he soothed. "It's OK."

In the darkness under palm trees he stopped the car and held out his wrist to me. "I'll stop you," he whispered. "Take some. I'll be all right."

Glancing nervously up at him, I bent my head and tried to bite through him with my teeth. They were sharp enough now, and they broke his skin with ease; his blood flowed slow and warm into my mouth. Oh, it was terrible. The blood never even reached my stomach; my mouth absorbed it like a sponge, like my entire body was a huge capillary gorging itself. I had never experienced such pure pleasure and relief in my life. I wanted to take all of him.

Too soon, Lovely tore his arm back from me and pressed his wrist under his arm. "Ouch! Enough, enough, already, OK? You're gonna break my arm." He lowered his head between his knees. "You've got to learn to control that shit."

I could see better, felt stronger. "I can't," I said, tears rising to my eyes again. "It's too good. I need too much."

"Yeah, well, you can't get it all from me, or I won't have any left for myself. We'll do something, all right? I know you were trying to get to Daniel's place. I'm looking for him too. We're all looking for him." Lovely cautiously examined his wound. It was closing, and the bleeding had stopped. He started the car again.

"Do you know what happened to him?" I asked.

"Nobody does. We've been calling him on his cell phone all day and all night, and it says that it's out of service. I haven't seen him for a long time—days now."

"How long was I—in there?"

"I would guess about twenty-two hours . . . which makes sense. I saw what you did to the bathroom. Pretty fucking amazing." He was smiling again already. "So how was it?"

"All I have to say is, *don't*. Don't do it. It sucks." I tried to run my fingers through my hair, but couldn't get my fingers through the mess. "It's like having your entire body eaten away with sulfuric acid. Everything—everything—I don't want to talk about it. Thinking about it makes me want to puke. I don't know how anyone survives it."

His eyes were starry. "Wow."

"Wow, bullshit." I was starting to recover my wits, and already I was thinking about it on a physiological basis. It seemed, then, that Daniel's blood was a violent poison, a corrosive, that destroyed my human body cells. But then how was I whole now? I wasn't sure what I looked like under the crust of my own dried blood. I was itching like crazy, but I knew if I scratched, I would tear my skin off.

"Are you better now? Did my blood help?"

"Yeah, it did. I can think straight now, finally. But I don't think I can ever listen to the Beatles ever again."

"How's that?"

I laughed quietly. "I'll tell you later."

In less than ten minutes we pulled into the street of Daniel's apartment. Lovely helped me out of the car, but I didn't need it; I could stand erect without cramps, and my legs were sure underneath me. Lovely stood a moment and gazed at me. "You look so cool right now," he murmured. "You look like something out of *Night of the Living Dead*."

"You're crazy," I muttered, walking up the courtyard. He shook his head and skipped after me.

Lovely unlocked the door and poked his head inside. "Daniel? You in here?" he called. I brushed past him and marched inside. If Daniel was here, he was going to get a god-almighty kick in the nuts. I stopped in the front room and looked around—he was here. I could feel him. He was very faint, but present, like a worry in my thoughts.

We found him in the bedroom closet, in the fetal position. Blood trickled out of his mouth to join a dark pool of half-dried, mingled blood and saliva under his head. All thoughts of how hungry I was, how much I hated his tape, or anything else fled in an instant. I cried out his name and knelt beside him, feeling his neck for a pulse.

He wasn't dead. He wasn't even unconscious. He turned dilated, glassy eyes at me, then at Lovely. Then he closed them again. *"Schlicht,"* he whispered. *"Bitte."* My shout had hurt his ears.

Lovely offered his wrist, still freshly marked. "Daniel, take it," he offered, his eyes overflowing with tears. "I don't care."

"Nein." Daniel gagged and spat more blood onto the dark carpet. With great difficulty, he gasped out, "It—won't help."

Lovely and I glanced at each other with trepidation. "Let's get him into bed," Lovely murmured.

I was surprised at how light he was, and how hot. He was flushed, sweating slightly as we dragged and carried him up to his black leather daybed. He collapsed onto it, limp, then curled back into his fetal ball, arms locked around his bare knees. I brushed his hair from his forehead. "What happened to you?" I asked.

"Poison," he said, smiling very slightly. His gums were very pale. Shock. I grabbed a leather coat from the closet and covered him with it. "The drug, the anesthetic drug. I took too much of it into myself. That traitorious bitch Chloe. I'm going to break her spine. And I gave you more blood than I could spare."

"Can't you just hunt?" Lovely asked, crestfallen.

"I need stronger blood than what you human cattle can give me," Daniel hissed. He had a laughing fit and tried to curl himself tighter.

"Can't you—*call* somebody?" Lovely fidgeted.

"Don't be stupid," Daniel said. "It's my own fault. No one in their right mind . . . it would be good for the others if I simply cease to exist. More for them. Only an idiot would make another vampire in this world. Only an idiot."

"Leave him alone," I said softly.

Lovely and I went out into the living room. Lovely lit a cigarette for me, and I inhaled deeply, intending to savor the nicotine rush that would inevitably follow a twenty-nine-hour cigarette fast—and nothing happened. I felt my lungs expand, felt blood rush in to fill the tiny sacs there; then I felt them take the nicotine, and then it was gone. It was almost exactly the same sensation as taking a breath of dirty air. "It doesn't work anymore," I sighed.

"What?"

"Cigarettes."

Lovely looked even more dismayed, wiping the tears off his cheeks. "I'm sorry."

I smoked the rest anyway. "I have to take a shower," I said, standing up.

"Aren't you going to save him?"

"Save him? How?"

Lovely gestured toward me with the cigarette lighter, then lit himself another one. "You're a vampire," he said. "Give him some of your blood."

"I don't think I have any to spare," I said.

"So you won't help him?"

"And kill myself? I've already died once today because of him. No, thanks."

Lovely said nothing. He blew a few crooked smoke rings in the other direction.

"All right, martyr boy. But I'm taking a shower first."

I remained in the shower for a long time, watching the reconstituted blood flow down the drain in a dark spiral. My hair took forever to wash, but even when the last chunks had been cleaned from it, I stood under the hot water with my eyes closed, absorbing the smell of the expensive soap, the water, even the tiles and the metal slides of the shower door. I could hear Lovely in the other room—pacing back and forth, looking in on Daniel, his mind a cloud of worry and impatience and guilt and grief. He really wanted to get stoned, but he didn't have any weed on him—it was all back in the room with Mimsy's body and Chloe outside propped up like a busted Raggedy Ann doll, bloody saliva streaking down in a tributary between her flawless white breasts. I saw it in his mind like a blurry snapshot. He finally settled on a bottle of Midori liqueur that Daniel kept on his mantelpiece because the syrupy green color almost matched his eyes. I heard Daniel too, even more strongly, the wordless anger and agonizing pain that drove all the sense from his mind. I would have liked to send him a comforting thought, but I was pissed off; pissed at how wrong he had gotten this, this simplest of acts, and put me in the position of having to, perhaps, give up my life to cover his ass. All I could think was, *You idiot, you fucking idiot, you can't do anything right. This is what you deserve.*

I came out of the shower at last and toweled myself dry, then came naked into the bedroom where Daniel lay, insensate and suffering, and Lovely stood, too wound up to sit, chaining yet another cigarette off his last one, and flinging the butt into the wastebasket. He gave me the once-over. "Wow," he said again.

"What now?"

"Look at yourself," he said.

I turned and glanced into the mirror. It was the ideal Ariané—well, perhaps not ideal, but a hell of a sight better than I'd looked in my life. I was somewhat thinner, and my skin was an absolutely perfect even tone all over, the color of pure cocoa butter. My neck was longer, my hands were longer, my feet were more arched, even my breasts were perky. "Jeez," I remarked. "I don't even have any scars."

"Get dressed," Lovely said, unable to supress a smile. He threw me a clean black T-shirt and a pair of jeans that I'd left there recently. Wordlessly, I put them on, and wound my hair behind my head.

Daniel opened his eyes. "What are you doing?"

I sat on the floor beside the daybed and held out my arm. "Try it," I said.

"I don't think—"

"Try it, or Lovely's going to guilt-trip me to death." I looked over at Lovely, and felt Daniel's hot, uneven breath draw up the fine hairs on my skin. "When I die, do you at least promise to make me a saint?"

"Who's guilt-tripping who?" Lovely drawled.

Daniel sank his teeth into the inner side of my elbow. It hurt like bejeezus, and I was indelicate about vocalizing that fact. He took a deep swallow, then another one, and then lay back onto the daybed, breathing hard. He was able to stretch himself out now, but he continued to shiver and sweat. He lay there for a moment, eyes closed, licking his lips.

I felt faint. I was glad that I had chosen to sit down. The pain traveled up from the crook of my arm into my heart, my belly, and soon I was curled up the way Daniel had been, moaning helplessly.

Daniel looked at Lovely. "It's not helping," he said.

"What? But you're—you're—"

"I can't," Daniel cut him off. "I'm still not me. I can't see into your head . . . or hers . . . and I can't smell . . . and I can't see . . . and I'm as weak as a baby."

"You look fine to me," Lovely bit out impatiently.

"Bullshit. If someone took your eyesight, you'd look fine to them, but you'd feel like shit, wouldn't you? My senses. They aren't my own. I'm not me!"

"Maybe you're not meant to be! Can't you just deal? Look at Ariane. She's fucked up. Look what she did for you!"

" 'Just deal'? Are you out of your mind?"

"Shut up," I snarled. "Shut up shut up shut up! Daniel, get him out of here. Now, before I kill him."

They left. They left me alone. I heard them going out the door and Dolores starting her massive engine. Maybe they were leaving me to die. There was shit I could do about it, in my state. I couldn't hear anything after a while, only the weak pulse in my ears, every second or so, then slower. I rolled to and fro on the floor, then slid on my side to the closet, where I touched my tongue in vain to the dried spot on the floor. It didn't give me much.

I spent an eternity there.

"Ariane . . . here . . . lift your head . . ."

Something against my lips—the smell overwhelmed me and I was nearly sick, but it was going into my mouth and I gulped at it desperately, hoping it was the right thing. It was. My mouth came alive and I was a swallowing machine, efficient as a parasite.

I sprung up and opened my eyes.

Lovely held an empty Big Gulp cup, stained to the brim with blood. He looked as startled as I felt. "Got damn," he said. "You drank that in, like, half a second."

"Where did you get that?"

Daniel stood behind him, in the doorway. I guess he'd had time to get dressed while I was writhing on the floor; he looked almost like his normal self, just without his brilliant aura and without his devastating force of personality. "I always hated that dog," he said with a smile.

"That was *dog blood?*"

"Well, it's eleven o'clock in the morning, what was I gonna do? It worked, didn't it?"

I shivered. "Oh, God, gross . . . and I could still use some more."

"It'll have to do for now. I really think it's time we got out of here."

"And go where?"

Daniel rubbed his palms against the legs of his jeans. When he looked at me again, he looked old and strung out. "I need help," he sighed. "The best thing for me, and it might be the only thing for me, is to go back to my source."

"What source?" I looked at him in confusion, and he hung his head. "You can't mean—"

"It won't take us long to get to San Francisco. I've got enough money."

I laughed out loud. "You're even stupider than I thought if you think that Orfeo Ricari is going to bail you out of this. He can't even say your name. What makes you think he'd do it for you?"

"He won't do it for me," Daniel said. "But he'd do it for you."

I looked at Lovely, as if he could explain this descent into madness. "Did you put him up to this?"

Lovely shrugged, and Daniel broke in again. "No, I know what I'm doing here. Risa told me about it. She lost a lot of blood once, a long time ago, and she never got better until she drank blood from Alex again. She even tried others—me, for example. It made her stronger, but she was never able to take care of herself until she drank from the one who made her. I can't even hunt, I can't feed myself. If the dog hadn't been chained up, we'd have never—"

"No. Don't tell me. This is insane."

"He can help you too," Daniel said. "There's really nothing else to do. I don't like it any more than you. We have to get out of L.A. anyway. Too many people know about me here. I'm in danger. You're in danger."

The dog's blood was wearing off already. I wanted to sleep, to escape this wretched cycle. I was hungry for food, for water, not this . . . this substance. I was slipping into denial, too tired and wound up to protest the idea of returning to San Francisco. "I need to sleep," I sighed, closing my eyes.

"Let's sleep," Daniel conceded. "Tonight we'll fly to S.F., and the next night we'll go somewhere else."

I closed my eyes. Always *we*. I didn't want to go wherever he was going. The honeymoon, as far as I was concerned, was over. Ricari would hate me for even going along with this scheme, and there was no way I could face San Francisco after all this. If I were even seen there, all hell would break loose. All I wanted right now was to go to sleep.

"I'll stay up and watch," Lovely said.

Daniel and I, clothed, lay down together on the futon in the front room, the drawn curtains making it as dark as midnight, and with our backs turned to one another, we both slipped away.

Chapter Fourteen

In the darkness someone was shaking me. I opened my
eyes to Lovely's haggard, pale, sleepless face. "Get up,
hurry," he begged. "Your flight's in two and a half
hours and we have to get all the way to LAX and the
traffic is a nightmare!"

I was awake at once. Daniel handed me one of his
leather jackets. He looked like hell—it was beginning
to wear on him, as if the loss of his supernatural powers
was sapping his will to live. "C'mon, Ariane," he said
wearily. "I woke up a couple of hours ago, but I
couldn't wake you up. You sleep like the dead."

I wasn't given time to dwell on this little crack; we
piled into the Caddy and Lovely tore away down the
road. Daniel put in a tape, then turned to look at me
sulking in the backseat. "Don't be angry," he said
mildly.

"Don't be angry? How can you possibly say that?

You've ruined my life, Daniel Blum, and I'm not supposed to be angry?"

"I didn't do anything you didn't want me to do," he replied. He sipped from a silver flask. "Granted, I made a mistake, but I was trying to correct an earlier mistake."

"With your other ventures?"

"I gave them too little. It's not as easy as it looks, Ariane. The balance is very delicate. Give them too little, and it kills them, or it makes them crazy, destroys their brains. Give them too much, and you yourself . . . you lose."

I shook my head. "I can't believe how right Ricari was about everything," I said bitterly. "About you, about me . . . everything."

He rolled his eyes. "Perhaps I'll be right for once," he said with a sigh. "And if I'm not, then great, I'm dead, and you can get on with your wonderful life which I so callously ruined."

"What did I do to deserve you!" I moaned.

"Will you two quit bitching?" Lovely snapped. "Just move on."

We were all silent for a while, listening to the moody tones of Bowie's *Lodger*. "Ever been to San Francisco before?" Daniel asked Lovely.

"Nope," Lovely said. "I flipped a coin between it and L.A. L.A. won. Plus, it was cheaper to get here."

"You'll like S.F.," Daniel said.

Lovely shrugged. "Wherever you're at, is fine with me," he said.

I put my head against the armrest. *So if we divide in S.F., I lose Lovely*, I thought morosely. *Do I have to be shackled to Daniel for the rest of Lovely's life? Do I have to wait patiently while Daniel louses up another transformation?* Then it occurred to me that the rest of Lovely's life was only three years, if Daniel was to hold true to his vow to take his life on his twenty-first birthday. This did not cheer me, but it limited my travels with Daniel to only three years, which, I figured, if I was going to live to be three hundred years old, wouldn't be so bad. What a great deal.

Daniel was talking some more. "I wasn't there for very long, and it was a long time ago," he said, handing the flask to Lovely. "It's very nice if you like fog. I rather like fog myself. I miss it. It was foggy a lot in Berlin. I miss Berlin. Should we go back to Berlin? Ariane, what do you think?"

"I don't know," I said.

He didn't seem to be really addressing me, or listening to me. "We should get on the freeway soon," he mentioned.

"I'm getting there." Lovely paused to sing along. "Red sails! Chain reaction . . ."

"I hate this song," I muttered.

"It's a great song! What would you rather hear?"

"I don't care," I said. "I'm hungry. I can't think."

Lovely reached behind him, searching for a tape amongst the heap on the backseat next to me. I closed my eyes and leaned back into the squeaky surface of the red vinyl, wishing the whole thing was over with.

"Shi—"

A jolt roused me, and before I could do anything but begin my fall forward into the space between front and back seats, another turmoil of G-forces lifted me off my seat into the air and then flung me back against the vinyl. I hit my head on the armrest and lay there, dazed, feeling a knot rising on my forehead, right between the eyes. "What the—"

Daniel began thrashing in the front seat ahead of me, tearing madly at the upholstery, wrenching at the door handle. It came undone and he fell out of the car, onto the road. Everything was very quiet except for the sound of my own breathing. Daniel's face appeared at the window above me, sideways. His mouth formed the phonemes of my name, but I didn't hear them at first. He opened the car door on my side. His face was a mess of blood, and he was digging a cube of safety glass out of the hollow just under his eye. "Ariane, get out of the car. Please get out of the car."

I spilled onto the pavement. I couldn't stand for a moment, but he held out his hand and helped me up. "What happened?" I murmured vaguely. I looked back at the car.

There was another car attached to our rear bumper, and the front left corner of Dolores had become an accordioned chunk of black and silver and rusty metal, half on the sidewalk. Gasoline and antifreeze ran down the road and pooled in the gutter. In a second, gleaming red joined the stream, and together they formed a swirling rainbow at my feet.

"He's gone," Daniel breathed. "Oh, God, he's gone."

I looked closer, my stomach in a shaking knot. I saw Lovely's white shoulder, streaked with blood, his black tank top absorbing it. Above that, I saw nothing. The strut of the front window had gone quite through his neck, pulling his head to the left, where, I assumed, it was partially out the side window. His fingers still moved feebly against the steering wheel, crushed against his chest.

I put my back to it. "This is bad," I said. I almost laughed.

"We have to go," Daniel said softly. "We can't be late. Especially not now."

"We can't leave him," I said. My voice was flat and distant, a desert voice.

"He's gone," Daniel shook his head. He grimaced as a tear stung the wound under his eye. "That's a corpse. That's not Lovely. We have to go, Ariane."

"No," I said, letting him lead me away, into the road. The old woman driving the car behind us slumped against her dashboard, dead or unconscious. The driver of the car who had hit us head-on cried out for someone to help him, his legs were trapped. "I'm gonna bleed to fucking death!" he yelled. Another man was trying to pry his door open without success; people were gathering on the street, standing around, gaping. At least no one was taking pictures. Yet. We *did* have to get out of there.

"Stop a taxi," Daniel said, wiping his face with a twisted hand. "Stop a taxi. You can do it. There's one coming right now. Just make him stop."

I stood in the center of oncoming traffic and held up my hand. A yellow cab screeched to a halt a inch away from me, so close I could feel the heat of the engine. "What the hell are you doing?" the cabbie screamed out the window. "I could have run you right over! Are you high or something?"

I stared at him and spoke with a voice that didn't feel like it was coming from my own throat. "Take us to the airport."

Daniel stared at him also.

The strangest feeling, this. I could almost see the chain between us, locked to his mind, the other end held in my hand. I could reel it in, bring him closer, make him walk when he didn't want to. I could make him kill himself, fall in love with me, or simply never think again—or, easier, keep him doing what he did all night, every night, just do it for me.

The cabbie blinked, and the traffic behind him began to honk and shout. "LAX?" the cabbie asked, as though he were in a dream.

I envisioned the center of his brain, thought of my words snaking their way from his auditory centers to all parts, and told him, *This makes sense.* "LAX. Take us there."

"All right," he said softly, reasonably. It made sense. In the road, people had gotten out of their cars; several people were calling for ambulances and police on their cell phones. I heard vague phrases that I recognized— *car wreck, dead people, two of them are walking away, blood everywhere*. I heard them, but I wasn't listening. Someone was having screaming hysterics about the blood and how sick it was making her. I almost looked back to see Lovely's face one more time, but I knew it wasn't Lovely's face, it was the startled, robbed face of a cadaver, probably horribly crushed, ripped to shreds, jeweled with safety glass. Daniel held the door of the taxi open for me, and we climbed in.

"Keep your eyes on the road," I said to the cabbie. "Don't listen to us." His eyes straight forward, he flipped the meter off and moved smoothly into traffic, leaving the chaos behind.

Daniel sank down beside me, his injured hand quivering. He took a bandanna out of one of the pockets of his own coat and wiped his face more carefully with it, wiped his hand, spat on a corner of the bandanna, and wiped his face again. He touched the knot on my forehead. "Ouch," he whispered. He had a huge bruise already forming, covering his whole forehead. "My head broke the windshield," he explained. "It's not going to heal anytime soon."

"Your head, or the windshield?" I took the bandanna from him and touched up a spot that he'd missed. "I'll do what I can when I can," I said.

"You scare me," he said. "You're strong. You're damn strong. Stronger than you ought to be right now."

I didn't feel strong. I felt like shit warmed over. But my head didn't hurt anymore, and my fingernails were on their way to becoming proper claws. All this from the blood of a dog, and a couple of friends, and a little girl. I began to break down, tearlessly. There wasn't enough fluid in my body to spare for tears. "Good thing too," I replied. "You certainly can't take care of us."

"Everything's going to be all right," Daniel said. "It has to be."

"Everything's not all right," I cried. "Lovely is dead."

Daniel was crying for me. Tears, streaked with blood from his cut, ran over his cheeks. He needed a shave, badly, and his lips were almost as pale as they had been when he was in the closet. He needed blood as least as badly as I did, perhaps more. "He didn't have the death he wanted," he choked out, "but almost none of us does. The best thing . . . the best thing we can think of is that he didn't . . . hurt . . . for very long."

"I'm trying . . . but it's so hard."

"We all have to live with this," he sighed. "We all have to see the ones we love die. Either they grow old, and gray, and die in a hospital hooked up to tubes and machines, or they die of accidents, or something takes them. War took a lot of the ones I loved. They were young and beautiful as Lovely, and they were sweet guiltless people who got shoveled into ovens or got blown to bits . . . or shot . . . and I had to watch . . . and it's hard, it's bloody hard. But we have to go on. We have to go on."

"We have to live on it," I said.

He nodded. "Yes, we do. We're alive. We have to feed on the dead. We always do. Everything does."

I let him take me in his arms, and took what comfort I could against his chilly, hard body, as light and bony as a dead bird's. He stroked my hair. "I don't know if I can stand this," I said.

"It'll be better when we're healthy. Nothing seems impossible then."

"Daniel, did you know Lovely's real name?" I asked.

Daniel smirked a little. "Sheldon Sherman Boyd," he replied. "Horrible, isn't it?"

"Oh, God, poor kid."

And we both managed to smile, if only for a moment.

That cabbie floored it the whole way to the airport, passing and merging like a madman. We gunned into the airport ticketing area, jumped out, and the cabbie picked up another fare as if he did this every night. I was completely unfamiliar with the airport, but this was one of Daniel's main pickup joints, and he dragged me along to the correct ticketing area. "Has Flight 445 to SFO taken off yet?" Daniel gasped out to the woman behind the counter.

She glanced at us, two ragged, somewhat bloody freaks in leather jackets and jeans, and examined her computer terminal. "It took off nine minutes ago," she told us.

Daniel squeezed his eyes shut as if he'd been shot. "Shit!" He rubbed his forehead and tried to think. "Next flight . . . I need to transfer these—two of these— tickets to the next flight. When is it?"

"It's at . . . one o'clock. Last shuttle of the night. What was your name?"

"Uh . . . Weiss: D-Donald Weiss."

I couldn't help smiling at his consternation. We had a good three-hour wait ahead of us; there was no point in getting impatient and forgetting your assumed name.

"Do you have a photo ID and a credit card? There's a thirty-dollar transfer charge per ticket."

Daniel produced a generic California ID and a well-worn credit card. "So that's your name," I murmured, amused. "Pleased to meet you, Donald."

He squinted. *Be quiet,* he thought furiously at me. I heard it like a shout through a tin can and a wire. The ticket agent calmly processed us, and handed us boarding passes. "That'll be at Gate G-14. Enjoy your flight."

Daniel and I staggered through the megaplex that was LAX. It was too bright in there, too vast, and even at this time of night, insanely crowded. "It's Wednesday night," I said under my breath. "Don't these people have anything better to do?"

"Ariane," Daniel said, wrapping his arm around me and speaking into my ear, "it's time."

Yes, that. In a brightly lit, insanely crowded, security-heavy airport. What was I supposed to do? I felt like a beleaguered lioness, forced to hunt on a vast plain with a hundred poachers ready to strike at any moment. But I needed it too. The smell of so many people, so much potential blood nearby, was driving me insane.

Daniel went inside a bar and grill and sat in a booth near the door. He worried at the cut on his face with the bandanna. "Go," he said simply. "Be discreet, be quiet, and for God's sake, be careful."

I wished I didn't look so uncombed, so stereotypically dangerous—a redhead, in a leather jacket, T-shirt, and jeans (all black), and fists clenched into balls in my pockets. I sucked some water from a water fountain, and it went down my throat and sat in my uncomprehending stomach like liquid mercury.

I went into ladies' bathrooms until I found one that wasn't particularly crowded. There were three women before the mirror and none in the stalls. I washed my face in the sink, drying it with paper towels. One of the women left. I turned on an electric hand dryer and roasted my hands in the blast of hot air, careful not to look up, not to look anything but bored and busy. Another woman left, leaving just us—me and a yuppie in her thirties, dressed in a summer suit and pearls and white tennis shoes. She was compulsively putting on lipstick, checking the contours.

I gazed into the mirror at her. She looked into it at me, then turned and looked at me. "Is there something I could help you with?" she asked, her voice crisp, guarded.

"Yeah," I said, "actually." I smiled.

I need you to do what I say.

"Sure," she said. "Name it." She capped her lipstick and put it back into her overnight bag.

I angled my head towards the handicapped stall, and obligingly she went towards it. "Go in," I said. "Sit down."

She did so. I brought her bag in with her, and set it down under the toilet-paper dispenser. The stalls here were brushed steel, anti-graffitti, easy to clean. Good. I closed the stall door behind us.

She smelled great. I'd never encountered that particular perfume before, but it was woodsy, smoky, intimate, like a men's cologne but lighter. And her hair was really quite nice. She had money. "I need some money," I said.

Obligingly she opened her overnight bag, took out her wallet, and handed me five twenties. She smiled as I took it and slipped it into my back pocket. If I wasn't positive she was under my control, I would have sworn she was just doing this on her own. She seemed so cheerful about the whole thing. I concentrated on this sensation, the sheer pleasure I was getting from being near to her, and how happy she was to be helping this down-on-her-luck young woman who was just trying to get home, and communicated it back to her.

"Hand me your wrist," I told her. "Relax." I rubbed the veins under the tan skin, tapped her thumb, making them rise a little bit. "This won't hurt." I put my mouth over the wrist, found the vein with my tongue, and bit it.

I almost didn't stop in time. Really, I should have stopped before I did; she was passed out cold when I finally lifted my head and took a breath. It all happened so fast. I just couldn't get how Daniel and Ricari ever managed to control themselves, to just take a little. I threw back my head and sucked in the air, feeling it mingle with the oxygen already present in the blood, and stood up. I took a moment to smooth the woman's hair behind her ear, dab the little wounds in her hand with toilet paper, zip up her travel bag, and take one last deep breath of her amazing scent, which, it was becoming apparent, was a combination of her particular cologne and the smell of her body. I knew I would never smell it again.

I returned to the bar, where Daniel had downed two shot glasses of what smelled like whiskey. He looked vaguely drunk. "Any time," I said casually to him.

I fed him in the darkest corner of one of the parking garages. He slurped at the wound hungrily, sucking at it even when the skin had closed over the blunt cuts his teeth had made. He finished with a weary sigh. "You're good for me," he said.

"You're not good for me," I told him, feeling the strength and security that I'd had so briefly gone, gone into sustaining him.

He smiled crookedly. "I'm not good for anybody."

"I wish I could have a drink."

"You can. It just has flavor. Though the ones I drank got me kind of foggy. I think my body can't just ignore it right now." His eyes were brighter, clearer, and his grip on my hand was strong and steady. "Not too much longer, dearest, I promise. Only another hour, and then forty-five minutes on the plane, and then—"

"Then we see Ricari."

"Then we see Ricari," he echoed. "And find out whether we're saved, or screwed."

That last hour in the airport was hell. I went so far as to buy us sunglasses to protect our eyes from the harsh lights, and I was humiliated to my toes to look so stereotypically like vampires. I wanted to hunt again, but there wasn't time. I lay with my head in Daniel's lap while he stroked my hair, winding the curls around his fingers. I had lost my best friend, my little brother, and my lover, all at one stroke. That, on top of the death of Mimsy and Chloe (at my own hands!), on top of the physical pain and fear and disgust, had brought me lower than I thought I could go.

Nonetheless, I wanted to see Ricari again. Simply for the contrast, if nothing else. The more time I spent with Daniel, the more I missed Ricari's simple piety and gentleness, his oversized morals, his protectiveness of me. So much he didn't tell me, since it was better if I didn't know, and I had found it all out the hard way. He had tried so hard. I had no idea how he'd react to all of this.

One A.M. shuttle flight to San Francisco International Airport. We got on the plane at a sleepwalk, got off the plane in a white-eyed twitch of anxiety. I got a taxi the conventional way, and let the miles add up. "I don't even know if he's there anymore," I said, trying to chew on one of my nails. It wouldn't budge.

"He's here," Daniel said, his eyes unfocused. "I can feel him."

I watched him slipping into reverie. "All the way out here? How does it feel?"

"You'll know when you're separated from me. I'm with you all the time now. But when I'm gone, you'll feel like a part of you has gone with me."

I looked away then. Was he aware, then, of my desire to get away from him? I knew he couldn't help it, he was just trying to stay alive, but I just couldn't forgive him for abandoning me when he knew I'd need him, when he knew I'd be vulnerable. I was in no mood to be noble.

"So odd," he went on, "to be in the presence of a father and a child, at the same time. An extraordinary feeling. Quite rare, I'd imagine."

"Yes," I said.

"Oh, Orfeo! How I loved you!"

I shushed him, anxious for quiet now that we were in the city.

It was strange to be back. It was the very depth of summer, and the streets were warm and a fog was rolling in slowly over Twin Peaks. It was beautiful, but claustrophobic, after the infinite space of Los Angeles. It no longer felt like home.

The cab driver let us off in front of the Saskatchewan, and I paid the thirty-three-dollar fare. Daniel climbed out and shivered in the chilly fog. "Saskatchewan," he sounded out slowly. "This almost looks beneath him."

"Is he here?"

"Oh, yes. I do believe he's anticipating us."

The desk clerk, the same old man as before, had fallen asleep watching TV. Daniel and I slipped silently past him to the elevator. I punched the button for the ninth floor. "I can't believe he's still here," I remarked. "I thought he'd have killed himself before now."

"It takes Ricari a million years to do anything. That's why he's so bloody old." We shared a dirty snicker. "He works on nineteenth-century time."

"I think this place is perfect for him," I said.

We got off the elevator. The door to Suite 900 was open.

Ricari was sitting on the edge of his gold chaise longue, staring at the floor, counting out the rosary. He seemed so tiny, a little dejected elf, hair tucked neatly behind ears. He wore all black, was barefoot. His old aura filled the room with a quiet hum.

"*Guten abend,* Orfeo," Daniel said with quiet respect.

Ricari looked up. "How could you?" he said.

Daniel did not react well. He tossed his head like a sulky teenager. "Oh, God, don't start."

"I'm not talking to you," Ricari said. He looked piercingly at me.

I blinked. "What?"

"Daniel, well, it's too late for Daniel. We all know that. But didn't *you* learn anything from me?"

"I did," I said. "I didn't mean it. Anything. I'm sorry. This shouldn't have happened. But it did. And now you have to help us." I went to him and took his hand. It felt remarkable—he had had less blood in the last month than either Daniel or I had in the last twenty-four hours, but he was very warm and alive and solid and smooth. His hands were like sunlit-carved alabaster. I had forgotten how beautiful his hands were. I rubbed them against my cheek without being able to stop myself, in love with their texture. I was in love with everything: the room, the light, the inexorable, subtle scent of him that I was too crude to perceive before.

He stroked my face for a second, then threw his arms about me. "Oh, Ariane!" he sighed. He covered my hair with kisses.

At the same moment, we both looked up at Daniel. He had quietly drawn the door shut behind him and was staring at it. Ricari gently edged me away, touching my shoulder, edging his fingers under the leather. "Daniel," he said. "You look like hell."

"I made a mistake," Daniel said.

Ricari folded his hands in his lap. "I don't want to help you. It's very tempting to let you stay like this, to feel pain and longing without release, for once. Perhaps you'll understand what I go through. What Ariane goes through. What everyone has to go through." He sighed and drew his fingers through his hair. "But then you'll just take that as an excuse to run amok and kill as many as you like, maybe betray all of us, out of revenge."

Daniel turned then, his eyes wide. "I wouldn't—"

Ricari stopped him with a subtle gesture of his hand. "I know you, Daniel. I know your nature. I'd rather not have that on my conscience. You nearly destroyed me once. I won't let you destroy me once and for all. I'd rather simply be rid of you. You're like a rat; you'll survive. You'll get through."

"Orfeo, you've never—"

"Shut *up*. I'm talking."

"You're having a goddamn monologue, you mean."

I stared at them, a smile darting across my face too quickly for me to do anything but cover it with my hand. The two of them! How in the world did they ever stop fighting long enough to fall in love? I could imagine their terrible fights, Daniel cocky with death, and Ricari growing more and more frustrated by the minute. I didn't doubt that it frequently ended with blows.

"If you'd be quiet, you'd hear what I'm actually saying. I'll give you just enough. Just enough to get you back to where you were before. And then you leave. You leave me, and you leave Ariane. You've ruined her life enough already."

"She's mine," Daniel said petulantly.

"Do you want me to leave you two alone?" I asked.

They ignored me. "You don't know the first thing," Ricari snapped, his cheeks coloring. "The first thing. You—you don't even know where to start. Haven't you got any sense? Let them draw four heartbeats of blood from you, no more, no less! I told you that."

"You didn't tell me it was a *rule*."

"I never thought you'd be so stupid as to reproduce! Let alone three times. And three mistakes. Thank God she's all right. Second—stay with her. That means you're there. You wash them, you help them understand their pain. I was with you. Wouldn't you give Ariane the same courtesy?"

"I was hurt. I was drugged. I was confused. I wanted to go somewhere and lie down and sort things out."

Ricari threw up his hands.

I stood up. "I'm going to go downstairs and buy a

gun and shoot both of you," I shouted, and both of them were silent and stared at me with astonishment. "Fuck it, OK? It's done. It sucked, but it's done. We need to maybe concentrate on the matter at hand. Didn't you just say you wanted Daniel the hell out of here? I think you want to keep him here so you can bicker with him a little while longer, live out the old days when it was just you two in a tavern throwing glasses at each other. Well, it's cute, but I'm just not interested. I'm hungry, and I'm tired, and I really want to either feed myself, or get some sleep, preferably feed myself. You guys can play Punch and Judy while I'm actually getting something accomplished."

"Wait." Ricari rose off the chaise.

I stormed out and left the hotel, shutting my mind to their demanding, confused voices. I was on my old turf, home or no home, and I had some money in my pocket, and there had to be something I could do. I bought a pack of cigarettes and a lighter and walked until I had smoked four cigarettes. The act of holding a cigarette, smoking it, comforted me a little. I was getting lightheaded.

I went to my old apartment. Someone else was already living there; I could see the red glow of their digital clock shining through the ground-floor window. Lighting another cigarette, I stepped forward and touched the grate. It was cold and slick on my fingers. It was as though I had never existed. I wanted to ring the bell, see who occupied my home, whether or not the tiny blood drops still stained the living room carpet. Nonetheless, I turned away and went back into the fog.

In Golden Gate Park, I took a sleeping homeless man, surprised that he didn't wake up as I pressed my teeth against his bearded throat. I didn't even find his smell offensive; it was strong and rank and his shirt collar greasy with sebum and sweat, but I appreciated it with savor. His blood was thick, but undernourished,

253

and I needed a lot. When I was finally able to tear myself away, he breathed once more and then was still. I stepped back, then bent forward and covered him again with his cheap blanket and plastic tarp. At least he was happy when he died. I clung to that notion; at least it was pleasurable, what I did. It hurt for a second, and then joy beyond compare shot through the body. I remembered that much. There had to be some reason why I let Ricari and Daniel have me whenever they wanted. I began to walk again.

I found myself in a phone booth on Van Ness, calling the only number that I could remember, the number to John Thurbis's apartment. It rang so many times that I nearly hung up and left him alone, but I wanted to talk to someone. At last the line connected, and I listened to the dull soft fumblings on the other line.

"Hello, it's three in the morning, you better have a good excuse."

"Hi, John. It's me, Ariane."·

There was a long silence. I said, "Hello, hello," at the phone, wondering if the connection had been lost. The quarter clanked into the machine. "John?"

"It's really you?"

"Yeah. Can I come see you?"

"You're in town?"

"Yeah. I'm on Van Ness."

"God." He began to laugh. "Yeah, I'll be here."

"I'll be there as soon as I can." I hung up, scanning the street for a taxi.

Seven dollars later I got out in front of the tall flat in the Duboce Triangle. It had a "FOR RENT" sign wired to the front gate, and John's number on it. I stepped up and hit the buzzer, and he came down to let me in.

He was wearing a bathrobe over a T-shirt and pajama bottoms, which he never wore when I was with him. His hair was quite long and it suited him, especially tousled from bed. He locked the door behind him and we went upstairs. I wanted to fling myself at his back and hug him to death, but I didn't allow myself to touch him. I sucked in the smell of him, the gentle purring of his blood in the quiet.

John turned on the lamp. "I want to make sure it's really you," he said, shining his glasses on his bathrobe and putting them back on again. "I keep thinking I see you in the street, but it's never really you. I've gawped at more women with red curly hair than I like to admit. I've been . . . I've been going mad."

I sat down on his couch.

"Where have you been?" he asked softly.

"L.A.," I said.

He looked confused, justifiably. "L.A.? Why?"

"I just ended up down there," I said. "It's actually a really long story."

He smiled. "You know, I got your letter."

"What letter?"

"The letter you wrote me. In April, I think it must have been. They found it in your apartment. You knew they were going to go over your apartment. Everyone thinks that you're probably dead. You've never just gone missing in your life. You haven't used your bank accounts, all your clothes were still there, you still had half a carton of milk in the fridge—we thought 'alien abduction' or something. Actually we were quite sure you'd committed suicide. The department's pretty much given you a funeral by now. Police have even practically given up looking for you. You're probably going to end up on TV sometime soon."

"No," I said, aghast. "No, no, no, that can't happen. If you've done anything to—if you've—"

"I gave up," he replied. "I determined that you could only be dead, because you wouldn't just disappear without telling me, without letting me know where you were."

"I couldn't." I shook my head. "I couldn't. It's such a long story."

"It's not a long story. You fell in love with someone else. You went away with him. He sounds like a real character. Want a cup of tea? I have a pot ready."

"Did you read the letter? Really read it? It was real. I tell you, it's real. All of it's real."

"All of what?" He was in the kitchen, puttering about with the teapot and coffee mugs and sugar.

I sighed. "I fell in love," I said slowly, "with a vampire. A real vampire."

He joined me on the couch and handed me the tea. "A blood fetishist? I read about those. Or just a tall, skinny guy all dressed in black? I remember you used to have a taste for those."

"No. I mean . . . pointy fangs, white skin, drinks blood to survive, *bleh bleh bleh*." I held up my hands and hunched my shoulders, Bela Lugosi style. "Could crush your skull with his thumb, can't die, the whole works."

John's forehead was wrinkling interestingly. "What?"

"Like this." And I lifted my upper lip to show him my fangs.

He actually jumped, spilled his tea on the sofa. "What the hell are those?"

"Those are my teeth, John."

Now he was shaking, nervously rubbing his hands together. "So let me get this straight . . . you fell in love . . . with a vampire . . . and he made you into a vampire . . . and then you went to L.A.?"

"Well, no, I fell in love with a vampire, and we had a fight, so he sent me to L.A. to this other vampire, and *he* made me into . . . well, you get the picture."

"No, I don't think I do at all."

"It's true," was all I could say. I sipped my tea.

"That's . . . that's insane . . . not to mention impossible . . . not to mention totally . . . totally incomprehensible . . ." He rubbed his chin, bit his fingernails, glanced about the room in a panic, as if looking for some device, some prop, that might help him explain this. "Ariane, tell me this isn't true, tell me I'm still asleep, I'm dreaming."

"I wish that were the case," I said.

"So you came back here just to tell me this?"

"No, I came to see you. I miss you. I love you."

"I thought you were in love with someone else."

I sighed. "I think I'm finished with that sort of thing for a long while. It seems to be nothing but trouble. I just left the two of them arguing. They used to be in love, you know?"

"The two bloke vampires?"

"Yeah." I couldn't help it. I laughed. "Exactly."

John stared at the ceiling and made jerky movements with his hands. "Homosexual vampire mutants," he intoned softly, "in Los Angeles. It really almost makes sense. If it were a movie, I'd go see it."

"So would I," I said. "Probably how I got myself into this mess."

"And you want me to help you," John said.

"No. Nobody can help me. *They* can help me, but they're too busy either clawing each other's eyes out in a classic catfight, or they're fucking right now. Either way, they haven't got time for me and my little problems." I yawned. "I think I just wanted to go someplace that made sense, even for a little while. I just want something to make sense." I glanced up at him. "You make sense. The way I feel about you makes sense."

John stood there a moment, looking at the phone, the door, the navy blue sky out the window, then at me. I didn't want to influence him in any way, but I couldn't help thinking, *Trust me. Please*. He cautiously approached the couch and sat down; growing bolder, he reached out to my face. "You're cold," he said, snatching his hand away.

"That's because it's cold outside." I shrugged out of my jacket. I took his hand, placing it inside my shirt and against my side, where I knew he could feel my heart beating. "I'm not cold there, am I?"

He shook his head. "Where's your scar?" he asked in a whisper.

I looked. Of course, now my appendectomy scar was completely gone, along with my freckles. "Now do you believe me?"

His color had come back into his face, and concentrated itself in his cheeks. "Congratulations then, I guess," he breathed. "I guess you've discovered a new life form, Dr. Dempsey."

"You can't tell anyone," I said, exerting gentle pressure on his hands. I didn't want to break any bones accidentally. "You'd be putting my life in danger."

"From whom?"

I rubbed my hands together. "I kill people, John. I have to. I don't want to, and I don't mean to, and maybe someday I won't ever need to . . . but at this point, I've killed at least three people and maybe a fourth one. Either I'll be classified an animal, in which case they'll kill and dissect me, or I'll be classified as a human, and spend the rest of my life in jail. And when I die, they'll dissect me. And then the others will be hunted down and exterminated, and John, I care about some of these people. I haven't met a lot, but the ones I met, I . . . liked."

"I know it's inappropriate at a moment like this," he said, "but you're incredibly beautiful."

"I thought you'd miss my scar." I blushed.

"I do." He smiled. "And I miss your eyes."

"My eyes?"

"They're quite different, close up. They're darker. But I can still see the insides of them."

I touched his face. His cheek was marvelously smooth, marvelously rough down the side and the chin. I was shaking. "I know it's inappropriate at a moment like this," I said, focusing my eyes on his mouth, "but I really . . . really want—"

"Ssh," he said, and kissed me.

There was nothing that could compare with this. I didn't know how much I missed him. I had forgotten how incredibly sweet it was to make love to him. There were none of the athletics that Daniel had engaged in; I had forgotten what plain old boring sex was like with someone who I was in love with. It was marvelous. And it was completely different than when I was human; every single simple touch curled me up with pleasure. It would be fruitless to describe it; there was nothing that you don't already know about, and the things that were new I can't express.

Overwhelmed in orgasm, my body reacted in the only way it knew how; I bent over him and pierced his neck with my fangs as I felt him nearly coming beneath me. His eyes popped open and he gasped; I drew my mouth away wet with blood. He went rigid, and then lay still, eyes closing.

He was silent for a very long time. "John?" I asked worriedly. "John? John? Are you all right? Say something. Please." I wiped my lips with the back of my hand.

A slow smile spread across his face. "That was," he purred, "the best orgasm I ever had."

I rubbed the mark on his neck. "Really?" He said nothing, awash in bliss. "God, I thought I'd killed you."

"I thought you'd killed me too." He finally opened his eyes. "How'd you do that?"

"Apparently, I can't help it. I'm glad you liked it."

"It hurt at first."

"Yes, it does that. I am breaking your skin, after all."

"Do I taste good?"

"Better than nearly anything I've had." I sat up and reached for the phone on the bedside table. "I have to make a phone call."

John was too content to make any protest. I called the Saskatchewan.

"Saska'tch'wan Hotel" came a dull voice through the phone.

"Suite 900, please."

A long pause, with the purling sound of an internal phone system ringing. At last the connection was made. "Who is this?" Ricari's voice could have cut glass.

"Good, you're still awake."

"Where are you?"

I rubbed John's shoulder, pulling the covers over him. He gazed up at me from the quilts with an expression I recognized; I had seen it in Lovely's eyes, in the eyes of all of Daniel's teenage lovers. It had been in my eyes. John was mine, for as long as I wanted him. "I went to John's apartment," I said.

"Who?"

"John. John Thurbis. The man I was going to marry."

"Oh. I think I remember you mentioning that . . . but it didn't seem important to you, so I forgot it."

That stung. "Well, it's important to me now. He's the only person I know that isn't dead, thinks I'm dead, or hates my guts forever."

"I don't hate you," Ricari said, defending himself.

"You know what I mean. The only . . . human."

"Oh, Ariane." I heard him sighing on the other end, clearing his throat.

"Is Dan still there?"

"He's asleep. He sleeps too much. Like a mortal."

"He eats food too," I added.

"Lord, preserve us. He's been changed for seventy years and he hasn't given it up yet? I hope you grow out of that. It's so wasteful it makes my skin crawl."

"Maybe it's soothing."

"Soothing. Debussy is soothing. Eating is perverse."

I found myself laughing. "Orfeo, Orfeo, Orfeo, how sweet you are."

John was looking at me strangely.

"Are you coming back?" Orfeo asked.

"Yes," I said. "Not right now."

"You can't go back to that, Ariane. Leave him. You'll only drive yourself mad this way. We'll go away together, you and I, and you can learn what you need to know from me."

"I love him," I said.

"Do you love me?"

I wished he wasn't doing this. "Yes."

There was a long pause. "Is he the sort that would come with us," he asked slowly, "and not cause trouble?"

"Like me, you mean?"

He made a quiet noise that sounded like a laugh. "No. You had too much will even for that. You were trouble."

"John's another scientist. He's a physicist, so he won't have some of my, er, troublesome qualities—"

Ricari was definitely laughing now.

"—but he will question. He won't be a slave. I could never tell him what to do in the first place."

"What are you talking about?" John asked sotto voce.

"I don't know what to tell you, Ariane," Ricari said. "But we do have to go."

"Is Daniel all better?"

"He fell asleep waiting for you before I could do anything."

"He's good for about eight hours," I told him. "Look. I need to sleep myself. I'll figure out what's going on when I wake up. I'll come as soon as I'm awake and alive."

I hung up, hoping he wouldn't unthinkably take off without me. Despite my cavalier attitude, I really needed Ricari; I did need to learn from him. I still didn't know half the things that even Daniel took for granted. John nudged me with his forehead. "What's the time?" he asked.

"Looks like—seven thirty-two."

"Hand me the phone," he said. "I'm going to call the Physics secretary."

"Calling in sick?"

"I'm not getting out of this bed for a while. . . ."

I lay there and listened to him leaving a long and detailed message, with instructions for each class that he would miss and each appointment that would have to be rescheduled. Before he was finished, I had gotten up, wrapping a blanket around me.

John hung up the phone. "Where are you going?"

"I have to go to sleep," I mumbled.

"Then come here, for heaven's sake."

"I can't sleep with you."

"Why?"

"I just can't . . . let me sleep in the study. And don't come in."

"You're not sleeping on a couch. You're exhausted. It's bad for your back. Really, Ariane, how bad could it be?"

I looked at him. "Do you really want to ask that?"

He went pale and swallowed. "I'll sleep in the study," he offered, getting up himself. "Let me get some things so I won't disturb you."

Back in bed, I watched guiltily as he gathered up a pillow, an extra quilt, jeans and a cardigan, and a book on Da Vinci. "Promise me you won't look," I said.

"Yes," he said. "I won't look."

"Thank you for believing me."

"I can't otherwise." He shut the door gently behind him.

I was asleep before I heard him reach the other room.

Chapter Fifteen

He seemed to honor my request; when I woke up into the late evening redness, the door was still shut, and he looked up from the television with surprise as I came out. "Hi," I said.

"Was watching the news," he said, turning back. He was drinking a tall glass of scotch and ice. "Wondering if any of your handiwork was going to make the six o'clock news. It seems that a few deaths here and there don't make a damn bit of difference."

"Actually, they might have made the L.A. papers," I murmured, smoothing my hair and sitting beside him. My hair would no longer smooth down; it was a mane of deep auburn ringlets, as bouncy as telephone cords. Only its weight kept it from surrounding my face like a clown's wig. I had stood before the mirror in John's room, vowing to never cut my hair shorter than shoulder length. "Our accident, that is. It was pretty huge."

"What accident?"

"Car crash," I said with surprising calm. "A very good friend of mine was killed in it. Some other people were too."

"When was this?"

"Um, well, it was last night." And the last glimpse of Lovely's face came to me; grinning, rosy-cheeked, the dark smudge worn off his great dark eyes, his rosy lips pursed around a joint. He'd winked at me in the rearview mirror, and I'd turned away, consumed in my own thoughts.

John wiped my face with a scratchy tissue. I'd been weeping without realizing it. "I can't believe it was only last night. I can't believe all this has happened so fast."

He gently kissed my cheek. "How long have you been—"

"A vampire? Um, this is my third day."

He made a face. "What?"

"You'd have never guessed, huh?" I stood up. "I have to go, John."

"Are you coming back?"

I stopped halfway into the leather jacket. "I don't know," I said, continuing, the other arm finding its place. I pulled my hair from under the collar. "It's probably best if you never saw me again."

"You can't do this," he said. "I'm going to go crazy. Everyone will think I've snapped."

"You probably have," I replied.

"I love you—don't go. Don't go back to them. Please. Maybe this is reversible. Maybe—"

"It's not reversible, John. Any more than you could be reversed into a chimp. Just because I look superficially like a human doesn't mean that I am. I'm not. I'm different. I'm like them, and like it or not, I have to learn to be what I am now."

"Then take me with you," he said. "I don't want to . . . be separated from you again."

I sighed. "All right then," I said, "come with me tonight, and see if you want to come with me. I don't even know where I'm going. Come with me and see the men who got me into this."

He put on his coat and his cracked, polished black oxfords, and we went out into the street and waited for a taxi to come by. We walked a bit, stood under the brilliant red light of the Church Street Safeway sign, watching a purple cloud come down over the hill and extinguish the feeble blinking of Sutro Tower. He bent over me and kissed me on the neck, breathing so that he could watch the hairs stand up.

I watched his eyes get big as we drove into North Beach, through the sleazy streets advertising every manner of voyeurism—watching people fuck, watching people eat, watching people shop, gamble, get arrested. I paid the taxi fare with what was left of my money. John smiled at me as I compulsively lit a cigarette. "I see you haven't stopped," he commented.

"For all the good they do me." I took another lungful, then tossed the useless glowing thing into the gutter. "Let's go, we're sort of in a hurry."

The door of Ricari's suite was closed, but not locked. I entered first, listening and smelling for the two of them. John stayed close behind me, hands jammed sweating into his pockets.

They were in the bathroom. Daniel raised his head from Ricari's wrist and regarded us with bright, calculating eyes. Ricari slumped drowsily against the back of the satin-upholstered chair next to the bathtub. "Ariane brought us company," Daniel declared, his voice slick with sarcasm.

I looked behind me at John; he was very pale, and his eyes didn't seem quite focused. I steadied him to the chaise longue, where he promptly fell completely unconscious. It wasn't like John to faint, but I guess he wasn't prepared. "Good work, Dan," I snapped, loosening John's shirt collar.

Daniel, quite restored, stalked out into the front room. "Is that where you've been all this time, love-nesting with this fine English wren? Now, now, don't be selfish, let Daddy take a good long look." He pushed me out of the way with startling ease. Now that he was back to himself, Daniel was ten times stronger than I was. He bent over John carefully, his nostrils sweeping through John's scent, poked gently at John's clean-shaven cheek. "Oh, I guess he's all right. You have good taste in men, Ariane. What . . . lovely skin."

"Daniel, don't fuck with me," I said.

"Who's fucking with who? Who asked you to bring your boyfriend? What kind of obstacle does this throw up? Oh, I bet Ricari said it was all right. Ricari can't refuse his precious Ariane anything. If I so much as ask for a drop of blood, it's 'You're evil, Daniel, you cause so much trouble.' I ought to slit this pretty throat. That would teach you all about trouble, wouldn't it?"

Ricari had come out of the bathroom, incredibly white and lissome in a simple blue linen shirt, rolled to the elbows and open at the neck. A few crimson drops stained the collar and sleeves. "Don't make threats," Ricari said with utmost calm. "I really don't care for them."

"I don't really intend to take John along with us," I said. "I only wanted him to see this, maybe understand why he can't come. Why it's better for him to just forget about me." I smoothed his hair off his forehead, where it had grown in so long that it more than covered his face. "Not to see me again."

Daniel moved away to the other chair and sat in it, brooding handsomely. In the dim light of the perennial candles, he was the incubus again, the dissatisfied angel. Ricari looked down at John, whose eyes were moving restlessly behind his closed lids. "It might have been the right thing to do," Ricari said, "and it might not. I suppose the evening will tell. There is no way to avoid hurting him. We all hurt one another."

John opened his eyes slowly, uncomprehending. "What happened?" he mumbled.

"You passed out," I told him.

"I did?" He had sat up and combed his hair back with his fingers before he noticed Ricari and Daniel and me all staring at him; I'm sure the effect must have been something like being a missionary in the middle of the cannibal village. He locked his arms about himself and squeezed into a corner of the chaise. "You're going to kill me, aren't you?" he asked in a very small voice.

"We don't want to kill you," Ricari said patiently.

"We can," Daniel added.

"But we won't," I said, staring Daniel down. He rolled his eyes at me. "John, this is Orfeo Ricari. That's Daniel—just Daniel. And this is John Thurbis."

"Charmed," John managed to say. I gripped his hand gently in mine, trying not to return his white-knuckled grip for fear of crushing his hand.

"I won't allow any harm to come to you," Ricari said. "Don't mind that one. He's got, as you might say, an 'attitude problem'?" He gestured. "He's been knocked off the top of the playset, and he's learning about what it's like to not be a god for a change. That is why I like to stay on the ground, yes?"

"Stuff it," said Daniel.

"You look tired, Ariane," Ricari said to me. "Do you need help?"

"It couldn't hurt," I said.

"You're new yet. You need as much as you can stand; gets you through it sooner. Though some, like Daniel, never lose the taste for blood every night." He put his arm around my shoulders and pulled me gently from John's grip. "Don't worry, John. Daniel would never be so bold—and besides, we can see him." He herded me into the bathroom.

First, a kiss. Our mouths met; my tongue was pricked on his teeth, and he sucked the blood from that for as long as it lasted. Nipping his lip brought forth a tiny trickle, barely perceptible to the taste, but enough to drive my body insane with wanting more of it. I took him at the neck and breathed in his blood. We held each other tightly; I crushing him down, he resisting with equal force to keep us in equilibrium. I drank for what seemed like an eternity. Then he pushed my head back and I breathed air again, my blood cells fattening with oxygen. I felt high.

What is he doing? came Ricari's voice clearly in my head.

Who? What?

Maria, Mother of God, I can't leave him for a second—

I had to steady myself against the wall to follow Ricari into the living room. By the time I got there, Daniel was on his behind on the floor, laughing, mouth a scarlet gash in his face, and Ricari was bent over John, chafing his hands. "You malicious dog," Ricari breathed.

"You can see me, huh? So you can see me, right?" Daniel crowed.

"He's dying," Ricari said to me sorrowfully. He let the limp hand drop.

Progressive hypovolemic shock. The term from first-year human physiology popped into my mind unbidden; the last thing I needed right now was a term for what was happening to John. He had fallen into shock with an expression of pure, sad terror marked clearly on his features; he was pale, his gums were pale, he was fading fast.

I acted almost without thinking, blindingly fast with Ricari's old blood inside me; I tore open my wrist and held it to John's pale cold mouth. "Drink it, stupid," I hissed.

"Ariane!" Ricari protested.

I whirled to look at him. "Help me!" I shouted to him.

Daniel had fallen silent, stymied, his expression bemused. He watched us with detached interest.

Ricari sighed impatiently, and obligingly opened his wrist as well. There was little blood left to spare in him, and it barely squeezed out of the four slits punctured by his teeth. I hadn't been keeping track of how many times my heart beat while my wrist was in John's mouth, so I counted two and then pulled back. John had swallowed at least twice, mostly mine, but a few trickles of Orfeo's as well. "Is that going to work?" I asked him anxiously.

"We shall see," he murmured. His eyes were very tired.

Daniel picked himself up off the floor. "Have fun, you two," he said.

"Where do you think you're going?" Ricari snapped.

Daniel shrugged and smiled. "You wanted me out of here, I'm going. Besides, I don't know the first thing, or the second thing, or probably the fifth or sixth thing . . . I'd just get in the way." He stretched his arms, admiring himself in the candlelight. "Please. Keep the jacket. And . . ." He reached into the pocket of his own jacket and tossed something at me. I watched as it skittered across the floor—my rat pocket watch, busted and dented and dirty with dried blood.

"Asshole," I muttered.

"No time," said Ricari, "look."

John was conscious again; his eyes rolled about in confusion. "What the hell . . . what did he do to me?"

"It isn't what he did to you," I said. "It's what I did to you."

John wiped his face, coming away with the fast-clotting, blackish vampire blood, leaving raw patches in the flesh. "God, no," he swore, "no, please, God, no!"

Between Ricari and me, we got him to the bathroom. John was staggering, looking around him with undisguised horror. "My heart," he kept sobbing, "my heart."

"It's only the beginning," I said, "but don't be afraid, I'm with you, Orfeo is with you."

"I'm not ready to die!"

"You're not going to die," I soothed him. *Though you'll wish you did.*

I don't know if the experience is worse when you're having it, or watching someone else go through it. It took longer than I remembered it; John vomited blood for a good hour before the rest of him started to change. Ricari held him down on the floor while he went through convulsions; sat patiently while John's soft short human fingernails tried to tear off Orfeo's skin. I held myself and cried. After a while, I took off all my clothes—no sense in them being destroyed in a tide of blood and body parts—and Ricari took his off as well.

Such a lot of flesh in a human body. I watched in sickened dismay as his skin peeled off in messy strips, his eyes turned to fluid and ran from his sockets, the muscles reduced to a gummy mass. After five hours, there was little recognizable in the bathtub; simply a human-shaped blob of tissue, with the sharpened bones protruding from the fingertips and kneecaps. "I can't believe I went through this," I gulped.

"Watch," Ricari said softly, a slick wraith gleaming with blood.

I watched. The bones were moving; the fingertips of bone were becoming longer, and the bluish gristle holding them together shone and then sprung together in a fetal fist. The mess of red tissue began to glisten brightly.

"It's complete," Ricari said. "If you want, you can go to sleep; I'll watch."

"Are you kidding? I wouldn't miss this for a million dollars."

He smiled at me from his scarlet mask.

John's body wasn't being put back together from the shed parts; it was growing back out of new tissue, almost buzzing as it arranged itself in neat, perfect, programmed pools and bunches and rows. His skin grew back before his body was completely filled out; he was quite loose, a bag of bones inside a sheath as thin and fine as spider silk. As his body grew itself out, wrinkles developed in the skin, and a fine sheen of dark baby-hair grew from his skull, growing thicker by the second.

I glanced out the bathroom door. "It's getting light," I murmured, yawning.

"Yes . . . we should go to sleep . . . this part's really boring. It's the inside of him that's organizing itself, and the fireworks are over. We should sleep so that we're here when he wakes up."

We washed ourselves and each other from the sink, since John was still occupying the bathtub. Ricari kissed me as he washed my hair and wiped the skin below my breasts and between my buttocks with a wet towel; I licked the shed blood from the skin under his chin. When we were reasonably clean, we went into the suite's bedroom, leaving the door to the bathroom open, and got into the bed, under the light summer blankets. Looking back into the bathroom, I saw the immaculate white porcelain and gilded paint streaked and smeared with blood, the floor slippery with bits of skin, shed teeth, mucous membrane. "I'm not cleaning it up," I mumbled, embracing Ricari.

"Me neither."

"I guess we'll have to call for maid service."

He almost giggled and fell into an acting mode. "I

say, goodwife, could you perhaps clear up some of this muck? I was thinking of having a formal tea in that room . . . there's a good girl."

I pulled down his head and kissed him.

We made love, and fell asleep.

I awoke still full of the sense-memory of his hips urgently feeding his cock to me with gentle, restrained thrusts; but he was not beside me in the cold sheets. I felt for him before opening my eyes, but finding nothing, sat up at last and pushed my hair out of my face.

Ricari sat crouched in the chair, back in his black clothes, knees drawn up to his chest. He stared intently down into the bathtub.

"Ricari?" I inquired.

"There's something wrong," he murmured.

I got up and pulled my T-shirt and jeans back on, and half ran to Ricari's side. He smoothed his hair back again. Down in the bathtub, John Thurbis lay still, as red as a devil, his hair grown back to a thick, short, even mane, his face covered with a gleaming, damp beard. It was startling—he had never worn a beard in his life. "What's the matter?" I asked. "He looks all right."

"I can't . . . hear him," Ricari explained. "I should be able to. He has my blood in his body. I should be able to catch his thoughts, though he himself is not yet conscious . . . but I can't."

"You're right," I said. "I can't get anything either."

Ricari shook his head. "I think we may have erred," he said. "I think we gave him too little blood."

"Is there anything we can do?"

"No." Ricari sighed. "There is very little time to do anything, once it's started. It is far too late to do anything now. Wait—he's coming to."

I moved behind Ricari and watched the creature in the tub stirring. His skin flushed, as all vampire skin does as it wakes from sleep, and it seemed so soft and flexible, like human skin. He took a great deep breath, and moved his head back and forth, gently, experimentally.

He sat up and opened his eyes.

Then he screamed.

We moved to quiet him immediately; his scream could have broken the windows and would certainly be heard. Ricari got his hand over John's mouth, and John promptly bit him, breaking his skin with his still-blunt teeth. As soon as he tasted blood, he became silent and still.

Ricari tore his hand back. The skin was in tatters over his knuckles. Like an injured boy in a schoolyard, he crammed his fist against his mouth. "Little bastard," he hissed.

"He's afraid," I said, feeling it flow out from John into me. "He's afraid of you." I went near him, held out my arm. "John, it's all right, it's Ariane, everything's going to be fine."

John jumped with a slosh from the tub, and pinned me against the floor. He tore at my neck with his teeth. "We're in trouble," I managed to say before he sucked the consciousness out of me.

I came to again on the floor, on my side instead of on my back, slowly making out the sounds of impassioned suckling. Ricari was beside me, steadying me. "Careful," he said, "you're going to be very woozy for a moment."

The sucking sounds were coming from John, who was swiftly and hungrily draining a middle-aged Chinese woman dressed in a tourist sweatshirt and madras shorts and the cheap sandals you can buy from bins in Chinatown. She was already dead, her short neat fingernails gone blue under the translucent keratin. "What happened?" I asked.

"I went out. I had to. He was going to kill you—

you're too young to sustain yourself with that much of your blood gone. He's looking better, though." Ricari gave a wry smile. "I'd better stop him, you'll need some of what's left."

Ricari detached John from the woman's body, and John promptly fell to the floor and puked. I crawled over, found a vein in her ankle, and drank the cooling, thinned blood.

Ricari looked at everything with delicate distaste. "What a dreadful mess . . ." He got John up. "John, can you hear me?"

John's eyes rolled, then closed. He gave a low, wordless moan.

"We have to clean you up, and then we must leave." I was able to stand. "That's a must," I agreed.

It seemed to take hours in the gore-soaked bathroom to get me clean, and get John clean; he seemed to soak the blood into his skin. "And get that silly-ass beard off him," I told Ricari, and I had to hold John still while Ricari went at him with the straight razor. Invariably, Ricari nicked John's chin and neck, but the wounds closed themselves almost immediately. John's eyes were already assuming that glassy texture that I knew so well from spending hours gazing at Daniel and Ricari; already he was stronger than I.

But there was certainly something wrong with him. He didn't seem to be able to speak. I opened his mouth and examined his tongue, his teeth, his palate; there was nothing the matter with them. He watched me with vague curiosity and an almost autistic indifference. All the time I got sensations from him—never words, always a formless turmoil of confusion, hunger, resentment, lust, impatience. When the lather had been completely rinsed from his face, I kissed him on the lips, and he returned it, going after me with his mouth afterward as though he wanted more. I put my finger against his lips. "John, we have to go," I said.

He stood up and looked at the door as if to ask me what I was waiting for.

"So he does understand," Ricari remarked.

John looked at him coldly.

"He just can't talk."

"I think he just doesn't want to," I said.

Ricari rolled his eyes. "Wonderful."

Ricari had no things to gather. He was materialistic only about the things that touched him: clothing, his razor and shoes. I put my jacket on John, since his shirt was ruined, and he was forced to wear his blood-stiff black pants, since nothing of Ricari's would ever fit on him.

I shuffled John into the street while Ricari settled his bill at the hotel desk. The old desk clerk never looked up. I felt Ricari's intent like a cold hand under my shirt, and I guessed that the old desk clerk wasn't going to remember this night at all if Ricari had anything to do with it.

On the street while I was looking frantically for a taxi, Ricari took my arm. "Ariane, I don't know if you wanted this or not," he murmured, pressing something cold and metallic into my hand. It was the rat watch. There was a huge dent right in the middle of the rat. I grimaced, and stuffed it into the pocket of my jeans.

We taxied to John's apartment, and I went through his closet, asking, "Do you want this? Do you want this?" and all of it was met with the same cold, haughty indifference. He was completely different—but I recognized this distance in him from when he had been human. Usually, when he was stressed out or angry, he would get expansive, going on drinking binges and tearing things apart; but at the very worst times, he would just relax, and take no more interest in himself or anyone else than he would in a passing cloud. In that strange apartment, looking at his piles of jeans and blazers, he was like a great cat, simply observing and giving no more reaction than a meaningful glance of his dark eyes.

Ricari was fascinated by him. He watched this static turmoil with great interest, studying John's features and every move he made. "He is a beautiful man, Ariane," he said.

"He's an annoying man. Fine, we're taking this and this and this, since you don't care, but I don't know where we're going, so . . ." I gave up and collapsed on the couch, clutching an armload of cardigans to my chest. "Where *are* we going?"

"I was thinking," Ricari answered. "I like this coast, this ocean. We should stay on this coast."

"What, the bay?"

"No, the ocean, I said. What cities are on the ocean?" Ricari idly fingered the sleeve of a fuzzy gray sweater draped over an arm of the couch. John watched his hands, some of the disdain passing from his face.

"Not the country?" I asked.

"I don't like the country. I like people and culture."

"I thought you hated people and culture."

"Yes, well, I'm alive now, I have to deal with it, and if I have to be alive, I would like to be somewhere where I can go to a museum or hear the opera if I chose."

"Yeah, being alive sucks, huh? Well, there's Seattle, Vancouver, B.C., Portland, I guess."

"Portland," he said, a dreamy quality coming into his voice. "Reminds me of Portsmouth, in England, where I stayed for quite some time. I liked it there."

"Well, it's not England. Portland's pretty nice, I've heard. Green. Rains all the time."

"Sounds marvelous," Ricari said.

I shrugged. "I don't care," I said. "Portland then. It's about as close to the country as I'm going to get. I suggest we take the bus . . . less security risk than flying."

"The bus?" Ricari murmured distastefully.

John smiled—a genuine smile—and almost laughed.

I sat up and put my arms around John, kissing the side of his head. He pulled away from me again, not roughly, but distantly again, as if he wanted to be alone inside his head without my touch. When I had touched him I felt something pass between us—something very strong and definite, a bond between us, like a sticky glue. It was enough to give me shivers. I wonder what it must have been like for him. "Bus," I repeated, keeping my mind on track. "It's cheap, it's boring, nobody will have guns and stuff there. If we just chill and act like regular folks, it'll be a snap. But we should go now."

"I've not traveled by bus since the nineteen-forties," Ricari said, rousing himself. "It was dirty and foul and noisy then—I can't imagine what it's like now."

"I'll make you a perfumed handkerchief, if it'll make it any easier."

John was already downstairs, in the street, tossing his long hair and taking great deep breaths of the foggy wind like some marvelous horse. Ricari and I followed more slowly, closing the door behind us and shutting off the lights. "Off we go," Ricari sighed.

I kissed him and pressed his hand, and he smiled.

Epilogue

Ricari left me some time ago.

He bought me this house in the west hills, furnished it according to his own dark, sad tastes, and dwelt with me there for a few years. In the meantime, he taught me the fundamentals—the hunt, the kill, how to learn control, how to talk to human minds. Under his tutelage I grew strong and infinite, learning new respect and wonder for life as I took bits and pieces of it into myself. To his disgust, he never did talk me out of eating people food and drinking alcohol, and even, disastrously, tried to do it himself once. We spent many very quiet evenings together talking and reading by candlelight, moonlight, even bare starlight. And he loved me well.

One evening he simply wasn't there; I searched and called for him for hours before I found his receipt for a one-way plane ticket to Toronto. That night I spent alone, sunk in despair, knowing that I couldn't keep him with me forever, and that living was still agony for him, opera or no opera. There was nothing that could be done about it. My heart calls out for him every day, and hearing nothing, retreats back into its hard, transparent shell. No one can see the shell, but it's there, protecting me. I hope that someday, before the end, he will tell me one last time that he loves me.

I am a scientist again.

I am still Ariane Dempsey, human molecular biologist. I do my work at the Oregon Medical Institute, researching and substitute-teaching the odd lab now and again. I feel about a million years older than my fresh-faced young students, but we still laugh together, still go for drinks after school. When they ask me about my personal life, I smile and change the subject and with a quick twist of my mind, they forget all about it.

Mainly, I study myself.

All my notes from my study of Daniel were lost; the Rotting Hall was razed not long after we left it, and everything within was destroyed. I'm still in touch with one of the little girls from the Rotting Hall—Genevieve—she works at a hair salon in Hollywood now and periodically writes me a long letter telling me all about the goings-on of those kids who survived that night and the area. There's a parking lot where *Verfaulenhalle* used to be, and the heavy-metal club has gone country-western. If I didn't know better, I'd be angry, but it just makes me laugh. I'd better get used to this—my favorite landmarks being made into minimalls, porno video stores, fast-food joints . . . parking lots. Such is L.A. Such is the world.

I know too much about myself; if my flesh didn't heal, I'd be crisscrossed with scars from samples, biopsies, attempts to brand myself, eat myself with acid, wear my skin off with diamonds. Not a whit. Everything I uncover leads to questions and more questions, and the more I see, the less I understand.

Daniel actually called me the other day. I hadn't heard from him since that night, and assumed I never would again. I finally opened the rat pocket watch after perhaps six months of living in Portland, and in it found the number of the bank account where he'd put money away for Lovely and me. I took some of it out, but left the rest there. It's quite a lot—enough to buy a different house, if that urge ever overcame me. Eventually I'm sure it will.

Daniel's somewhere on the other side of the world; I'm not sure where, but it's not England. The connecting operator had a British Empire accent, but it sure wasn't England. The first thing he said was, "Do you still have my jacket?"

"I wear it almost every day," I said truthfully. "The kids all think I'm some kind of dominatrix."

"No, it's just style. Do you miss me?"

"I've begun to miss you. It's been long enough. I was thinking that the Van Helsing Society had caught up with you or something."

"Van Helsing was a vampire. Anybody who's seen enough Christopher Lee movies knows that. Guess what? I'm writing plays!"

"Great."

"They're all filled with sex and damnation—you know, fun stuff. I've got these actors who are dying to perform them . . . mainly we just put them on in the front room, you know, over some iced tea and cucumber salad."

"Have you heard from Ricari?"

"No, why? He's gone, isn't he."

"Yeah, he took off for Toronto a while ago."

"I doubt that he's there actually. He tends to hop around, hoping he won't be found. It's ever so Ferdinand Marcos of him. I haven't heard from him, heard of him, or anything . . . that's probably for the best. He really hates my guts."

"He doesn't. You just freak him out."

"Do I freak you out?"

I smiled against the pillow. He'd interrupted me in the middle of my late afternoon lying-abed, not asleep, but staring at the pinkened peak of Mt. Hood out my bedroom window as the sun went down behind me, out of my sight. "Pleasantly."

"I was afraid you'd answer the phone and say 'Fuck off!' " He laughed. "You'd only be right to do so. I'm a terrible, terrible person. I should have died a long time ago."

"Hush up, none of that. You can't help being alive any more than a baby can."

"And I seem to have no more control over myself. Ah, Ariane. I've been trying to change. I've been trying to be a good boy and not fuck shit up. But how do you do it? Destroying things comes so naturally to me. I've always been this way. In Berlin, in the twenties, I was a madman! I lived to drink, fight, and fuck. I don't know how else to do it."

"I don't know, Daniel."

"Oh, God, did I wake you up? I didn't even think."

"No, it's fine. It's fine. You know, there's a parking lot where the Rotting Hall used to be."

"Marvelous, that's the way it should be. I can't wait until it's *all* parking lots. I should go. Can I call you again sometime?"

"Sure, Dan. Anytime you want."

"You're the best," he said softly.

"I know," I smiled.

"I must run. Take care, look out for the sun."

"I'm looking out," I said.

"Bye." He hung up before I could respond.

* * *

John, now still, lies beside me in bed. Neither of us is asleep, though the sun is beginning to brighten the gray rain clouds. This is the longest he's stayed with me in a very long time; usually, he comes in, ravishes me, and before the sweat has cooled on our bodies, he kisses me and disappears, well before the dawn. "The sun's coming up," I say to him. "You should go now, before it's too late."

His eyes are closed—his thoughts swirl around me, amazingly calm for him. Usually his brain is in a state of psychotic turmoil—a tangle of anger and loss and compulsive recall of physical principles. I've learned a great deal about particle physics, just being inside his head. "John?" I prod again. "You don't want to go out in sunlight."

He opens eyes at last and smiles at me. "No sun," he murmurs, his voice a scratchy wreck. He almost never speaks. "Gray."

"Doesn't mean it can't hurt you, love."

"I'm not going," he whispers. "Not yet."

I don't let the excitement and pleasure show on my face, which is pointless, as he can read my mind as easily as I can read his. "You can always stay," I tell him. "You know that."

"Not forever," he sighs, and buries his beautiful face into the pillow.

"Forever as far as I'm concerned," I say.

"Sleep," he says into the pillow.

He takes me into his arms and presses me to him, his flesh already starting to lose its warmth, its color. I relax and let consciousness and life drain out of me until I'm as good as dead.

When I wake up at sunset he is leaving. He's put on his still-wet, still-muddy, cast-off clothes, dumpster wear, appropriate for his hideout underneath the Pioneer Courthouse post office, but shameful on his body. Already his head hangs down; his hair obscuring his face. "Don't go, please," I plead, knowing it's useless. John is not mine. John is John's.

He glances up at me for a second. "Come with me," he offers.

"No, John, I like to have a *house*."

"And I like to have a *road*," he explains. "I like to have earth. Earth . . . and . . . sky." His eyes flutter closed for a second, and he slips into a beautiful, untouched, heavenly reverie; then he is back, and the pain in his mind takes over again. "I love you . . . but I can't . . . forgive you."

"I know."

He touches his temple and smiles apologetically. "It . . . doesn't work anymore," he sighs. "G'bye."

"Wait—another kiss—" I start half out of bed.

He stands at the door and kisses the back of his hand. Then he waves the hand, and he is gone. "I'll be back . . ." His voice floats faintly to me. I roll over in bed and stare out the window.

Such is the world.

BITE
RICHARD LAYMON

"No one writes like Laymon, and you're going to have a good time with anything he writes."
—Dean Koontz

It's almost midnight. Cat's on the bed, facedown and naked. She's Sam's former girlfriend, the only woman he's ever loved. Sam's in the closet, with a hammer in one hand and a wooden stake in the other. Together they wait as the clock ticks down because . . . the vampire is coming. When Cat first appears at Sam's door he can't believe his eyes. He hasn't seen her in ten years, but he's never forgotten her. Not for a second. But before this night is through, Sam will enter a nightmare of blood and fear that he'll never be able to forget—no matter how hard he tries.

"Laymon is one of the best writers in the genre today."
—Cemetery Dance

Elizabeth Massie

Sineater

According to legend, the sineater is a dark and mysterious figure of the night, condemned to live alone in the woods, who devours food from the chests of the dead to absorb their sins into his own soul. To look upon the face of the sineater is to see the face of all the evil he has eaten. But in a small Virginia town, the order is broken. With the violated taboo comes a rash of horrifying events. But does the evil emanate from the sineater...or from an even darker force?

___4407-2 $5.99 US/$6.99 CAN

Sips of Blood

MARY ANN MITCHELL

The Marquis de Sade. The very name conjures images of decadence, torture, and dark desires. But even the worst rumors of his evil deeds are mere shades of the truth, for the world doesn't know what the Marquis became—they don't suspect he is one of the undead. And that he lives among us still. His tastes remain the same, only more pronounced. And his desire for blood has become a hunger. Let Mary Ann Mitchell take you into the Marquis's dark world of bondage and sadism, a world where pain and pleasure become one, where domination can lead to damnation. And where enslavement can be forever.

___4555-9 $5.50 US/$6.50 CAN

Dorchester Publishing Co., Inc.
P.O. Box 6640
Wayne, PA 19087-8640

Please add $1.75 for shipping and handling for the first book and $.50 for each book thereafter. NY, NYC, and PA residents, please add appropriate sales tax. No cash, stamps, or C.O.D.s. All orders shipped within 6 weeks via postal service book rate. Canadian orders require $2.00 extra postage and must be paid in U.S. dollars through a U.S. banking facility.

Name_____
Address_____
City_____ State_____ Zip_____
I have enclosed $_____ in payment for the checked book(s).
Payment <u>must</u> accompany all orders. ❏ Please send a free catalog.
CHECK OUT OUR WEBSITE! www.dorchesterpub.com

Quenched

MARY ANN MITCHELL

An evil stalks the clubs and seedy hotels of San Francisco's shadowy underworld. It preys on the unfortunate, the outcasts, the misfits. It is an evil born of the eternal bloodlust of one of the undead, the infamous nobleman known to the ages as . . . the Marquis de Sade. He and his unholy offspring feed upon those who won't be missed, giving full vent to their dark desires and a thirst for blood that can never be sated. Yet while the Marquis amuses himself with the lives of his victims, with their pain and their torture, other vampires of Sade's own creation—are struggling to adapt to their new lives of eternal night. And as the Marquis will soon learn, hatred and vengeance can be eternal as well—and can lead to terrors even the undead can barely imagine.

___4717-9 $5.50 US/$6.50 CAN

Dorchester Publishing Co., Inc.
P.O. Box 6640
Wayne, PA 19087-8640

Please add $1.75 for shipping and handling for the first book and $.50 for each book thereafter. NY, NYC, and PA residents, please add appropriate sales tax. No cash, stamps, or C.O.D.s. All orders shipped within 6 weeks via postal service book rate. Canadian orders require $2.00 extra postage and must be paid in U.S. dollars through a U.S. banking facility.

Name_____

Address_____

City_____State_____Zip_____

I have enclosed $_____ in payment for the checked book(s).

Payment <u>must</u> accompany all orders. ❑ Please send a free catalog.